Marcus Bird

SEX, DRUGS AND JERK CHICKEN

2

Copyright © 2013 by Marcus Bird

Cover design © 2013 by Marcus Bird

Author photograph by Marco Vasquez

ISBN 978-0-615-84968-3

"We do not look in great cities for our best morality."

- Jane Austen

SEX, DRUGS AND JERK CHICKEN

Chapter 1

She was a brunette. Her name was Cindy, Samantha or Candy. Tony couldn't remember. These parties were so familiar; the names, the faces, the beer, the noise. He had heard about the party from Cool Asian Dude. He had met Cool Asian Dude at some dive in Adam's Morgan. This wasn't however, Cool Asian Dude's house, it was his boss's house. Or was it his high school roommate's house? It didn't matter because all was going well. She was for the moment, Brunette Chick. He and the brunette had a brief thrilling conversation about the platitudes of niceness.

"You're nice, like *reeeally* nice," she said.

"I'm nice? You just met me."

"Yeah but," she said, placing a hand on his chest.

"Trust me, I *know* nice people, and you are nice."

"*C'est la vie,*" Tony shrugged.

Her mouth opened with surprise and she slapped his chest.

"Get out! You speak French?"

"Well no—"

"I went to France on a language exchange for a semester in college."

Immediately, Tony's saw an image of her in a similar situation, talking to a well handsome French guy dripping with stubble.

"College?"

"Well not really college, but University. I went to American."

Tony chuckled to himself. He hadn't met any American Alumni who ever added "university" to the end of their school. American U was simply *American.*

"Did you live on hall?" Tony asked.

"No, I had a place nearby. It was so nice, you'd have loved it."

Hand on the chest again.

"I got some help from my parents to have some interior decorating done. I had all these weird Rorschach-style paintings my friend Elmer did. He was super talented."

"Elmer?"

"Yeah, he hates his name too. We call him Duke."

"Did he go to Duke?" Tony asked.

"No he went to NYU," the girl replied.

Tony sipped on his drink.

Two guys in matching grey shirts that read "Boston" walked past, cheeks flaming red. Tony wondered what that would feel like, to have red cheeks. They started throwing them back, vodka cranberry mixes and Bud Light beers.

"Hey man, I heard they have a Guinness keg somewhere in here," a short guy with a cherubic face said.

"Seriously? That would be awesome," Tony replied.

The cherubic guy walked away awkwardly.

Five minutes later, Tony was upstairs with Brunette Chick. It started out with the hand on the chest again. Obscenities flew from her mouth like a frightened flock of birds. They were in a closet, jostling about with tongues flailing and arms groping. Every now and then, Tony felt the wobble; a state of mind he and his friends described as halfway between drunk and "fucking drunk". Did that have anything to do with fucking *while* drunk? With a mischievous smile on her face, Brunette Chick interrupted this mental diatribe.

"I want you," she cooed.

He could smell and taste the sweetness of all her vodka cranberry drinks. Mumbling a brief reply, he fiddled with her jeans. They were in mostly darkness, with only a yellow line of light at the base of the door for guidance. He followed the trail of the girl's open zipper and felt around. His fingers brushed against a soft bed of pubic hair. No panties. She came to this party with a plan. With a surge of strength, she thrust him into rack of clothing. Something sharp and cold scratched him on his back. He grunted in pain.

"That's right," the girl said eagerly.

For a brief moment, a sliver of light hit her face, exposing her blue eyes. A wisp of dark hair hung over her nose. Feeling as if he were on a merry go-round, Tony listened for the *shhlp* of her pants hitting the floor. Her hands were strong and penetrating. His pants were off as well, though he didn't remember when that happened. Brunette Chick straddled him, slim arms like steel around his neck. She expertly grabbed his throbbing manhood and stuck it in. With her legs propped on the wall and Tony somewhat leaning back to support both their weight, she began pounding him mercilessly. Such organized sex didn't seem like the behavior of two drunken people, but Tony reasoned they were working mainly on instinct. The girl groaned an octave or two deeper than her usual voice and Tony felt a chill go down his spine. As she used her seemingly inhuman strength to maintain a sexual position most likely not in the *Kama Sutra,* Tony stifled a laugh. He still didn't know her name. Outside, people in the party shouted in unison about something, an inadvertent rally cry for another Tony victory.

Winston had seen Tony go upstairs with the cute girl. Dammit! Earlier that night he had said hello. Maybe if he hadn't been so hesitant he'd be up there doing God knows what with her. That Tony. Legendary! *What was her name again?* Shrugging, he looked around to see if there were any more willing participants. He walked into the living room, where two dozen people floated about in various stages of inebriation. Near a set of large windows that faced a well-manicured garden, two guys with matching Pools and khaki shorts were laughing at nothing in particular. An angry orange couch was swaddled with people. A tall Italian-looking guy with thick eyebrows and a sleepy expression kept whispering into the ear of a cute girl with brown hair. Each time he said something, her cheeks would flush and she would glance at her friend.

"Save me!" her eyes said.

But her friend was throat-deep in the mouth of another Italian-looking guy. A few girls walked back and forth, holding hands and talking loudly. More animated fellows in Polos ran around, shouting strange phrases, downing beers and doing shots. Winston left the living room and walked through a hallway into a dining room. Red cups lined the floor like ants and wet spots dotted the soft carpet. Three girls were sitting in the room, drinking quietly and bobbing their heads to the music. One of them turned towards Winston and flashed a bright smile. *She's cute,* Winston thought. She had shiny black hair and was well tanned. At a glance she looked European, or possibly Brazilian. Most of the people in the house were white, but this girl was from somewhere else. Winston gave a conciliatory gesture to the smile; raising his drink a la "cheers" and smiled. She laughed and rattled off something to her friends in a foreign tongue.

"So she is from Europe," Winston said to himself under his breath.

A huge guy straight out of an Abercrombie and Fitch advertisement strode into the room. He had broad, all-American features: sandy blond hair, high cheekbones and the look of someone who's never had a bad day in his life.

"Ladies!" he shouted.

They smiled and waved at him. He ran forward and picked up the girl farthest from the girl with the dark hair, a blonde bombshell with a ridiculous tan. She squealed and he left the room with her, his massive footsteps audible even with the loud music playing in the background.

"Big guy huh?" said a voice from behind him.

Winston realized he was still looking down the hallway where the large guy had just taken the girl. He turned to see the girl from before staring directly at him.

"Oh, yeah," Winston replied nervously.

He walked over to her. His heart leapt a little. She was more than cute. She was strikingly attractive, with thick black hair that appeared hand-polished, cloudy green eyes and flawless skin. Her face was very symmetrical and she had a straight, sloping nose with the slightest bulb at the tip.

"Where are you from? I hear an accent," she said.

"Take a wild guess," Winston answered.

"I dunno, Trinidad?"

Winston winced as she said this.

"Aww, did I say something wrong?" she asked with a soft smile.

Winston being Jamaican, felt like explaining that the two accents sounded nothing alike and the countries were hundreds of miles apart over a huge gulf of the Caribbean Sea, but he decided not to.

"I'm from Jamaica," Winston said.

At the sound of the word 'Jamaica' her eyes lit up with excitement and a broad smile spread across her face. Her teeth were perfectly white and straight.

"I love Jamaica!" she said, taking a small step forward. She turned to her remaining friend.

"No, *we* love Jamaica!"

They both laughed loudly and sipped their drinks. Winston, not sure whether to feel flattered or a bit confused, tried to work his angle.

"So where are you from? I heard you speaking what sounded like a foreign language earlier."

"Oh, that's Spanish. I was born in Barcelona, but I've been living in the states since I was nine."

"Interesting."

"Why is that interesting, Mr. Jamaica?" she said.

"Oh, no reason. What's your name?" Winston said.

"Elsa," She replied with a smile.

Winston sipped on his drink and noticed that her friend was also gorgeous. During the party he had seen many girls, but these two seemed like a pair of the hottest ones. Why were they inside by themselves? Her friend seemed to be European as well. They shared similar features; well chiseled faces with a peculiar cloudiness in their eyes. Her friend had brown hair. Winston chuckled nervously. At five foot eight and a half, he wasn't close to being strapping. With a moderate physique and a shaved head, he often thought he looked like an escaped convict, or a high school student with an old grudge.

The music that was playing in the background stopped briefly. For most of the night the selection had been quite random; mostly hip-hop tunes playing from someone's Ipod. The noise of fifty conversations floated through the air, and then the speakers came back to life. A familiar score flew through the airwaves.

"Yeah yeah!" came a voice from the speakers.

Sean Paul.

Both girls almost dropped their drinks. Elsa grabbed her friend's hand and Winston's as well.

"I love this song!" she shouted.

With surprising strength she pulled them both into the living room, where most of the people had started dancing.

Winston watched them for a brief moment. Elsa was wearing a body-hugging black skirt with silver trim. Her body was very curvy, and she moved with a practiced rhythm to the music. She closed her eyes, fantasizing as she danced. She grabbed her friend's hand and they both danced with each other erotically. The two drunk guys with the Polos wandered by.

"Yeah!" one of them said, raising his arms in the air.

"Oh yeah!" the other one chimed.

Both guys were short and looked fresh from a *World of Warcraft* marathon. With alcohol fueling their confidence, they started to dance with both girls in a stilted fashion, all shoulders and no hips. Winston laughed loudly as he watched the spectacle. The girls weren't pleased. Elsa opened her eyes and gazed at Winston. She stepped away from the guy trying to dance with her and put her arms around Winston's waist.

"Show me how they dance in Jamaica," she whispered.

This is not real, he thought, but didn't waste any time. Holding on to her softly, he rolled his back, occasionally grinding her pelvic area. Elsa followed suit, following him with exact rhythm. As the pounding bass from the dancehall song vibrated in their feet, Winston could feel Elsa becoming more attuned to his motions. Her body was firm and with each movement they made Winston felt that natural closeness that comes with the unison of music and woman. Then, the song stopped. Elsa looked at him with her powerful eyes.

"You're a good dancer," she said leaning forward and giving him a kiss on the cheek.

"Come," she said. "Let's go outside and talk a bit."

Winston walked outside with her, smiling as he walked past her friend who was still dancing with the first of the two short polo-clad guys.

Chapter 2

Bishop was grasping at straws. He was sitting on the sidewalk, chatting to two red-faced Asian-American girls, trying to maintain some semblance of conversation. They were Elaine and Christina, each holding a large blue cup in their hands, having a buzzed conversation. A few minutes earlier, Bishop had had their attention, but after the usual introductory banter, whatever they were chatting about had dwindled down to almost nothing. Bishop smiled as he sat there, even though his proximity to the girls made him feel awkward. He tried to squeeze back into the discussion.

"So Elaine, where do you work?" Bishop asked.

"Dupont," she replied.

Turning her head back to Christina, she continued her conversation. "So I went to Georgetown the other night and it was so shi-shi—"

Bishop sipped on his drink and felt a flash of trepidation go through him. The girls were very cute, but this situation didn't seem salvageable

"I know what you mean. Can't beat the shopping though. I got this skirt at the French Connection store last week," Christina said.

"French connection? Wasn't your ex working there?" Elaine asked.

"He works in Bethesda somewhere now. I'm back in the F-C."

"Oh there's that guy from earlier, he's cute."

Bishop listened to the conversation, while looking at them closely. Christina was tall, with long smooth legs, silky skin and an oval face shadowed by an outcropping of bone straight hair. Her breasts were small but proportionate, and her eyes—slanted slightly upwards—were dark and mysterious. The first time he saw her, a sensation of desire rippled in his stomach and an erection threatened to show in his pants. Her friend Elaine was attractive as well, in a different way. She had a sharp, angular face, a button nose, large eyes and a stylish haircut. A purple streak ran down a rogue bang of hair that covered most of her right eye. Unlike Christina, she was short, with skinny legs that protruded from a tiny blue plaid skirt. Her breasts were larger.

Something solid hit Bishop on the back and he coughed on his drink.

"Big man! I leave you for two minutes and you have the cutest girls at the party?"

It was Kevin, his best friend. Kevin had come to D.C for a visit. This was the tail end of a two-week stay. The slight commotion distracted the girls, and they both looked up. Kevin was tall and broad chested, with thin eyes and a large face. He looked like the ex-athlete who gets the law degree and the hot wife.

"So ladies! Do you mind if I sit?" Kevin asked.

Without waiting for a response Kevin sat down, squeezing his large frame between the two girls. He and Bishop now both had a girl beside them.

"You're tall," Christina said with a smile.

"It's been said," Kevin replied.

"Wow, you have a strong accent. Where are you from?" Christina asked.

"Jamaica," Kevin replied.

Bishop sighed inwardly. He was from Jamaica as well, but he spoke with a crisp inflection that always belied his origins.

"Very cool. Hey, isn't there another Jamaican guy here tonight? Tony? Is he your friend?" Christina said, looking at Kevin and Bishop between glances.

Kevin shook his head. Bishop nodded. He had seen him around, Tall, with his chocolate-dark skin, big head of hair and disarming smile. Apparently the dude had quite the reputation.

"He's hot," Elaine said with a chuckle.

Kevin laughed and said to Bishop in rapid Jamaican patois. *"These girls are ready."*

Bishop nodded in agreement. Ready indeed. To stop talking to him and disappear with Kevin down a dark alley. Kevin launched into a story about a guy that hit on him once in Jamaica. The ladies were spellbound by his words. His voice, deep and well projected, made even Bishop pay attention, even though he had heard the story a dozen times. A guy wearing a Red Sox cap turned backward gave Kevin a light tap on the shoulder almost falling to the curb as he passed.

"Dude you fucking rock," He said while stumbling off into the distance.

"Yeah man. Respect!" Kevin said with a smile

"Sorry about that ladies. So I was saying, this big guy comes over, think Arnold Schwarzenegger with man-tits, and then standing this close to me," Bishop puts his index fingers an inch apart. "He says: Jiggle my titty."

The two girls erupted into high-pitched peals of laughter. Elaine laughed so hard she spilled some of her drink on Christina, who stopped laughing.

"Jesus Christ, Elaine!" Christina said.

Elaine, still laughing, tried to compose herself. Bishop came to the rescue. "Don't cry over spilt beer my dear. At least she didn't throw up on your shirt."

At this statement, Elaine shot Bishop a nasty look.

"Not that you look drunk or anything," Kevin said with a smile.

Elaine smiled. Christina looked at the sticky shine of beer on her left arm briefly, and sat back down. She chuckled. The annoyance was gone. "I can't believe that guy said that to you!" Christina said.

"So how did you feel? I mean, guys have said weird stuff to me before, but that must have been creepy," Elaine asked.

"What kind of weird stuff has a guy said to you?" Bishop enquired.

"Well, it depends on the situation," Elaine replied, taking a sip of her drink.

"Indulge me."

"Well this guy asked me if he could come in my shoe one time."

Christina turned her head rapidly towards Elaine, her hair swishing like the hair you see in a television commercial.

"What? I've never heard that story," she said with a slight frown.

"Well, it was some random guy on the bus, it was very awkward."

"That beats my man-tit story by a mile!" Kevin said with a laugh.

The group laughed.

Chapter 3

Winston was in a dream world. For the last hour, he and Elsa had been talking as if they were old friends. It was always fun to meet someone you had an immediate connection with, but it was different when the person was freaking gorgeous. Elsa had a warmth to her that spoke of that Winston imagined was from her fast-paced Spanish lifestyle. He could imagine green rolling hills, pastel-colored houses and exotic food when she made certain gestures. Through her cloudy eyes, he could see the landscape of a place he'd never been to. Maybe her with her family walking through a quiet forest, her gleefully running towards a babbling brook as her father, a handsome Spaniard looked on in pride. She represented the beauty and fire, the addictive and stereotypical allure of a European woman. Then there was the laugh. In her laugh, he saw her life, a whirlwind of treasured experiences: happily erotic nights with boyfriends, trips to Mallorca and sun tanning on the beach. Maybe, Winston thought, it was possible for a person to be sucked in by these fantasies based simply on how a woman looked. Maybe she could be the one. It's hard to meet someone and see so much in them so quickly, but if he weren't careful, he'd get lost. Right now, she was telling a story about where she came from.

"So, there was this man, and he was very tall, big and strong. Not like you. You are smaller, yes, but sweet," she said, pinching his cheek.

Winston didn't know how to take this. Blushing inwardly, he listened attentively.

"He said he was a prince, but he was actually some kind of gardener from Italy."

"This guy was your first boyfriend?" Winston asked.

"In a way, yes. We did not make love, no, no. It was more like, a fantasy," she said, her eyes looking briefly reflective.

"But that's the past," Elsa said. "If I asked you, would you come with me to Barcelona?"

Winston paused. As if sensing his hesitance, Elsa continued.

"Have you ever done something on a whim? You know, like gone somewhere just for the heck of it, or eaten something disgusting just to see if you could? I like those things... I like unknown territory. My family's like that. They've lived in England, New York and even Hawaii. Then they decided to come here a few years ago. "

"To Washington D.C?" Winston said.

"Yes. It might sound weird, but they felt like they had a home here. For them, it felt right. Sort of how this moment feels right now, with us."

She touched his arm, and Winston felt his heart race.

"I'm sorry, I hope I'm not being too forward."

Winston smiled and nodded, "It's fine."

He felt trapped. Even though this was a small conversation at a party straight out of an *American Pie* movie, there seemed to be some cosmic significance to their meeting. Her rapturous energy and his burgeoning need for companionship.

"So, would you come with me? It would be wonderful. I would show you all the beautiful sights. We could take a look at the Gaudí buildings, the Cathedral and swim in the sea. I'm sure you love the beach, since you are Jamaican."

"I haven't been to the sea for a while... but I wouldn't mind," Winston said.

"I just invited you to go across the world, and you didn't say yes?"

She gave him a hard slap on the shoulder as she said this, and let out one of her laughs again. A sea of fingers tickled Winston's back, settling into the base of his spine. At that moment, her friend May, the girl with the brown hair, came over.

"Bettany left with David," she said, looking wistfully at a small vase of roses tucked away in a dirty corner.

"Oh, I see," Elsa replied.

"Winston, can you excuse us for a moment?"

Winston nodded and Elsa walked off with Maria. Winston felt his left leg trembling. He was giddy with emotion. This was by far the hottest girl he had ever had such a nice vibe with, no—connection with—and he wasn't going to fuck it up. He took another sip of his drink, and coughed as a tiny piece of ice slipped down his throat. He glanced up at the sky briefly. He had been alone for stretches at a time. He hadn't felt a woman's touch in months now. On top of a thin feeling of loneliness that hung over his head like a drape, the tiniest spark of hope was echoing from his consciousness.

Chapter 4

The smell of coitus lingered in the air. Behind them, through the closed door, the dull throb of hip-hop music and meshed voices trickled through a small gap under the doorway. Brunette Chick was putting her clothes back on. Tony sat near a tiny window, with his shirt on and his pants off. In the dim light he could see the faintest outline of her body. Nice posterior, supple breasts. She slipped into her jeans and shuffled beside him. She gave him a wet kiss.

"I'll see you downstairs."

"Definitely baby," Tony replied.

For a second, bright light flashed into the tiny room, and the roar of voices and music spilled inside. Then, it was gone. Tony was alone, on the floor. As he stood up and put on his pants a sickening feeling hit his stomach. Tiny hands grabbed at his intestines, and he was hit with a wave of nausea. He clenched his eyes shut and took a few deep breaths. This happened to him sometimes. It had nothing to do with alcohol, but a lot to do with something from his past. He often felt this way, at the most ill timed moments. He looked out the window and his mind went back a few years when he was—

"Whoa! Sorry buddy. I didn't know anyone was here!"

A short fellow wearing baggy jeans and an awful t-shirt was standing by the door. He had a drink in his hand. Behind him, a red-faced guy with a shaved head and a goatee mumbled, "Dude, this isn't the bathroom."

The door clicked again. Tony chuckled to himself. He took another deep breath, zipped up his pants and headed back to the party. He stepped carefully past people sitting on the stairs, and made sure not to spill some drinks precariously perched on the stairway railing. If his feet made a sound on the carpeted stairs, he couldn't hear it over the din of the party. The crowd was a sea of white faces with a sprinkling of color here and there. Tony headed towards the kitchen. Inside, twelve people hung around a central kitchen counter. One guy in a chef's apron that read, "I'M THE BOSS" was mixing drinks. Another person was fumbling through the fridge.

"Hey man do you know who has any blow?" asked a short, well built man with a buzz cut and designer prescription glasses.

Tony shook his head in slight annoyance. He never did drugs, or even liked the idea of doing drugs. His therapist had recommend Xanax for his infrequent anxiety attacks, but he couldn't bother to take the medication. These people at parties always seemed to think he knew where the blow was, or the weed, or whatever.

"Hey, Mr. T!" a voice chirped.

It was the girl from upstairs, with three of her friends. Wow, Tony thought, her friends were really cute.

"Cindy *lovvves* you," One of her friends purred, rubbing Tony on the stomach.

Tony laughed. Brunette Chick must have told them about their upstairs frolic. He did some quick math. In their entire interaction, the girl from upstairs had never said her name. Without missing a beat, Tony replied to the group. "No, Cindy *lovvves* you."

This tickled the three girls and they all started laughing.

"Shots?" the same girl said.

"Sure," Tony replied.

"But I get to pour!" the girl shouted.

"Sure thing," Tony said, holding out his glass.

"Me too Cindy," Brunette chick giggled, putting her hand back on Tony's chest.

Shit, Tony thought. Cindy was the other girl. He still didn't know Brunette Chick's name.

* * * *

I and I is a artical.

I and I is a don.

I and I is irie.

Kevin tried to remember where those lines came from. Probably some dub poetry session he had attended years back, or maybe when he was listening to that roots rock mix CD when he was high. The lines always popped up when he was close to sealing the deal with a girl, He became *artical.* He became *irie.* A man in charge.

He was inside with Christina. He couldn't help grinning, a few more chit-chats and a few more thinly veiled innuendos and she would be his. He could smell the scent of her body wash. Some kind of raspberry vibe. She peeked back at him as they were walking, smirking. She became intensely attractive in this moment. A wisp of her hair tickled his forearm, and he gave her a peck on the cheek. He liked the party—the people and the environment always felt so different from what he was used to—and he entertained the thought of actually living in the States. Jamaican parties were a bit different. For one, he probably wouldn't randomly be at someone's house, drinking all their liquor and chasing the hot girls around. He'd be hanging with friends, high-fiving people he knew already and scheming for girls he had probably slept with, or for friends of girls he had already slept with.

The only new girls in Kingston were usually college girls, and they could be damn annoying sometimes. He'd probably pop into a hole-in-the-wall bar, high five some more people he knew, drink two Heinekens and then go to The Quad, or Fiction Nightclubs. There wasn't anywhere else to go. Then maybe one of his boys would meet him at the club, and if it was lame then they'd end up at Lucky 38 and he'd drop money for a blowjob from a grimy stripper. But here, in the States, sitting on a sidewalk he met a tall version of Lucy Liu without needing to spend any money. He could escape around complete strangers; gain high status without shelling out any cash. He knew all comparisons between countries drew lines on cultural norms. As he glanced at white guys in Khaki shorts and backwards caps, open toe slippers and faded Polos, it was a different vibe. No one was dancing really, and if they were it was a complete joke. Who could dance like Jamaican women? It was a cultural thing they learned as little girls.

They walked into the Kitchen. Tony was there, laughing with a group of cute girls. Kevin gave him a perfunctory nod.

He hadn't liked him the first time he had seen him. His smile was a little too self-assured, his walk too confident. A weird feeling ran through his chest when Tony had shaken his hand when he introduced himself. It was as if he was melting, all six feet three inches of him. He didn't know why, but Tony made him uncomfortable. On the table were cups with varying levels of leftover liquid. Little pieces of ice had formed into a small puddle in the middle of the table, which Kevin noticed, had a dent. Christina said she wanted to have a vodka cranberry. He poured the drink and smiled at her again. She reminded him of a girl he had slept with a few months ago. She was Jamaican-Chinese (She was actually mostly black but loved harping on and on about her Chinese grandfather). There was some familiarity though; the slim body, captivating features. But Christina was full Asian, no dilution. She said something funny and they laughed. Holding hands, they walked to the makeshift dance floor.

Chapter 5

The girls were gone. Brunette Chick had left so drunk she could barely walk, while Tony gave her a perfunctory smile from the couch. Maybe he would see her again, maybe not. He was sitting there with his new temporary friend, a slim guy with a red face. He talked a lot.

"These girls man, I tell you, every girl is the same. Every girl is the same. You know what I mean?"

Tony nodded.

"You pamper and you prod, I mean, if I say would you like a drink? Why are you gonna look at me like I don't speak English? I speak English, don't I? Am I right?"

Tony nodded again.

"Every time, I mean at bars, at clubs, it's the same man. Such a waste. But man, girls are so beautiful, I just want to— yeah!" He made a forward thrusting motion while sitting down.

Tony chuckled. He was half-listening to the guy's drunken banter. What was really funny was the fact that the fellow worked at a local think-tank in a high position. To their left, a tall young man with a short beard walked down the stairway. Tony vaguely recognized him; earlier he was dressed in a sharp polo shirt and slacks. Now he was in a faded t-shirt and crushed shorts. He must be one of the tenants.

"Hey man, did you enjoy the party?" he said to Tony.

Tony stood up. "Yeah, it was pretty cool man."

"Cool man, we're having one next month, same time!"

"I'll be here," he said, shaking the guy's hand.

Tony walked into the street. It was quiet and devoid of life. In the distance, large houses stood like sleeping giants. He flipped open his cell phone. Black letters on a soft LCD screen read: *4:05 a.m.* This was a problem. Trains don't run at four a.m. in D.C, and this was the twilight hour for taking cabs home. Especially in an area like Tenleytown, taking cabs are so-so if you are black. Tony lived no less than twenty blocks away, which was at least a thirty-minute walk. He sighed and turned and looked at the house once more. It was like many houses he had been in. These neighborhoods of khaki and Polos, alcohol and cabbies that pretended not to see you. He started walking home, alone.

Chapter 6

The BMW roared to life, with Kevin and Bishop in the front seats. In the back, Christina and Elaine chatted to themselves. Bishop hit Connecticut Avenue, and headed towards his apartment. He didn't live too far away, Georgetown. Just off M street, he rented a nice row house that came chock full of furniture fit for a nightclub. His father's business friend owned the place, and he lived there for a pittance of what people around him were paying for it. Not that he couldn't afford it. In Jamaica they called that "links". Here it was known as a "the hookup".

Kevin had successfully set up the after party. Bishop knew that Kevin was going to sleep with Christina, but he warned him not to go into his bedroom. "So we'll have sex...on di' dirty floor...", Kevin had said, with a laugh, quoting a raunchy line from a popular dancehall song. He was happy to see his friend. It had been six months since he went to Jamaica, and they had partied every night until his departure three weeks later. Their energy overlapped into their thought patterns and actions. They liked almost all the same things, and only differed with specific kinds of women. Sometimes Kevin would like girls who were a little thicker. Bishop called them chubby, but Kevin would vehemently deny they were big. Other than this dispute, everything else had a symbiotic continuity between them. Their manner of dress was similar, the way they spoke, and even the things they found funny. Bishop would make arbitrary references that would leave them laughing and choking for air. Kevin was his storehouse of recollection to the past, a vessel that represented the sum total of his childhood, high school and partially adult experiences. It was good to have him here, even though he was slightly worried about Elaine. Experience had shown him that he was a bit fawning at times, and would mess up even a sure thing.

"I've never seen a man toss so much pussy into the rubbish," Kevin always said.

The first time he had mentioned this to Bishop, he laughed until tears came into his eyes. It was a small revelation. Kevin was the playboy and Bishop pulled women mostly because girls knew who his family was. It was slim pickings in Kingston town. They rolled down M Street, past old street lamps and cobblestone streets. At the stoplight, an old Benz growled at them as it drove past.

"Wow, what do you do?" came the voice of Christina. "Georgetown is so expensive."

"It's not that bad," Bishop replied.

"I live in Columbia Heights," Christina said.

"What's Columbia Heights?" Kevin asked.

Bishop wanted to explain that it was the young person central of D.C, that everyone that lived there with their degrees and mixed level incomes were squashed together in a horribly convenient location with lots of time to hook up and shop at the nearby Target.

"It's up the road," Bishop replied.

The ladies were pretty wasted, and in the few remaining minutes before they reached the apartment, Bishop learned Elaine was only in town for a few days, visiting from California. He turned the car onto a back alley and parked behind a locked garage with a rusty padlock on a thick chain. He punched a code onto a small panel beside the back door. Something beeped and a loud click sounded. Bishop walked inside, the smell of the apartment wafting through the air. The floor was black marble. They entered through the back, leading through a small walkway with an office to the right. Bishop slipped off his shoes and stepped onto soft, fuzzy carpeting. Behind him, he heard the shuffle of feet, and giggles from the girls. He tapped a small button and dim lighting came on.

"Beers are in the fridge. Vodka is in the freezer and I have snacks in the cupboard," Bishop said, flopping on the couch.

Everything had a black finish, from the kitchen-top appliances to a little remote holder built into the wall. The fridge was a black behemoth with exotic features Bishop never used. He rarely cooked. The walls were a cool red brick with black-framed photos of famous architectural buildings, each one recessed into small four by four grids. The guy who helped him to move in explained that the size of the pictures forced people to look at them. Elaine was standing by the wall, staring at one of the photos. The guy was right. Kevin was standing near the fridge, awkwardly pressing panels on the walls. The lights flickered from bright to dim a few times, then dancehall music played through speakers hidden in the walls.

"Yeah, the party start now!" he bellowed.

Kevin's voice resounded with passion, and Bishop felt himself transported for a split second back to Jamaica, in the middle of a sunny day in high school. He and Kevin were walking in their uniforms with big smiles. In this memory was Kevin still taller than Bishop, with thinner features, before his ears matched his head. Before he wore bigger shoes.

"Welcome to La Casa Chung!" Kevin boomed.

Christina stood quietly in the kitchen, statuesque in the soft light. Above her, one of the lights shone directly on her hair, making the top of her head look white. She was beautiful. She stood up a bit awkwardly, coolly trying to keep her balance. Bishop knew she didn't need any more alcohol. Kevin was excitedly chatting about what the meaning of "bloodclaat" (a Jamaican curse word) was to Christina. She watched him quietly while pulsing music roared in the background. Bishop watched her behavior with quiet envy. A hand touched him. It was Elaine.

"Why are you so quiet all of a sudden?"

As she said this she looked around, her eyes scanned the room. "This place is so nice."

Bishop shrugged. It *was* a nice place—but he lived there. Elaine was cute, pretty even, but he wanted Christina. He could imagine her long legs in his bed, swimming under the black sheets. Her hair would rest on his chest, swishing and swaying while her tongue resolved to explore his entire body. Elaine sat close to him, resting her head against his shoulder. She smelled nice, and he could feel her left breast pressing against his arm near the elbow. She was warm and soft.

Then, she was on him. Her tongue felt cold and wet against his skin, and the sensation sent tremors into his stomach that made him quiver. She was kissing his neck, and then their lips met sloppily. She pulled away from Bishop with a sound that went *smack*.

"I'm not drunk," Elaine said. "Not that drunk anyways."

Bishop saw the kitchen in his peripheral vision. Kevin and Christina were gone. Bishop looked at Elaine, with her small button nose, silky straight hair and passionate eyes. A groundswell of excitement surged through him. His best friend was having a good time, so should he. Their lips met again, and he felt her tiny hands feeling around his stomach. His roamed as well, touching the wet softness under her plaid skirt. He was surprised. Elaine sensed this.

"My last boyfriend hated hair down there. I guess it's an old habit," she said with a chuckle.

"You like Christina don't you," she said, in between kisses.

"What? No," Bishop replied.

"Shh," Elaine whispered. "She's beautiful, but she wouldn't do this. Not in a million years."

The tiny fingers Bishop felt before were on his belt buckle now, deftly pulling the belt off. It was a weird, double buckle belt he had picked up on a trip to New York. He had trouble taking it off sometimes. It fell to the ground. Clink. Then Elaine growled. With a few strong tugs, she pulled Bishop's pants off. Elaine's lips found their mark, and as Bishop closed his eyes, he heard a loud giggle and a laugh float from downstairs, mingling with the dancehall music in the kitchen. It was Cristina's voice, and she sounded happy.

Chapter 7

Winston was sitting with Elsa at The Diner. Her friend, May, was sitting with them. They were eating breakfast. In front of them, large steaming plates of food rested between tall glasses of water. Behind them, early morning patrons in various stages of inebriation happily ate food and chatted about the night before. One set of girls, all brunettes with silky dresses on, chatting in excited tones about the happenings at Madam's Organ. Directly beside them, three girls with chocolate skin and natural hair smiled as they sipped on orange juice. Further back, a scruffy fellow in a Braves cap was trying to kiss a red-faced girl in between bites of his omelet.

"Hello... Earth to Winston," came Elsa's voice.

"Oh, sorry about that," Winston said with a laugh.

"You are the dreamy type aren't you? Always in your head?" Elsa asked.

"Well," Winston said.

"Of course he is," said May. "Everything about him screams an artist or a writer."

Winston smiled. He was neither.

"Why do you say that? " Winston asked.

May chomped into a mean sausage and continued.

"Aren't all Jamaicans like, musical and artistic?"

Winston groaned internally. Stereotypes like these never made any sense. Elsa seemed to sense this.

"I mean I LOVE Bob Marley, don't you? He was Jamaican. He was artistic," May said, speaking in a quick, frantic way.

"Well, I think Bob Marley's okay," Winston said.

In reality he preferred Peter Tosh, but rarely had the chance to tell anyone this.

"One love!" May shouted. "One heart! Let's get together and feel all right!"

The whole diner fell silent for three seconds. May's face reddened and she put her face in her hands.

"Sorry, I guess I'm drunk," May said weakly.

Elsa rested a hand on her shoulder and whispered something in her ear. "We'll be right back," Elsa said to Winston.

As she got up, she gave him a pinch on his thigh. They went to the bathroom and were gone for the next twenty minutes. During this time, Winston felt annoyed and impatient. Why did these girls always get so drunk? He asked himself. He rarely drank, and if he did, only mixed drinks. Beer was tasteless and too fizzy for his palette. He sipped on his water and picked at his food. Outside, the dull glow of the early morning started to creep in through the windows. He felt very tired.

"Winston?" a voice said.

He turned to see Elsa standing near the table. Her slim figure and her long hair hit Winston like a soft slap on the cheek. His annoyance evaporated.

"We're going to get a cab home. I'm so sorry that this happened."

"No problem," Winston said, beaming a smile. "Is she okay?"

"Yeah, throwing up usually helps these situations," Elsa said.

"Is she still—?"

"No, she's just freshening up in front of the mirror," Elsa replied.

"Cool, well I guess I'll head home then."

Winston stood up and felt in his pockets. House keys, check. Wallet, check. He was good to go.

"Aren't you forgetting something?" Elsa said.

"Oh, I'm sorry!" Winston said. He glanced at the menu. Mumbling to himself, he tried to remember his meal. The turkey and mashed potatoes, eight bucks. He dropped a ten on the table. He felt a hand on his shoulder.

"Not that silly. You are too cute," Elsa said.

She was smiling, and Winston felt the tug at his heart again. He could smell her body.

"Give me a hug."

Her body was soft and womanly, firm in the right places. She gave him a wet kiss on the cheek. Her lips felt like heaven.

"Call me," she said. "Let me go check on May."

"Okay. I'll see you."

Winston watched her walk back to the bathroom gracefully. The doors shut behind her and Winston sighed. He walked outside and waited for the 92 bus. Images from the night played through his mind. The party, then Elsa, now The Diner. He didn't trust anyone with his feelings, but why did she make him feel so good? Was this really going somewhere?

Chapter 8

Whole Foods Market was a few blocks away by bike. He and Kevin were riding towards Dupont Circle. Bishop rarely rode any of the three bikes stacked behind a set of storage boxes in the basement, and it showed. His bike, a rusty black Schwinn squeaked with each revolution of the pedals. Kevin got the better deal, calmly riding an old but more functional mountain bike. He came from a family of tall men, and his long brown legs pumped powerfully as they careened through the streets. Bishop's father and brother's were both tall, but he had inherited his mother's height and delicate features from her Chinese ancestry.

"So, where's the spot to get some food in di morning?" Kevin said.

"Nuff places around here still... but mostly sandwiches," Bishop replied.

"Sandwiches? People eat that for breakfast here?" Kevin said with a laugh.

Yeah you would be surprised. Especially in New York, that's sandwich central. People pay like, ten dollars for a sandwich."

Kevin slowed down the bike and came to a short stop. He was mouthing something.

"Seventy dollars to one U.S... wait. A man will buy a sandwich for Eight hundred dollars Jamaican! Rass!"

Bishop laughed. Kevin's currency conversion was off by at least one hundred Jamaican dollars, but whichever way you looked at it, a ten-dollar sandwich was a little pricey. And they could both afford it.

"No man, I need some real food. I need some dumpling, some chicken, some fish you see it?"

"You are hilarious, big man. I'm not sure where we can get that. Actually, what time is it now?" Bishop asked.

Kevin glanced at his watch. "Ten to twelve."

"Oh, well we can go to this Jamaican place I know. Its not that close, but I'd say twenty minutes we can be there and have a man-sized lunch."

"Forward!" Kevin shouted.

He sped forward on his bike.

"Wrong way boss!" Bishop shouted.

Kevin laughed and spun around, almost getting hit by an SUV.

The food place was small and simple. It had a white tiled floor, a small counter and a regular-sized display case for pastries. The people working there looked distinctly Jamaican, with dark skin and heavy accents. Kevin and Bishop sat at a small table, looking a tad awkward in small pairs of shorts and crushed t-shirts. Kevin, true to form, had ordered the biggest meal on the menu, a twelve-dollar monster that mixed three different meats, rice, dumplings, yams and bananas. Bishop had ordered a more modest brown-stewed chicken lunch. Kevin was sipping on a *Ting*, a popular Jamaican grapefruit soda drink.

"This is wicked man. You mean to tell me I've been here almost two weeks and you didn't tell me about this place?"

"You have to save the best for last," Bishop said.

Kevin hissed his teeth. "You know I can barely function on the McDonald's and all that crap. That sort of food can't do anything to help a man boss."

Bishop chuckled.

"Why you think so many women around the world love Jamaican man so?" Kevin continued. " We eat some good food. None of that fried business that make your dick stop working when you turn thirty!"

Now Bishop really laughed, nearly falling off his chair. He loved Jamaican theories on male sexuality. It seemed everything boiled down to food, church and odd concoctions like Guinness mixed with Red Bull.

"Yeah man. Real Jamaican food. Real vibes," Bishop said.

Kevin eased back into his chair comfortably, though his chair was a little too small for him. His legs were too long to fit directly under the table, and he had them stretched out a few inches past Bishop's side of the table. They both sat for a few moments, not saying anything. On a flat screen TV in the background, the movie *The Matrix* was playing without sound. The doors clinked as a new person came into the establishment.

"Last night was hype," Kevin said.

"Most def," Bishop replied.

"That girl, Christina… man, she look good! Wish I could take her back with me," Kevin said. "She even said she might want to get a plane ticket to come look for me in a few weeks."

"Oh?" Bishop found this interesting. "What happened? You kill it?"

"Boy, the most I did was feel it up still. The girl said she was on her period, so I didn't really want to mess with that. You ever link a girl when she on her period?"

Bishop paused for half a second. He had once, when he was drunk, with an ex-girlfriend. This however, was extremely taboo, even between best friends.

"No."

"Exactly! All that blood and what not! But the girl nice man, she still run some heads," Kevin said this last part with a chuckle.

As Kevin said this, the image of Elaine's head between his legs came to the forefront of his vision, then their subsequent couch frolicking. He felt himself getting hard in his shorts, and adjusted his position.

"This is the life man. Woman and good food. *Nuh true?*" Kevin said, raising a fist.

Bishop pounded his fist with his. "True, true."

A calm feeling washed over him, the kind that only a good conversation with a friend can stimulate. Bishop knew a lot of people in D.C—parties and schmoozing throughout the city did that—but not a lot of those people knew much about him past his schooling and where he lived. They didn't know anything about his childhood, his favorite music or what pissed him off. He was just another smiling face in a sea of faces in a city of mixed races. They couldn't make esoteric jokes that made him choke for air, nor could they reference girls he had been with, or give him much advice on the future. Kevin was one of his few beacons, a glimpse into himself through another person's reality.

Like Bishop, Kevin came from a well off family. While his father had a miniature empire dealing with imports and exports, Kevin's family was a double threat on the parent side. His father had studied at NYU where he received his MBA. His mother was a gynecologist. About eight years ago his father opened a financial consulting firm, now one of the most respected in Kingston. Kevin had leaned towards medicine for a while, and then gave up after seeing human cadavers. He was experimenting with his own business ideas while helping his father out. Now he was doing promotion for parties and launching a clothing line. They lived only two houses from each other, on the same avenue in a tucked away street in Jack's Hill, Kingston. As boys, there were few days he didn't see Kevin. Either they were playing games at his house, going to a party at his house, or going somewhere together. Until Bishop had left for the States, you hardly saw one person without the other. Last night was a reminder of an aspect of the weird beauty of friendship. He initially felt a twinge of envy when Kevin scored with Christina, but he realized Elaine was nice as well, and it's always better when two people score instead of just one.

Living in D.C with his nice apartment and car afforded him enough girls without too much work, but there was nothing like having your friend around to jab you, piss you off, make you laugh and remind you that you are alive. Each time he saw Kevin now, he was reminded of that specificity of his existence; the idea that some of the simplest things are the most important.

"Six thirty one!" a voice shouted. It was their order. The food was ready.

Chapter 9

Tony hated Sundays. They felt empty, like a huge warehouse that once buzzed with life, filled with the sweat and energy of dozens of workers, which had become a relic of the past, filled with the ghosts of old curse words, coffee breaks and forgotten drops of machine oil. Sundays made Tony remember why he felt alone, how disconnected he was from the people and things around him. On Sundays the walls of his apartment seemed to be closing in on him, their stucco frame sliding inwards at a slow rate, reminiscent of a popular Star Wars scene. He, Han Solo (of course) would be unable to escape, until the zero hour hit and he was saved. But he was never saved. There were Sundays he flipped open his cell phone and dialed almost everyone he knew. Friends from the past, current friends, girls who had flaked, one-night stands, but no one picked up. He would frantically send out text messages into the void of the wireless realm, and like a one-sided canyon, but he would never hear anything come back. On Sundays Tony felt frightened, as if the world was reminding him that he had to keep trying, that questioning his purpose and reason for existence couldn't be measured by the number of girls he had slept with, how well people interacted with him, or his creative talents. Sunday reminded him that he felt empty. The weekend was a roller coaster, with Friday being the high point and Saturday being the point of no return. If nothing happened by Saturday, he would have another lonely Sunday. He had a headache. He popped two aspirin and flopped back into his bed, staring at the ceiling.

Last night as usual, he went too hard. He had too much to drink, didn't get the girl's number and ended up walking too far to get home. Sunlight leaked into the room from underneath a curtain. It hit his eye, and he sighed. He couldn't stay inside. He needed to take a long walk. He slipped in his ear buds and listened to loud, aggressive dancehall music. The kind that made him want to grab a rifle and run to the hills, scattering the clouds with bullets while dancing with a girl at the same time. He went down his steps and outside.

Reading helped a little. He grabbed his latest novel, an Anne Rice book about the underworld of sadomasochism and headed out. Thirty minutes later, he was at the National Mall. It was a beautiful clear day, and in the distance, hundreds of people were walking around. Thick rays of light shot down from the sky and illuminated the leaves on the trees around. Tony felt calm whenever he went to the Mall. He would walk around, people watch, and sometimes meet someone. Most of the time, he just sat somewhere on a patch of grass, staring up at the sky and waiting for the day to be over. The night was his domain. His was a world of dive bars, clubs and happy hours. The night energy fed him. His days felt slow and awkward. He sometimes wondered if it was because he didn't have a girlfriend. Maybe if he had one they'd be watching a movie, going to a botanical garden or having afternoon sex. He had girlfriends occasionally, but they always disappeared or acted weird. Casual sex was the order of the day.

He continued his stroll down past the Washington Monument, watching sweaty bodies in the afternoon sun. Sun burnt kids played soccer passionately, barking at one another. In the distance Frisbee and kickball games were in full swing. Tony never understood kickball. What was it? Baseball with kicking? He walked past another group of people playing a casual game of soccer and stopped for a moment. A bench was near them. There he could sit and read, occasionally watching the progress of the game. His eye caught a thick-legged brunette chasing down the ball. *Varsity girl*, he thought. He flipped open the book, and started reading.

Chapter 10

The highway flashed by in a quiet blur of steel and concrete. On the horizon, the rippling surface of the Potomac was visible, between the dark shapes of cars driving to and fro.

"You ever thought about immortality?" Kevin asked.

"What?"

"Immortality. You know, ever-lasting life," Kevin said.

"Like vampires?"

"Hah, yes. Like vampires."

"Not really."

Kevin shuffled in his seat. He was wearing a close-fitting t-shirt, slim jeans and large dark glasses. With his tall legs bent slightly inwards, he looked like a rock star squirming after a hard question on late night TV.

"Why do you ask that?" Bishop said.

"Well, " Kevin said. He looked out the window, quiet for a few seconds.

"If we die, isn't all that's left of us what we did in this life? You know, the kids, the houses, the cars."

"I guess. Where is this coming from?" Bishop asked.

"Nowhere really," Kevin replied.

"No, tell me."

Bishop glanced at Kevin briefly. He was still looking out the window, his eyes invisible behind the large dark lenses of his designer glasses. The car was quiet, save the humming of the engine, and the occasional rattle of some loose change in the ashtray.

"When I die, I want hundreds of people to be at my funeral," Kevin said, his voice was flat and unemotional.

"I know when my father dies... what! Man, when he dies, there will be so many people at his funeral. He's the man. I want my funeral to be like that. I want people in high offices, owners of businesses and regular folks to be there."

"Well, I guess that's reasonable. Sort of like a state funeral," Bishop replied.

"No! More like just when a popular person dies. Nobody too famous, but a person famous in the right kind of way, you know?"

"Not really, but okay."

Bishop turned the car onto a ramp that had a display of a large airplane on it. They were approaching the Reagan National Airport. It loomed in the distance, a monolith of gray stone and glass.

"Either way, forget about that. This was a wicked trip boss. I had fun! Next time we tear up Jamaica again. Negril? Montego Bay?" Kevin said.

"Not sure about Negril... remember what happened last time with those German girls."

"Haha! I remember that. Well, we'll figure it out the next time you come. Big party in a few weeks. Grab a ticket and come through."

"No problem man," Bishop replied.

They pulled up to the American Airlines terminal. Bishop hopped out, meeting Kevin on the other side. He already had his bag; a sleek suitcase his father had purchased on a trip to Italy.

"All right big man! Next time!" Kevin clasped Bishop's hand in his, and they patted each other on the shoulder. The man-hug.

Kevin walked through a pair of sliding doors and disappeared. Bishop went back to the car, sitting for a few moments. The BMW purred quietly as he thought about Kevin's statement. What did it mean?

He pulled the car away from the curb and drove off, heading back to the city.

Chapter 11

The room was quiet and cold, beside him Elsa lay sleeping, her dark hair spilling over the cream colored pillows in their hotel room. Winston stood shirtless by the window, looking at the colorful vista of Barcelona in the early morning. A sea of brown buildings stretched into the distance, their rooftops slightly illuminated by the rising sun. Far away was the faintest outline of a mountain, and the tip of the sea. He took in a deep breath, wondering how he had ended up here. Only a year ago, he was at a party with a drink in his hand, and happened to say hello to Elsa. Now he was in Europe, looking out at the sweeping display of a foreign land, with her beside him. A slight draft squeezed under the window, and he headed back to the bed. Winston reached over and held Elsa close to him, her warm body causing goose bumps to rise all over his arms. Outside, the sun was rising, with soft rays of light trickling in. It was exquisite. Winston hadn't known such euphoria.

Winston was laughing as they walked down *Las Ramblas,* the most famous street in Barcelona. Thousands of people were walking about, shopping, laughing, and eating. That morning, they went to a small restaurant to get something to eat. The server spoke rapid Catalan, the language of this region of Spain, and it was a struggle to get the food. Winston spoke broken Spanish as best he could, and Elsa, even though she was from Barcelona, spoke little Catalan. A meal and a cup of coffee later, they were walking down Ramblas, hand in hand. A man dressed like Michael Jackson was standing frightfully still nearby.

"I want a picture!" Elsa said.

She ran over and Winston snapped a picture of her with her prized camera, a Leica. Today their destination was the waterfront. They were going to see the *Mare Magnum,* a large, very touristy mall that overlooked the Mediterranean Sean. First, they walked into a farmer's market. The smell of wine, fruit and gourmet cheese wafted into Winston's nose.

They ate some bread and cheese, sitting on a bench and people watching. They laughed together. Earlier that morning as they made love, Elsa had pinched Winston's nipple, which had caused him to erupt in a cacophony of laughter mid-coitus. In fact, Winston had no memory of ever laughing so much in his life. The days, months and years before all seemed to be a cold shroud from which he had emerged, with Elsa's face as a beacon of light leading him forward. It was pristinely intimate, pristinely valuable.

They walked past dozens of people selling souvenirs. Many of them were miniature Gaudí replicas. There were also miniature versions of the Cathedral and other large sites. There were flags, t-shirts, necklaces and rings. A store that sold discount clothes was a stop. They had everything inside for twenty euros and under. Winston had smiled with himself as he tried on a tight t-shirt while Elsa tried on two summer dresses. Each time Elsa came out, he felt pride tingle in his stomach. Whenever Elsa asked him how she looked, he would tell her she looked beautiful. She bought a bright orange dress. After the store, they walked carefree, toting their little plastic bags in their hands.

Sometimes as they walked through the crowd, Winston would see people walking with a single cane and a leg brace. *Polio?* There were huge throngs of people from all about walking around. Elsa would constantly point out the Americans. *They are the guys with the short haircuts*, she would say with a smile. Most of the time, she was correct. The Barcelona crowd was a colorful, exciting bunch. Kids with shaved heads with three thick locks at the back, or yellow and blue dyed hair wearing six-inch platform shoes seemed to be everywhere. The people looked like Elsa, darkly bronzed with black hair and distinct facial features. Painters of beautiful art hawked their works at the side of the road. Some men juggled while singing in Spanish, and everywhere, people were handing out flyers for parties later that night. The buildings were also beautiful as well, each with astounding attention to detail. Everything seemed hand touched by a sea of artisans.

They continued walking down *Las Ramblas*, looked at some more human statues, talking about how small the cars in Barcelona were, until they reached an open square. In the middle of the square was a statue of Christopher Columbus, pointing forward, to the "new world". A passerby snapped a photo of them at their request. In the background, the monstrous castle, *Montjuïc,* was visible, as well as a part of the air tram that took you up there. They went to *Mare Magnum* afterwards, and strolled through the mall, looking at clothes, and nibbling on bits of the cheese Elsa had bought. They stopped at a Starbucks—the largest Winston had ever been in—and talked. In this moment he looked at Elsa, her face reflected quietly against the well-polished glass of the opulent establishment, and she smiled back at him. In that moment, he felt truly, happy.

Then before he knew it, the trip was over. For him, the images and passion of the trip had rested a heavy weight on his shoulders; one that was now growing inside him. There was a new spark in his heart, a feeling of euphoria and attraction that didn't feel normal to him. Elsa had changed in his mind. She was *more,* and he wasn't sure what it meant. He thought about it the entire way back to D.C, while she mostly slept in her seat beside him, and he idly watched one of the in-flight movies.

Shortly after returning to D.C, he told her in a phone call he loved her. There was a long pause on the phone, to which Elsa replied, "That's sweet Winston."

After this, things became gradually awkward. The idea of his love invaded their relationship like a phantom, creating shadows and gloom where there was none. When they hung out, made love or ate together, if Winston looked at her with a smile in his eyes, there was something different in hers. The previous lingering curiosity now held questions, trepidation and elements of fear. She started doing more things with her friends, occasionally calling Winston drunk early in the morning, saying she wanted to see him. More time passed, and Winston realized he was losing her. Then one night she told him she wanted to travel for a while. Probably Europe, or South America, but she didn't want to do it with a boyfriend. That night felt like a brick to the head for Winston. He didn't say much that night, simply nodding quietly. There were no tears, no heavy-handed goodbye filled with kisses and hugs. The phantom was still there, lingering in the background, watching the proceedings. Elsa had become a stranger immediately, not cold, but distant. Her eyes had that same look of trepidation, and it would be the only thing Winston would remember on the walk home that night; the eyes of a stranger.

Chapter 12

It had been a while since he'd been in this part of Jamaica. Only two weeks before, after his phone buzzed a few times more than normal, did he make rapid plans to depart D.C.

"The flight is already taken care of," came the solemn voice of his mother.

Bishop nodded at the time, scrambling to pack a suitcase.

Now, Bishop was driving down a road covered in two feet of water. It had been raining heavily earlier that morning and the streets were partially flooded. Beside him in the passenger seat, was his cousin Shauna, and in the back seat were two of her friends. They were laughing.

Boy bands from the nineties was the hot topic. Bishop spoke frankly about the top Backstreet Boys songs, mentioning how some of them had great staying power. Shauna had argued that the NSYNC guys were cuter, and then Bishop asked Shauna to play a track from one of his play lists. The music blasted through the radio, and as they drove along, they were singing the words to "I will love you more than that". Some distance in front of them, the hazard lights of a dozen or more cars were flashing. The cars in front of them trudged ahead through the muddy water. The dense foliage of small forestry broke into a wide-open view of a sprawling estate dotted with small specks of grey as far as the eye could see. Bishop had seen this place before, with its tombstones and grave markers as far as the eye could see. This was the Dovecot Cemetery, a sprawling estate where people came to bury their dead. He was going to Kevin's funeral.

Bishop was still singing along to the song on the radio, with his cousins and their friends laughing along with him. He squinted to see the hazard lights of the cars in front of him, and saw that they were quite some distance away. A sense of urgency clamped around his throat. His mind flashed back to the Church earlier, to the moment after the sermon.

Kevin's childhood friends (his as well) were all crying and could barely function. They held onto his large coffin weakly as they carried it to the hearse. Bishop was a tower of composure. He wasn't sure how to react, and so didn't. He did however; want to be one of those carrying his friend's body to the grave. It was a quiet sermon, with three hundred or so people in attendance. He was one of the men that held on to the massive coffin holding Kevin's body.

"I remember Kevin," A tall lady with curly hair had said. "He was so tall and handsome. The first time he came into the office for a summer job, he was wearing a full suit and tie, I thought he was the new boss!"

The congregation had erupted into laughter. Bishop had laughed too, remember how seriously Kevin had taken small jobs a few years back. As the laughing died down, the lady raised a handkerchief to her left eye, dabbing a tear. "He will truly be missed," she said quietly.

A splash of water on the windshield brought Bishop back to reality. His car was trailing behind the group because of the water, and a frightening urgency filled him. The pallbearers were those people who held the coffin, usually four to six men. It was the most important role of any funeral; the men walking grim faced and solemn with the body to the final resting place. If he arrived a few minutes later, he wouldn't be one of those men.

He pulled into the cemetery, cursing at a series of speed bumps that stretched for a few hundred feet in front of him. In the distance, he saw the rest of the procession already walking toward the gravesite. The car was quiet now, and no song played from the radio. He quickly parked the car and hopped out, running into wet, red mud. The hearse was parked about forty feet away, and it was empty. Another fifty feet away, a huddled group of people in black stood in a circle. Between some arms and legs, he could see the slight movements of something being rested on a series of poles, ropes and planks: Kevin's coffin. He ran towards the gravesite, cursing himself for reaching late. Around the grave, faces were grim. Kevin's father stood there, silent as a stone. Bishop's father stood a few feet behind him, looking at Bishop with a sadness he had never seen. Bishop breathed heavily, flustered. The coffin was already on the ropes to be lowered into the grave. Dammit! He wanted to be a pallbearer. He was supposed to be one of the procession taking his friend to his final resting place. He felt hot under his suit. The preacher, a man of medium height with a large stomach expertly contoured to his funeral garb, was holding a bible. He said it was time for the final hymn. A mournful song began, and Bishop felt a crushing sadness hit his system. For the week or so that he knew his friend was dead, there was no shock within him. He had operated normally, had slept normally and didn't even feel sad. When he got the news that Kevin had shot himself in the head with a 9mm pistol, it seemed weird. It seemed as if it was something that had happened to someone else, somewhere else, far, far away. It was today that he saw the body for the first time, seeing how grey and cold his friend looked. His head was distended in a strange way. The skin too tight, the shape of the head different. Kevin's nose, normally straight and prominent, was flat. His sandy brown skin color was now the color of death. It looked nothing like him. If it weren't for his broad chest and the familiar large hands now resting on his midriff, Bishop would almost be able to lie to himself and say he wasn't dead. That wasn't his friend in front of him. That was someone else. Something else.

He could hear Kevin's voice echoing in his mind from the last time he had seen him, a few months before. They had laughed and spoken about normal things. Bishop had fallen asleep on his couch, as he always did. At some point he had woken up, laughing and slightly embarrassed. Kevin had walked over, given him a hearty slap on the back and beamed his thousand-watt smile. "We'll see each other later," Kevin had said. That was the last time Bishop saw him. Now he was standing at the graveside, and the funeral home men, men with skin shined black from years of burying bodies, began the slow process of lowering the coffin. Then, from a place deep within him, Bishop was hit with a cascade of memories. Him and Kevin partying around Kingston, traveling to America, arguing about video games, counseling one another about women, working out together, laughing, fighting, greeting and smiling. The thoughts pounded him in the face like the final blows of a heavyweight match. Each memory hit him with a bright shock, and he felt his body shudder. Kevin really is gone, Bishop's mind said. The coffin started to move lower, and then Bishop knew he would never see him again. He instinctively reached forward, as if to stop the men from taking his friend away, and there was his father, resting his hand on his shoulder. His father's hand felt like granite on his flesh and Bishop became manic. He started to scream and tears burst from his eyes. "Kevin can't be gone!" he shouted. "Kevin was my boy. He was my boy."

A quiet fell over the entire congregation as Bishop wailed with the intensity of a newborn. Kevin was his best friend, his confidant, and now he had been ushered into a place where everyone goes, but he had gone too soon. As the men started tossing dirt on top of the coffin, he rushed the graveside, falling to his knees, smearing his suit with red mud, clutching his head in dismay. He started talking to the dirt. "How could you do this to me!" he screamed, "Why didn't you talk to me?" he asked. "God dammit why didn't you say anything!" he shouted, as tears and snot fused into a wet stream on his face. "We were supposed to do things, and go to places," he wailed. "We were supposed to do things."

As he knelt there in the mud, an overwhelming emptiness hit him. The sounds and images around him faded and for a while, he wasn't at the cemetery. He felt distant, hidden within the folds of grief and shock. When he stood up, the lights around him felt different, the sky had a different luminosity, and the faces around him, those of his friends and family, seemed strange and distant. He was no longer the same person. The past echoed in a cacophony that fell into some unseen chasm inside him, and Bishop knew that he would never be the same.

Chapter 13

Tony walked down the wide strip that was 18th Street, navigating his way expertly through the crowd. Behind him was his friend Ben, a short Italian guy with a penchant for curse words, rapid conversation and a taste for African-American women. The night was unseasonably warm and people were out in droves. There were so many people milling about, the street had been closed to traffic and bodies moved to and fro like a colony of ants. Drunk people roamed the streets, and every few seconds a person with a slice of pizza too large to fit on one plate would traipse back and forth. They walked into a bar near the top of the street. A tall bouncer with a shaved head and dark eyes took their IDs. He spoke with a heavy African accent, and smiled at Tony and Ben as they walked inside. Ben went straight to the bar.

"What are you drinking?" he asked.

"Get me a Bud Light," Tony replied.

On the dance floor, under the intermittent flashing of strobe lights, were a few dozen tightly packed bodies. The thick smell of sweat, perfume and cologne had fused to create what Ben called "Bar Smell". In the middle of the dance floor, a girl with a tiara with a long strip of white cloth attached to it, danced with a few friends. *Bride-to-be*, Tony thought.

He saw these women around occasionally, faces flushed from Tequila shots, eyes darting rapidly around the bar almost chanting *this is it*. They would float on an air of inebriated uncertainty about their respective futures with the bridesmaids bringing up the rear with verbal tokens of goodwill chased with Jagermeister. Standing near to her, with calm, protective smiles were three cute girls. Beside them, two frat boys stood up, both of them in pastel polo shirts, with baseball caps turned backwards. A few feet away from them, a set of girls danced with practiced rhythm, their dark bodies moving expertly to the club music. One of them had locks that flashed around seductively. One of the others seemed entranced by the atmosphere, dancing with her eyes closed as a man held her from behind. People were stuffed into every iota of space; hidden in the shadows, or scrunched on the dance floor. There were too many people to look cool, too many people to relax, not sweat, or chill out. Ben came back with the Bud Light, and Tony took a sip. Without hesitation, Ben moved towards the girl with the locks, flashing a smile. Tony watched him say something to her. Their voices were muted by the noise of the music coming from the speakers. Already, she was laughing. Now she was shaking his hand.

"I'm Ben," he could see Ben say to the girl. Now they were dancing, and Ben gave him a rapid wink of his left eye. A hand touched Tony's waist. Beside him, was a short girl wearing a very plain grey dress. Her face was average, but she had well toned arms and a fiery intensity in her eyes.

"Why aren't you dancing with anyone?" she asked.

"I don't really dance," Tony replied.

She smirked.

"My friends were wondering who the tall, attractive guy was, and I said he'd dance with us," she said.

She gestured towards a group of girls standing near the speakers. They all had the same well-toned look, and the giggly energy of a group of best friends out for a night on the town. They smiled and waved. The girl held Tony's hand and led him through the crowd. Sweaty hands, wet dress shirts and all types of hair touched Tony's hands as he walked through the crowd towards the group of ladies.

"I'm Susan," the girl said. "This is Mary, Bethany and Misty."

"Hi, I'm Tony."

Susan began dancing and gripped Tony's hands with the strength of a gym rat. Tony moved against her, her body lithe and firm. She moved around him and slid her body up and down his from behind, and Tony could feel the firmness of her breasts go down his back and rest briefly on his buttocks.

"We think its wrong for the hot guy to stand there by himself," Susan said into his ear, her eyes twinkling.

Tony smiled with her. One of her friends came over and said something into her ear. "We're getting drinks, what would you like?" She asked.

"I'll have whatever you are having," Tony replied.

The four women walked in a line easily through the crowd. A tall man with dark eyes said something to Susan. She laughed and kept walking. A hand touched Tony. It was Ben.

"Who are these girls?" he asked.

"I don't even know," Tony replied.

Tony asked Ben about the girl he was talking to.

"She's nice man. Just hanging around a bit because she went to take a piss. Let me know what's up with these girls."

Tony told him he'd shoot him a text message. At the bar, the ladies were doing shots. The girl in the grey dress had one in hand for Tony. By the better light of the bar, he noticed her features. Auburn hair, with cloudy grey eyes. She had a nice smile. They did shots and returned to their original spot. Ben was there.

"She bounced with her friends, but I have her number."

Tony introduced Ben to the group. One of the girls, a tall brunette in a tight fitting black dress gave him a lingering smile. As time passed, the music got better and the Tony gave the DJ a high five on a trip to the bathroom.

The dancing between him and the girl had been escalating erotically and he knew it would be time to leave soon. The Brunette, Misty, had the two other girls staying by her place for the weekend. Apparently they were all friends from school in Minnesota. The crowd started to thin and Tony whispered into Susan's ear: "What's the plan?"

"I have drinks at my place," she replied.

"What about the girls?" Tony asked with genuine concern.

"Oh, we live three blocks from each other. We'll stop at Misty's place first and then head back to my place. Is that okay with you?"

"That's fine," Tony replied.

They left six strong and started the ten-minute walk towards Mount Pleasant, where Misty lived. Ben entertained Misty with interesting conversation and Tony chatted to the group about nothing in particular. He felt Susan's hand squeeze his, and could feel her eyes undressing him. He wondered how her body looked in the soft glow of a night lamp.

At Misty's house, the games continued. Ben and the girls started a rousing game of beer pong. In a hallway nearby, Susan kissed Tony passionately. He felt himself getting hard and so did she. He broke the kiss.

"Let's go and play some pong," he said. She laughed and replied, "Yes."

"Your friend is so cool!" the girls said as Tony and Susan walked into the room. Ben laughed.

The night became dull as the beers kept pouring. Tony felt his body soft with alcohol, the sounds around him somewhat muted. Laughter from the group echoed slowly in his ears, as they drank and high fived one another. Ben's face was red now, covered in a smile laced with innuendo. Susan was smiling too, occasionally giving Tony a peck on the neck. Some of the ladies started feeling sleepy and Ben was overjoyed to get Misty's number.

"Oh my God she is hot!" Ben said as they left the house.

Tony laughed and told the group goodbye as he walked with Susan to her place. She lived in a row house a block away. It was a quiet, clean apartment that smelled like potpourri. Immediately she was on Tony, and in moments they were naked in the hallway. Her body was firm; her scent mixed with perfume the slightest hint of alcohol. During the jostling, Tony found a condom from his wallet. They never made it upstairs.

He woke up the next day in the living room, curled up on the carpet. He felt cold and slightly sick. The night before was a blur, and the girl sleeping beside him felt like a stranger. *Susan, that's her name,* Tony said to himself. He walked to a nearby bathroom, and looked at himself in the mirror. He felt sick again, and gritted his teeth. A light sadness enveloped him for a few minutes. Outside, a car rolled by in the early morning. With Susan still sleeping on the ground, he slipped outside, into the light of day. Tony sighed.

Chapter 14

Bishop wasn't like this. He didn't do coke. Ever. Everything about him felt far away, locked into the box that went into the ground months before. On the table in front of him, the three lines of cocaine lay alongside one another like bleached sand dunes. Eddy, to his left, was playing Guitar Hero and missing every note. Behind him, Kelsey was chatting gibberish, her face bright pink from alcohol. "I have no FUCKING BUDGET!" she screamed, darting into Roy's room. Roy was a DJ in town who Bishop had recently met. He was a tall Italian-American from New York with a thick Queens's accent. This was the after party for an event at a Bar on U Street. Kelsey was screaming about her parents cutting off her allowance, even though she had a job that paid her a hundred thousand a year. Roy looked at Bishop and mouthed "Cokehead" with a sly smile and followed her into the bedroom.

"Fuck me, and fuck Guitar Hero," Eddy said, dropping the guitar controller on the floor with a clatter. He stumbled over to the table. "Hey, you wanna do a line?"

Bishop thought about where he was. In the middle of D.C with drunk people he barely knew, hanging out in the nice apartment of a girl who was apparently, a cokehead.

"Okay," he replied.

Eddy leaned over with a rolled up bill in his hand. With a swift gesture and a quick snort, one line disappeared. "Dollar bills are the best," he said. "Sometimes a twenty will fuck everything up."

"Yeah, I know what you mean," Bishop said, lying.

Bishop leaned over the table and took Eddy's bill. He snorted a line, feeling the little crystals travel up into his nasal passage. Bishop waited, but nothing happened. He made himself a vodka cranberry and walked over to the couch. Mary, Eddy's girlfriend, was asleep. She wasn't very cute, but had a great sense of style. The video game was blinking on screen, with the prompt "NEW GAME?" flashing at regular intervals.

Bishop walked into rear of the apartment and found a small, but clean bathroom. He flipped a switch and was blasted with light. Eight bulbs were on the mirror, four on each side. He looked at himself. His skin was faded and he looked yellow, but it could have been the light. He ran the water and doused his face with some icy water, and felt nothing.

Outside, Kelsey was screaming again. A door slammed and Bishop jumped back in shock, almost falling into the tub. The lights in the bathroom seemed brighter, and he was very awake. The coke was kicking in.

Outside the couch was empty now, and Eddy was gone. Roy was standing near the table, sipping on a drink. "Fuck this place man. Let's go."

Bishop felt a pulse of life surge through his veins. His mood was neutral a few minutes ago, now he felt like going to the gym, having sex and watching a Lord of the Rings marathon all at the same time.

"You gonna take that before you bounce?" Roy said, pointing towards the last line.

Why not, Bishop thought, and snorted it quickly.

Roy was out of the door in seconds, and Bishop followed suit. The night air, a thick cloud of humidity, felt different. A hip-hop song trickled through the air from somewhere; an odd vocal inflection over dull bass-beats. Was it the rapper, T-pain? Roy pulled out a sleek phone from his pocket.

"Uh huh. Where? Nah I'm not doing anything. I'm with my man Bishop, this cool fucking dude from Jamaica. Nah, he doesn't have any weed haha! Okay man, see you in a few."

It was a party nearby, a few blocks shy of Kelsey's apartment in Adams Morgan. Roy said there would be more girls and more drugs. Bishop felt a cold surge of regret. He had never taken drugs. Was this the wrong thing to do? *It felt so good,* his mind replied. It was a six-block walk to the party. On the way, two cute blonde girls tugged on Roy's shirt. "I like your shirt," One of them said. Bishop could smell the vodka on her even from six feet away.

Roy laughed and wished them goodnight. Bishop eyed the friend on the left. She was pretty cute, but they were both toasted and he didn't like drunk girls. Something about the second girl made him stop. Then, he remembered.

Kevin had a girlfriend from Norway once. Her name was Marta. That girl looked like her. It reminded him of a night they had gone out in New Kingston. It was Marta and her friends, six exchange students living in Kingston out for a night on the town. Kevin and Bishop had looked like serious pimps, strolling down the road with eight tall, attractive white women. That night he had felt powerful, in the same way he felt now. But Kevin was gone.

The other party was mayhem. The terrace was packed with people, and the din of music and voices inside spilled out into the night air. A smile was plastered across Bishop's face. They went inside. The crowd was mixed, but mostly white. The smell of alcohol and sweaty bodies lingered in the air. A hand pinched his buttocks. Bishop turned to see a cute girl with a beer in her hand. "Why'd you come here so late?" the girl said.

"You know I had to make an entrance," Bishop replied.

A weird feeling quivered through his system. He never spoke like that. It sounded like something a dashing TV actor would say.

"What's your name?" she said.

"It's a mystery," Bishop said with a laugh.

He twirled her, and she acquiesced, spinning a little too quickly. He walked quickly into the crowd. The kitchen was chaos. Spilled chips and beer had coalesced into a sticky puddle on the counter. Hundreds of red cups, most half-full were everywhere. Bishop made himself another vodka cranberry. He felt tall, very tall. He leaned against a wall.

"Hey, didn't I see you last week?" a voice said.

Bishop turned to see a girl staring at him. She was short, with mocha colored skin.

"I don't think you did," Bishop said with a grin.

"Let me ask you a question. Do you believe in fate?" the girl asked.

Bishop took a moment to size her up. There was an immediate quality to her that floated into the mix of his senses. Her eyes were large and captivating; they were voluminous and questioning, but not strange in their appearance. Her face was a light oval shape, and a lip ring was nestled in the lower right section of her bottom lip. She had a flat button nose. She looked almost fairy-like in the dim light.

"Fate, I wanna live forever," Bishop sang weakly.

"Haha! You are funny, but I think that song is "fame", not fate," she said with a smile.

Bishop had seen her before. These days he went to Starbucks a lot, idly surfing the Internet on his laptop, drinking cup after cup of coffee even though he had stacks of gourmet at his house. He saw her sometimes, walking in with a pair of plaid pants on. They fit her nicely. Tonight, she was wearing a black skirt with a huge white belt. Sparkly.

"So what's your name?" she said.

"Bishop."

"Bishop? wow, that's different."

"Yeah, and my last name is Chung!"

"Chung? "

"Yeah, my mother is Chinese. Well, half-Chinese."

"You don't look Chinese."

"I'm from Jamaica, anybody with a drop of Chinese blood is called Chinese."

"You're Jamaican? You don't sound Jamaican."

"Wait till I take you to my bedroom."

Bishop laughed awkwardly. He felt sexual power raging through his thin frame.

"Okay, a little weird Bishop. I'm Monica by the way, thanks for asking!" she said, slapping him on the shoulder. The slap felt like a moth landing on his arm.

He glanced for a second into a bedroom, through a door that had opened near him. Bishop could clearly see a floor with smooth, spotted tiles and light furnishings on the inside. The room was large and bare, save a tiny futon and a very old television. In this room a few girls were standing around idly. One girl was standing on the bed, even though she was wearing a pair of dirty Chuck Taylors. She had a very sharp haircut. A huge guy in a white t-shirt walked by the girls, and then the door shut.

He looked back for Monica, but she was gone. He looked at his cup; it was already empty, even though he had no memory of drinking it. He went back to the kitchen. Roy was in there.

"Yo Bishop! What can I get you man!" Roy said with a bright smile.

"I guess a vodka cranberry," Bishop said, his voice trailing off. Outside the kitchen, a lot of people started murmuring. A guy with a baseball cap walked past.

"Look's like the cops are shutting the party down," he said.

"Ah, dammit, I just met this cool chick too!" Roy said. "Here you go, man."

He handed Bishop the drink and darted into the crowd. Bishop sipped on his drink as the crowd began to thin. The music had stopped and the sound of meshed conversations bounced off the walls. A few feet beside, him a familiar figure emerged from a hallway. She stood beside another girl with a drink in her hand.

"Monica," Bishop said.

"Hey!" Monica replied, walking over.

Her eyes froze for a second and a frown broke on her face.

"Oh shoot! I am so sorry, I already forgot your name!" she said.

Bishop smiled at her for a few moments. Monica kept talking.

"I swear this doesn't happen to me, tell me your name again please."

Bishop didn't reply.

"Oh come on, man," Monica said, her voice half-laughing.

Bishop held out his hand for her to hold it. "This a memory exercise I'm going to teach you. You ready?" He said.

Monica nodded.

"Okay, I'm going to hold your hand like this. Now, look into my eyes. My name is Bishop. Bishop Chung. Repeat it."

"Bishop. Bishop Chung."

"One more time."

"Bishop. Bishop Chung."

"Okay there you go."

Bishop loved the way her hands felt. They were soft and smooth and had an elegant richness. Monica turned to her friend and excitedly told her about the memory trick. Bishop felt his arms trembling slightly. Time to leave. He started walking away. He heard Monica's voice.

"Hey Bishop, are you on Facebook or something?"

"No," he replied.

"Maybe I'll see you around?"

"Maybe."

"What's my name again?"

"Bishop. Bishop Chung. Wow that trick really works!"

"There you go. Later gator."

Later gator?

Bishop walked outside, coasting on the last of his cocaine. Roy was nowhere to be seen. He walked quickly to 18ᵗʰ Street and hopped into a cab. He flopped into the back seat. "Georgetown please," he said to the cab driver.

The driver, a middle-aged man of Middle Eastern descent turned around. "If you are drunk, please do not throw up in the cab. It will be seventy dollars."

"I'm not drunk," Bishop said with a laugh. "Just, happy."

The cab pulled off, with the lights of D.C screaming by as Bishop floated in and out of consciousness. He pulled his cell phone out of his pocket and dialed a phone number. A voice answered.

"Big man I have to tell you about tonight!" Bishop said. "Kevin, if you only knew how the girls in America are, you would piss your pants."

"Kevin?" the voice interrupted.

"Yes, this is Bishop. Am I speaking to…" his voice trailed off.

Bishop looked at phone in horror and clamped it shut. He let out a groan, and a cold feeling spread across his chest. Kevin was dead.

"Are you all right, sir?" the cab driver said.

"Just take me home," Bishop replied, with his eyes closed. "Just take me home."

Chapter 15

It's easy to float in D.C, Winston thought. Floating between purpose, ambition and reality. He fiddled with the handle of his portable laundry basket, which was actually a small grocery cart. Swamped in the thick heat of the Laundromat near his apartment, he deposited coins into various machines. He sat directly across from one of the washers, watching it come to life with a *sssswish*. The machines hummed a relaxing cacophony of soapy notes. Through the large panel windows at the Laundromat's entrance, Winston looked at the long stretches of asphalt leading endlessly into the distance, the mark of man's architectural brilliance. A girl ran by, pale and sunburnt, ponytailed and sweating profusely in running tights and a yellow sports tank top, jamming to some unknown album through white ear buds. In her Winston saw an MBA, an NGO or a close end to an undergraduate degree. Her eyes had steely resolve as she ran in place at the stop light. It changed and she was gone.

Winston sometimes ventured to Georgetown to see these types run, the glow of an evening sun baking pale or dark bodies, people running to nothing and from everything. In Georgetown, he could smell the difference in society. The intermittent cobblestone streets, the upscale stores. The waterfront with its yachts idling on the Potomac, bakeries with prices that made him blush, nightclubs with expensive drink sand places that one needed *savoir faire* to access. It reminded him of the first time he had ever visited Devon House, an old mansion in the heart of New Kingston that now served as a hangout spot. The place had screamed upper class and bourgeoisie, and there was this *scent* about it all. Ancient Oak trees and carefully manicured wood, people with lighter complexions and energies hanging about. For little Winston, it felt like a screening room for the elite. It was as if places like this and Georgetown were living, breathing entities, able to ooze pheromones that attract their ilk, and warded off those unfamiliar with such territory. But just as easily you can float over to parts of Southwest D.C and see dangerously dilapidated buildings, people with the marks of a tense daily life etched into their faces; the roar of sirens in the distance; music streaming from cars and houses. There, Winston didn't smell society as much; he just smelled a situation. It was an area, plodded down on fields and valleys as man had always done, etching his signature on the art board of the world.

Winston's apartment was on a sleepy street in the Northwest Ward of D.C, near Howard University, U Street and the rest of gentrification's burgeoning landscape. But D.C was simply D.C, a place he called home. The bi-weekly trip to the Laundromat was a two-hour exercise in idle reflection, as he mentally drifted in between the different wards of D.C like an angel, creating a thesis no one would ever read. As he dropped the freshly washed clothes into a dryer, he knew these were the least of his thoughts of late.

Some say there is an equilibrium that exists in each person; an appropriate division of emotion, feeling and purpose that allows them to function every day. This equilibrium develops into psychology, wants and needs, regrets and desires, fears and phobias. He had been thinking about his equilibrium of late, because relative to the past, it felt so, so different. Some time ago, Winston sat on a bench somewhere in the city, looking up at the sky. The world around him had felt different, almost empty and he wondered where the feeling came from. It seemed that the past was a blanket of dark space, and where he was sitting in the present was a completely new reality, some shifted paradigm that had produced a new him, birthed fully grown; a man.

His mind floated briefly to his teenage years, and for a moment, his left hand trembled with thoughts of the past, his memories peppered with dark voices and flashes of red. In those days things had density. The time spent dreaming about getting a video game, the affection of a girl or just the idle free time of summer—these things all had a specific weight that children could touch and hold. But now, everything felt ephemeral and misty.

This dull haze of thought enveloped him for a while. Eventually, the machines made a dull *hrmmm* and came to a stop. Winston came back to reality, took his clothes, stuffed them into a small duffle bag and started wheeling them back home in his shopping cart. The apartment screamed with silence, and he decided to go for a walk. He remembered there was an event somewhere on U Street, some kind of poetry thing. In fifteen minutes, he was in front of the place, *Latte Life*. He stood quietly by a column, watching people speak their minds about life, love and the tortured history of America. The small coffee shop was a sea of mixed faces enamored by the passionate speakers. At some point, a hand touched Winston. He turned to a see a short woman, with a head of curly hair pulled into one, strong eyes smiling at him through rimmed glasses. "I'm glad it was you," she said. "Or else that would have been really awkward."

Winston felt a rush of familiarity. It was Amy. She was a college friend, the kind of girl who was cool with both girls and guys. She had been in a few organizations, ran for a few positions. She gave him a strong hug, and Winston could smell her skin, rich with the scent of some kind of fruity shower gel. Time slowed and his mind flashed back. *Amy, Amy, Amy.* There had been something there perhaps, a hint of possibility in their mutual naiveté. There were nights she would fall asleep in his dorm room, her hair mussed on the pillow, the soft rise and fall of her chest like music to his eyes, but he was too shy to make a move at the time. Did he try? A man's college experience tends to be riddled with stories of failure, perceived or otherwise.

"I have to leave right now, but hit me up sometime," she said, whipping out a cell phone.

Winston took the number.

"Good to see you," he said, trying his best to smile.

She nodded and stepped out of the shop, into the night. The sounds of the poetry cipher faded as Winston racked his brain. Had there been something between them? A night when he said something about his feelings? Maybe she didn't reciprocate. It could have been anywhere. In front of the school cafeteria, behind the bleachers were people would smoke and occasionally play cards, or it could have been in the city at a fast food eatery. Whatever it was, that was years ago, lost in a mosaic of frozen moments in time. But she was a friend, a friend he hadn't seen in a while.

He could still smell her on him, and as he thought of the hug, he realized that was the first time someone had touched him in what seemed like forever. It was almost funny, the idea that physical touch could become a foreign thing. After another hour, Winston stepped outside. Some eager patrons had taken the festivities to the sidewalk. A small group was huddled around a young man playing his guitar. While he strummed a beat, a group of young men did freestyles. As they stood there, their voices and lips moving in tandem with the notes, he thought of communities of old, where people sat around bonfires chanting and enjoying the pleasures of knowing each other, happy in their knowing.

Winston stood to the side, quietly watching them. Every now and then, someone else would join the group. People would laugh, hugs would be exchanged, and the tempo of energy would increase. A part of Winston wanted to step into the circle and start rhyming along with them. He wanted to sing his heart out, relishing the rush that would come from the positive energy of the group. He watched the smiles, laughs, adlibs and gestures, fading more and more into the background. *These people know each other*, he told himself. *They've known each other for years. They don't know you.*

He walked away, hearing a roar of laughter from the group. Whatever happened, he would never know. Walking back home, he thought about Elsa. In his mind, he was back in Barcelona. It was a slightly chilly evening, and they were standing on the beach, looking at huge black rocks jutting out into the sea. Elsa was wearing his sweater, her body lost in the slightly oversized garment. The sun had started to set, and a creamy reddish orange glow was softly painting the city skyline. He never forgot her eyes that day, the contentment in her expression. Winston wished he had said it, that he loved her, but he had held it in, hidden behind the folds of his mind.

He could hear her saying "Can you believe we are here!" and he could feel her fingers massaging his neck, something she did for no real reason. He could feel her stand close, feeding off his warmth as they stared at the vast expanse of the Mediterranean in front of them. Then, the sunset vanished and he was back at his apartment, looking at a brown door set in red brick. A sudden sadness enveloped him. He pulled his phone out and scrolled down to E. There it was, her name and number. His thumb trembled as it hovered over the send button. He shut the phone off.

As he walked inside, he heard someone in the opposite apartment laugh. The sound echoed throughout the emptiness of his apartment, bouncing across the dark walls, and gradually, outside, into the evening, where the sound dissipated into a low hum, joining the frequencies of the melee outside.

Chapter 16

Friday night. A time when the suits and ties got tossed into crumpled heaps on the floor, old rock music blared from the air conditioner vents of European cars, and people ran to happy hours with arms flailing. Tony's Fridays were the same; a blur of music, bodies and drinking that was missing a theme song. After eating a late dinner in Chinatown, he headed to the strip. The scene was the same. Lots of frat boy types, ivy-league girls, Ethiopians and every other minority with an advanced degree. Even now, people were walking into the used mom-and-pop shops, looking for an old gem, a dirty magazine, or foreign food. Tony headed to Bubble, a small dive bar. He saw Mick, the bartender. He was a tall, bronzed guy that resembled the lead singer of an Indie Rock Band.

"Tony my man, how's it going?" Mick asked.

"Same old, you know," Tony replied.

"What are you drinking?"

"Ah, Give me a Guinness."

Tony pulled a crisp ten-dollar bill out of his pocket. Mick waved it away.

"Don't worry about it man. This one's on me."

"Thanks man," Tony said.

Tony walked up a set of faded brown steps, listening to his foot creak on wood. Upstairs, a few people stood by the bar, and the DJ, a fat guy with a huge white t-shirt on, ardently paid attention to his laptop. The crowd was thin but groovy. He stood in a corner for a few minutes, quietly observing the crowd while listening to the music. A set of girls came up the stairs and a familiar face caught his eye. Casey.

He had met her six months ago, at a bar in Columbia Heights. That night, he and his friend Andrew were standing near the dance floor, somewhat bored. The DJ was playing some funk music, and the patrons, decked out in clothes fit for a day of TV and ribs on a Sunday, danced feverishly to the music. Casey came by, talking to Andrew first.

"Do you mind if I hang with you guys? My friend totally ditched me," she had asked, glancing at them quickly with a dart of her eyes.

"No problem," Andrew had replied.

Andrew had launched into what seemed to be quite interesting conversation with Casey. As they talked, Tony noticed her eyes float over to him every thirty seconds or so. At some point, he had said hello, then went downstairs. That night he toyed with the idea of playing a song on the jukebox. Maybe that hit Orgy had back in the day—Blue Monday—or if he could find it, some poppy reggae song that everyone knew, like "Heads High" by Mr. Vegas. He decided not to, and grabbed a beer at the bar downstairs, trading a few stories with a cute bartender who did part-time school at Maryland. When he came back upstairs, Casey's friend had returned (a thick-legged girl named Charlotte who worked on the Hill) and Casey was dancing with Andrew.

They had rocked slowly to some funk song that sounded like James Brown and Tony caught her eyes watching him again. In fifteen minutes, they had switched partners. Tony felt Casey's arms slip firmly onto his waist, and she brought her face within inches of his. She had a shy, endearing nature to her. Her cheeks were small put prominent, her eyes watery and filled with a strange quietness. Her body was curvy and she had amazing rhythm (it must have been because she was from California) and Tony had wanted her. Usually he'd lean forward, staring directly into her eyes and initiate a kiss, but he didn't. He was as hard as granite, and she playfully thrust her hips on him. That night, they never hooked up.

Like a lot of cute girls he met, she had completely flaked. Tony theorized it had to do with her being new to the city at the time (girls like that generally like to mess around a bit before they got settled) but he wasn't ever sure. He called her twice and left two voice messages. She picked up the first time, saying something about "Are you sure you're going to call me back?" After that, she didn't answer any more calls. It didn't matter, later that week Tony had met another girl, a History Major from Howard named Sarah, and Casey was all but forgotten, until now. Tony walked behind her and pinched her neck.

"Can I buy you a drink?" he said in a high, nasal voice.

"Tony!" Casey squealed, giving him a hug. She paused in mid-hug. "By the way, that was really creepy."

Tony laughed. Casey was wearing a grey and black striped dress over a pair of skinny jeans. A long necklace made from fat green beads hung between her breasts. She had a drink in one hand. Tony looked into her eyes and felt a chill run through him. He still liked them. They were warm, and calm. Her hair was a little longer than last time, but she looked the same. This time, the chemistry worked. After a few drinks and sweaty dances, they stood by the bar. There, Tony turned to her when ordering a drink.

"Why do I want to kiss you right now?" he said.

"What's stopping you?" she asked, looking directly at him.

He leaned over and kissed her, pulling back for a few seconds. Her tongue was strong and well trained, and Tony knew she wouldn't flake this time.

"Wait, not here. Not yet. Let's dance a bit," he said.

They had their drinks and danced to a few poppy songs with Casey's friends. They were two tall girls with bright smiles and breaths laced with alcohol. As he danced, Tony asked the fat DJ to play him a song, but he didn't. His phone vibrated. Someone had sent him an invite to a club.

"Do you know Mini? That new spot in Dupont?" he said to Casey.

She nodded.

"I feel like going over there. I'm on the list to get in. Me plus three."

"Sure, let's go," she said.

"Your friends?" Tony said.

"They are going somewhere else. It's cool, don't worry," Casey said, giving his arm a squeeze.

Her friends hugged her goodbye. "My roommate is spending the night by a friend," Casey whispered into Tony's ear.

They walked to an ATM and grabbed some cash. Tony hailed a cab, and in moments they were in Dupont Circle. A bouncer at least six-foot eight was standing at the door. Before Tony had even taken out his ID, the bouncer warned: "Fifteen for you, ten for her."

"No problem," Tony said with a smile.

Inside the soft throbs of hip-hop music floated down from upstairs. In a few moments, Casey was standing beside him. A small chubby guy was sitting in a booth at the end of a short hallway.

"Fifteen for you, ten for her," he said flatly.

"Hey, I'm on the list, last name Edwards," Tony said.

He looked at the list. "Tony Edwards?"

"That's me," Tony replied.

"Where are your three?" the man said, raising an eyebrow. Then he noticed Casey standing quietly behind Tony. "Okay, just you two. Go ahead."

"Thanks," Tony replied.

As they walked up the stairs, Tony turned to Casey. "Isn't it cool hanging with me?"

"Yes, it is," she replied, her face laced with sexual innuendo.

Upstairs opened into a huge space. The place was classy, with marble top counters, plush chairs in a lounge area in the back, and a dance floor that showed the DJ spinning records two levels up. They walked to the bar, and Tony recognized the girl behind the counter. Her eyes opened to twice their normal size.

"Tony!" she chirped, and ran from behind the bar, giving him a bear hug.

"So great to see you!" she said.

Shyla, the bartender, was a gorgeous blonde with a face fit for modeling. She was wearing an outfit straight out of a bondage catalogue: a leather midriff, nonexistent tights and webbed stockings. Tony bought a few more drinks for himself and Casey and then went to the dance floor. They kissed in a dark corner while strobe lights flashed overhead. The alcohol in his system made everything sound dull, and as the bass tickled the bottom of his feet, he wanted to see her naked and hear her moan. She licked his lips while he occasionally kissed her neck, fingering the necklace.

"You want to get out of here?"

"Yeah," Casey replied, the cast of overhead lights giving her Goblin-like eyes.

He held her hand and headed outside. Within seconds they were in a cab. Casey told the driver where to go. Her place. After a few minutes, they reached her house. She lived somewhere near Mount Pleasant in a modest-sized apartment. Her room was small.

"Wow, nice place," Tony said.

"Yeah, its nine hundred bucks a month, but the area is pretty convenient," Casey replied, tossing her handbag to the floor.

Her laptop, a dusty well-aged MacBook, was open. She pressed the spacebar. One Republic's "Too Late to Apologize" blared through the tiny speakers. Tony chuckled. He would get laid to a breakup song. They began kissing heavily and flopped onto the bed. Casey reached behind her and shut off her lights. Tony slowly took off her shirt revealing small, firm breasts, with coral nipples. Her necklace still hung gracefully between them, and something about the necklace made Tony more excited than he had been in a while. He was ready, but his wallet had disappeared. No condom.

"Whoa. Where's my wallet?" Tony asked.

Casey laughed and fumbled in the dark through his clothes to find it. She was drunk, and so was Tony.

"Well, here's your passport," she noted with a laugh in her voice.

"A lot of good that will do," he said.

The wallet resurfaced and Tony found the condom. His head spun a bit and his bladder growled.

"Where's the toilet?"

"Just take a left and go straight."

"Cool. I'll be right back. Is anyone here?"

"No, my roommate is spending the night at her friend, remember?" Casey replied.

"Oh yeah, I forgot," Tony nodded.

Tony strolled out of the room in his underwear, his pulsing erection straining against his briefs. Images went through his head in a repeating sequence. Him half-naked in a strangers apartment going to a bathroom he'd see one. Maybe twice if he got lucky. As he washed his hands, he avoided looking into the mirror in the bathroom. He returned to the room ready for action. He slipped on the condom. The foreplay wasn't glamorous and he entered her quickly. Casey's bed was small, and with each thrust Tony made, her head kept sliding into the bed head. A bluegrass song started playing in the background as Tony and Casey try to reposition for proper coitus. They both breathed heavily, then she rested her hand firmly on Tony's chest. He pulled out.

"I can't do this right now. I'm too drunk," she said, sighing heavily.

At that moment, Tony's head became light, as if the last bits of oxygen in his system were gone. He was more drunk than he had thought.

"It's cool babe," he said, flopping beside her. In moments, he was asleep.

Tony woke up the next day extremely alert. He was rock hard (and magically, still wearing the condom). Casey was still sleeping, and he picked up a book on her beside table, *Working Stiff*, and read a few chapters. In his peripheral vision, Tony saw an assortment of books on another small table where the MacBook was; a tiny Buddha statue in the corner and a few pairs of shoes in front of her closet. The walls were bare, and other than the bed and two small tables, there wasn't much room for much else. When Casey woke up, they both talked for almost an hour about nothing in particular. As time passed, her fingers slowly touched Tony's thighs, then his shoulder, then his neck. This time, everything happened for real. They kissed frantically as the early morning light illuminated the room. He slipped the blanket off, and looked at Casey's body. She had soft, even skin. Her pubic hair was a landing strip about two weeks into regrowth. They started having sex. About five minutes in, she laughed. Tony, still thrusting, laughed too.

"What's so funny?" He asked in between breaths.

"These... oh... these walls, they are so *thin!*" she replied with a giggle.

Tony just nodded. *Doesn't she live here?*

The orgasm he had was incredible. The kind where he *buckled,* his thigh muscles would threaten to cramp, beads of sweat would pop quickly on his forehead and the sensation in his groin spread to the rest of his body like sweet fire. A bit later, they drank green tea in her kitchen and spoke for another hour or so. The conversation was light but interesting, filled with anecdotes and laughs.

"I'm going to New York for the week," she said.

Tony said they should meet up before she left. She agreed. Tony walked to the door and Casey had followed him. She gave him a wet kiss on the cheek and told him a soft goodbye. The early morning light greeted him like a lecherous cousin. The brightness of everything around tony had made the morning sex feel even better. The night before, the conversation, the chapters of that book—all of it had made Tony bristle with power. Circumstance more than sex was the intrigue. Those soft watery eyes of hers, her cute little room and her choice necklace.

The next day Tony called her and the phone went to voicemail twice. Before heading out he called her again. She answered the phone, and then hung up. Tony sighed, watching the LCD on his phone blip and fade as the call disconnected. The night before was a faded memory. Tony breathed out deeply and left his apartment. Time for Saturday night.

Chapter 17

Bishop stared at the easel. He held a pencil in his left hand, while he rested his hand on his nose. He stared at the white surface as if it were about to come alive. He was trying to jumpstart his creativity. Before, he would simply see the blank surface and ideas would hit him like rain. He would draw; he would paint, and lose sense of time and space. In his apartment, was a small studio. It used to be an old bedroom, but it was impossible to tell; the walls were bare save a few spots of paint here and there, and a single chair was in the center of the room, in front of the easel where Bishop worked. He never sat on the chair. Since Kevin's death, it had become increasingly harder for him to draw and paint. Staring into the face of his mortality had an effect on his creative perspective. At first, he drew dark, melancholy images shrouded in deep blacks with coarse textures. Then he would start procrastinating. His mind would have an idea, or an image, it would sit on his tongue and tug at his brain, but he wouldn't follow through. After a few months, he realized he hadn't drawn or painted anything. Since he was a child, Bishop had drawn something almost every day. That aspect of him started to close slowly but surely. As the days around him felt more like a void, and his life shifted into a different gear. Art seemed weird, pointless, even. He stared at the easel, and hissed.

"Fuck."

This precipitated his Starbucks outings. Which one never particularly mattered, but lately he settled on a Starbucks just outside Dupont Circle. It was small and cozy, and he would spend hours in there, reading blogs on the Internet and chuckling at grainy YouTube videos. With high-speed Internet back home, a bigger desk and a cozy designer chair to lounge in, spending hundreds of dollars on sketchy Starbucks Wi-Fi would seem like a waste, but the cost was unimportant. Bishop didn't care about money. He never did.

Only weeks before Kevin's death he had been planning an exhibition. An art group, WeSense, had received a million dollars of funding. They opened a half hostel, half studio and held regular events there. One of those events, "Kulture Shock" was the kind of event Bishop liked. It was a casual setting, a little dirty but real. People from all walks would come through. He could sell some art, meet some girls and take steps towards the future. It didn't happen. After he returned to D.C, he didn't answer his phone for a month, leading many to think he probably offed himself too.

Now he was at a sushi restaurant on Karaoke night, nibbling on a fat Meguro roll, watching a lawyer type singing a Foreigner song. A few cool Japanese guys who loved reggae ran the restaurant. Every now and then they'd ask Bishop (a regular) to sing a song. Tonight, they were busy, and Bishop didn't get more than a nod. After finishing the sushi, he thanked the guys and took a stroll outside. The night air was warm on his face. The bus to his street would be a ten-minute wait. He burped. Then, someone said hello. It was a person with large eyes, and a distinct voice. Monica. This time, Bishop was surprised.

"Wow. We keep running into each other. Not following me are you?"

"Not unless you like Japanese food."

"What?"

"I just came from a Japanese restaurant."

"Oh, I see. What are you doing right now?"

"Waiting on the bus."

"Cool, I'm going to pop into Starbucks for a second. Want to come with?"

Monica smiled at him, and Bishop felt a tingle in his stomach.

They stepped inside the star bucks, and a blast of cool air made the hair on Bishop's arms stand up. Monica walked up to the sales clerk.

"Cup of hot water please," she asked with a smile.

"Right away," the attendant replied.

Monica took her cup of hot water and walked over to the condiment station. From her bag, she pulled out three packs of green tea. Bishop smiled, "You are hilarious."

Smiling but not saying anything, she dropped two packs of green tea in the cup, and then mixed in a few sugars. She added a touch of milk from a packet.

She turned and faced him, her large eyes temporarily shrouded in a thin film of steam as she sipped from her cup.

"Do you still believe in coincidences?" she said.

"I'm not sure."

"What are the odds of me and you meeting at that bus stop, on this night at the same time?" she asked.

"Seems random to me. Are you saying it was *meant* to happen?" Bishop said.

"I don't think anything is an accident. Think of the times. How big is D.C? How many factors play a role here? You could have missed your bus by a few minutes; you could have decided to take some other way home. Slight variations in the smallest details would have prevented us from meeting," Monica explained.

"Seems a little out there," Bishop said.

"I've seen you like, four times now," Monica said.

"Where?"

"Two times here, the party, and today."

"This place is pretty popular," Bishop said.

"Yeah, but I don't live anywhere near here. I just came here randomly."

"Where do you live?"

"Mount Pleasant. See what I mean?"

"Again, I'm not sure. What are you, a philosopher?" Bishop asked.

"I don't know really. In college I floated through so many different majors, but I ended up studying art history. I was gunning for anthropology but I hated the size of those textbooks."

"You don't like reading?"

"No I *love* reading, but those books were all like big, fat and hundreds of pages... a little dense. I guess I wasn't that motivated."

"You seem like a motivated person to me," Bishop said.

"Really? Can I tell you a story? It kind of relates to my whole "chance" and "fate" argument. I promise this is the last time I mention it."

"Okay."

Bishop wondered about her. She was so interesting and quirky. Each funny question or inquiry was like a spark on a horizon far away, a flash of light in the blackness of his mind. Could she be a ray of hope?

"Okay, let's sit down."

"Can I get a sip of that?"

The warm liquid felt good going down his throat. Outside, a bus groaned as it passed by. He stared at Monica curiously. She was rapidly looking through her purse, taking out items and replacing them.

"Everything okay?" Bishop said.

"Yes," Monica said not looking up.

On the table now was a huge pack of gum, a small mirror and what looked like a really old stuffed doll.

"I'm sorry, I'm not really looking for anything," she said. "I'm just fidgety." She started to replace the items.

Bishop chuckled.

"Okay, so here it is. I had this friend of mine back in my hometown. He was this really cool kid named Jim. A little weird looking because he had these huge—" she made her hands into tiny saucers "—blue eyes and he was really thin. Like Somalian thin."

"Hey, this is D.C you have to be politically correct," Bishop said.

"Sorry, that's all I ever heard of growing up. He was pretty skinny, right? So he tells me one day that he can sense things about people and its scaring him. This was maybe eight years ago... we were both like thirteen, fourteen. So I ask him what he means. He says that sometimes he can just feel when people around him are in pain, and he even said to me that he knew I was feeling bad recently about something. I lied and said I wasn't, but it was true. A few days before my grandmother had died and I didn't tell anyone, at least, not yet. So maybe a week or two later I see him after school and he says he's having a bad feeling about a class trip. It was just a trip into the city to checkout a museum. But he's having this weird feeling inside he says, and its eating him up. So he figures out a way to avoid going on the class trip."

Monica stopped speaking.

"And?" Bishop asked.

"Just checking to see if you were listening. So he dodges the class trip and then the next day, something bad happens. Trust me, it scared the crap out of me."

"Did the bus crash?"

"No, it didn't crash. It's what happened before the trip. Ahh! Look at my hands they are trembling! Every time I tell this story I get these weird chills. So here's what happened. The next day the kids are all in line to get on the bus, which is across the road. So they are at a pedestrian crossing. The walk sign comes on, but a crazy drunk driver flies through the red and smashes into some kids, including Devon McIntire."

"Who's he?"

"He's Jim's best friend. It was pretty bad. One girl lost all her front teeth; there were a few broken arms and legs. Devon broke one arm and both legs because the car ran over him."

Bishop felt a cold feeling settle in his stomach.

"So when Jim told me this, I didn't know how to react. But it was true; it was in the papers the next day. But he says to me: "Monica, if I was with them, I'd be right beside Devon. What would have happened to me?" I didn't know what to say, I just looked at him and started crying."

"Wow, that's some story," Bishop replied.

"Fuck yeah," Monica said. "I don't really spend much time thinking about all the possibilities and variations of life you know? But when I run into someone I find interesting over and over in a large city it seems a little more ... planned?"

"So you told me this story just to let me know you are interested in me?" Bishop smiled.

"Of course not," Monica said with a smile, and sipped on her tea.

Outside, another bus rumbled by.

"Listen, I have to go. We should meet up later," Monica said.

"Sounds like a plan," Bishop replied.

They walked outside, and Monica hailed a cab. As it slowed down, flashing bright lights on the sidewalk, Monica pinched Bishop's hand.

"Bye, bye, Mr. Moody," she said.

Then, she was gone. Bishop watched the cab roll away into the distance. Something felt funny in his palm where Monica had pinched him. He realized he was holding a piece of paper. On it was her number.

"Nice," Bishop said to himself as he walked back to the bus stop, watching cars drive by in the quiet of the evening.

Chapter 18

Faceless people sat looking through the stained glass windows at the blur of concrete going by at sixty miles an hour. Winston stood quietly near a large man with thick wire rimmed glasses on the metro. This early in the morning people didn't speak. They merely stood quietly like statues, shuffling around in a militaristic fashion to allow people to enter and leave their train stops. For him it was four stops to his work place, somewhere in Dupont.

After exiting the train, the morning brightness hit his eyes. Clean, wide streets with people walking rapidly came into view. Tall skyscrapers with huge panes of glass reflecting the sun encircled him. Whenever he came to work in the morning, for a minute or two he felt progressive. He was a part of this engine, a fixture in D.C's workforce, even if his role wasn't that large. The huge law firms and government agencies, National Geographic building and Museums were nearby. His office was a small company that performed video library storage management. He was a file keeper. The records would come in; tapes would be logged and sent to a huge air-conditioned underground basement. His station, half of a room he shared with a graphic designer, was always chilly and even in the heat of summertime he brought a sweater to work.

It was cold and quiet down there, and often he would be surprised when he'd take his lunch break, marveling at how bright the clouds were, and how the light seemed to awaken a light in his heart, until he returned to his dungeon-like office. Dupont had a pulse that he liked. It was different from the quiet area in which he lived, somewhere near U Street. *This must be what progress is*, Winston always thought. The suits walking briskly to work. White-collar jobs in the belly of the most powerful country on Earth. He, the little Jamaican, was merely scratching out an existence like a subterranean creature, underground and out of sight. Burrowing and hovelling, hoping for a better day.

Todd, the designer, was talking.

"You like video games right, Winston?" he asked.

"Sometimes."

"I'm reading a review here of the top ten games of all time, and I wanted to get your opinion on something."

Todd was reading a video game blog. Sometimes between the long stretches of inactivity, they read blogs, chatted about existentialism, or sat quietly back to back, listening to their IPods.

"It's say here the top game of all time on this review is *Resident Evil.*"

Winston furrowed his eyebrows. "Sorry I don't know it."

"Are you kidding me? Flesh eating zombies, Raccoon City? You know, one of the coolest games to come out in the last fifteen years?"

Winston thought it sounded vaguely familiar. He imagined himself as a teenager, quiet and mysterious, reading Jules Verne novels and keeping mainly to himself. He never got into the Play Station or Nintendo battles.

"Sound's like a good game."

"What? It was a good *concept,* but it had one of the worst control schemes in history. Your ass would be half-turned before a zombie started taking a bite out of it."

Todd chuckled and turned back to his screen, reading and muttering to himself. Winston was watching the clock, as the second hand pulsed with its programmed rhythm, signaling the movement of time. Lunch was the usual affair. A variety of restaurants, and small eateries were everywhere to support DuPont's work force. Day to day you could have delicious Pad Thai, fat Chipotle sandwiches or Chinese food. Today, Winston felt like having Chinese food. He walked three blocks away from his building and turned onto M street. Laughing and smiling faces were everywhere. Girls in summer dresses with sandals and bubble glasses sipped lemonade under the limited shade of restaurant umbrellas. Scruffy errand boys with tattooed arms snaked through traffic with messenger bags securely fastened to their bodies. It was the same sequence of images he had seen every day since it got warm. Winston walked quietly, listening to his iPod, the movements of everyone around him synchronized with their own theme song. Sometimes he would see a co-worker and give them a friendly nod. Mostly, he saw no one, and shared brief conversation with the people who served him daily at the various food places he visited. It was never anything important, just a "hello" or "how d'you do?" Or maybe they'd laugh about a current event. Whatever it wa—

"Winston?"

Winston froze. It was Elsa.

"El-Elsa?"

She was in a summer dress, with a black tank top on. In the summer sun her skin was bronzed and shiny, flawless. Her hair, normally in a ponytail, was loose and hanging past her shoulders in a wild throng of curls. Her eyes, cloudy and sensual as before, struck Winston like a brick to the balls.

"Good to see you," she said.

Neither of them had moved forward. Winston's mind was spinning with questions. What was she doing in D.C? The last time they spoke she said she was living in Barcelona again, or traveling through Europe for a year.

"Good to see you too."

They both stood there for a few moments, and Winston felt his heart racing. He hadn't felt much since she had left, and suddenly standing in front of him, was his happiness.

"Listen, we should have a drink sometime. Take my number," Elsa said.

Winston punched her number in slowly, making sure all the digits were correct. Then with a wave of her hand, she was gone. Winston stood his ground, fascinated by the emotions spinning around in his stomach. At first he felt happy to see her. It was such a pleasant surprise to see her in the middle of the day. Then, after he ate his lunch he felt disappointed, even angry. How long had she been in the city? Why didn't she even let him know she had returned? The rest of the day was a blur, as these thoughts burned at the forefront of Winston's mind, pinching his face like a sharp veil.

That night, he had the first dream. In it, he was walking beside a river. In the distance, yellow blue skies painted a beautiful vista of some faraway place. Near him, somewhere, was Elsa. He could hear her footfalls in the distance, and he could almost see her. In the dream, he was trying to run, but his feet felt like they were encased in cement blocks. The harder he tried to run, the further away she felt. He woke up with his heart thundering in his chest, flooded with sadness, as he reached out into the darkness with no one to hold.

Chapter 19

Vampires, werewolves, bats and ghosts. These are creatures of the night. They live in the shadows, prey on the lonely and weak and are the stuff of legend. A creature of the night always knows its territory. Tony knew his. D.C was a land of dive bars, happy hours, movie screenings, art shows, Indie concerts, kickball leagues, barbecues, clubs and the occasional festival. There were numerous places to meet people, interact, spread social networks and generally have fun. Tonight was a trivia night at a bar in North East. Trivia Thursdays.

Tony walked in, the familiar bar smell hitting his nose. No matter where it was, that telltale mixture of beer suds, sweat and wood never seemed to go away. The scene was the same, mostly young white professionals hanging out at the tables. People laughed and smiled as a skinny guy with a red beard announced from a platform.

"Okay, and the team with the funniest name is…. WEHAZCHEEZBURGER!"

The crowd laughed. Tony laughed as well, and in mid-laugh, caught the eye of a brunette. She gave him a shy smile. Tony smiled back.

Beside him, three young guys that seemed fresh from the office were sitting down. Three beers were on the table.

"Hey buddy you need a team?" one guy said.

"Sure," Tony replied.

The team was I AM LEGEND IN BED. One of the guys, baby-faced in a crisp blue collared shirt, handed Tony a slip of paper and a pencil. The guy with the red beard started speaking again.

"Okay everybody, so here's the next category. Famous leaders, or as I like to call it, the "who am I?" part of the game."

The audience buzzed with excitement. Tony watched them casually. This was a city of academics, really smart people with Master's and PhD's. He only had a Bachelor's in English.

"Okay guys and girls, here's the first question. I'm Russian, and I hated Stalin."

The crowd buzzed like flies. People whispered loudly.

"Is it Trotsky?" a voice said.

"Quiet! It's not Trotsky. Well, maybe," another voice said.

"Hated Stalin? that could be anybody. You think he was Marxist?"

"Who says it's a guy?" came a girl's voice.

The guys at the table thought it was Trotsky too. Tony didn't know who the hell this Trotsky guy was. At the bar, the brunette was still there, sipping on a tall glass of draft beer. She laughed inaudibly while speaking to someone beside her. Tony caught her eye again briefly. In the background the microphone screamed feedback noise through the speakers.

"Sorry about that folks, when this trivia night gets national syndication, we can afford better equipment," the red-bearded guy explained as he shuffled through some papers in his hand.

"So let's hear it! Who is this guy?"

A few people shouted various names, all Russian ones that Tony didn't recognize. The guy at his table said Trotsky.

"Okay, and the answer is… Leon Trotsky. He hated Stalin, was Marxist and apparently dressed in drag on Sunday evenings. Yes, that last part came from a last minute Wikipedia entry."

Tony chuckled and played the game for another twenty minutes or so. Soon, they took a break. Tony went to the bar and made a beeline for the brunette. She was standing beside another girl.

"You guys don't have a team?" Tony asked.

"Not really, we didn't know it was trivia night," a girl beside the brunette said.

"Oh?" Tony said.

"Yeah. We came out to celebrate. She's my new roommate!" the girl said.

"Ah, always a good reason to celebrate," Tony chimed in.

The girl, who had wide shoulders and rosy cheeks, jiggled as she laughed. The roommate (the brunette) had a button nose, large lips and captivating eyes. She gave Tony another shy smile. Roommate number one went to the bathroom, leaving Tony with the brunette.

"Correct me if I'm wrong. Did I catch you looking at me?"

"Maybe," she replied.

"Well, I see a cute girl smile at me, I usually say hello."

"Usually?" she asked.

"Okay, always," Tony revealed with a smile.

In his assessment there were three kinds of women. Women that immediately don't like you, women that like you and women that want you. This one seemed like a category three.

"I live twelve blocks from here," she said, pointing east. "Do you live nearby?"

Tony told her he lived ten blocks in the opposite direction. It was more like Thirteen, but who was checking?

"Where are you from?" the brunette asked.

"Guess," Tony said.

"Trivia night and guessing games? I guess tonight I got the two for one special."

"Wow, that's incredibly corny," Tony said.

The girl turned bright red.

"Hear what. If you get the correct answer, you'll get a special prize."

She flashed a cute smile. He wanted her right there.

"Well, you have an accent. I'm thinking… Jamaica?" she asked.

Tony stood up and spread his arms wide, almost spilling the drinks of three other people sitting at the bar. He grabbed the girl in a bear hug, lifting her slightly off the floor.

"Yes! Right answer!" he said.

He put the girl down, giggling along with her.

"My name's Molly," she said, extending a hand.

Tony kissed the back of her hand.

"I'm Tony," he replied.

"So tell me one really interesting thing about yourself."

Molly looked up at the ceiling for a few seconds, and then turned to Tony.

"I traveled to Machu Picchu."

"Wow," he replied. "That's amazing."

"It *was* amazing. I love to travel, I love to see fresh and new things all the time."

"It's a three day trek to get there, right?"

"Back in the day probably, but now you can just take the train to the main site. Yes, it was one of the best trips in my life. So, what's a really interesting thing about you?"

Tony laughed inwardly. He had no idea how to top Machu Picchu.

"You globe-trot. I occasionally read trashy novels," Tony replied.

"Nice," she said.

" … and thank god for iPhones and discreet Asian massage parlors," came the voice of the guy with the red beard over the loudspeakers.

The crowd laughed and Tony sipped on his beer, closing his eyes temporarily as the suds fizzled and popped down his throat.

The night started to wind down. Molly was rubbing Tony's hand and her roommate looked on with a sly grin.

"What are you doing tomorrow?" Molly asked.

"Nothing," Tony said. "Nothing at all."

* * * *

Molly's house was in a quiet section of Northeast, where the streets were dark, and the drone of traffic was indiscernible. Tony had taken the bus to get to her house.

"Four twenty two," Tony said to himself.

He walked down a few dark streets cursing slightly as he forgot which direction he was going in. Then, he saw the numbers were going up. Four hundred, Four hundred and two, he was on track. A large man on a bicycle quietly rode by, like a specter in the night. He was getting closer to her house. How many houses had he been to? How many neighborhoods?

Molly opened the door. She smelled fresh, like Juniper breeze, or any of a million kinds of heavily scented soaps. A strand of dark hair clung to her forehead. She had just taken a bath. Always a good sign.

"Hey there," she said.

Tony walked into the house. It was large and very clean.

"Hey, would you like something to eat? We were sort of having a little wine party here," Molly said.

She strutted over to the kitchen, where a bottle of wine and a few slices of gourmet cheese were on large brown plate. Tony didn't like gourmet cheese, but bit heartily into a chunk. The roommate emerged, happy and jiggly as before.

"Hello sir, how are you?" she said.

"I'm great," Tony replied, knowing he meant it.

They sipped on wine and played Nintendo Wii. Tony, not the best gamer, was killed by Molly's superior hand/eye coordination. Jiggly played pretty well, too. Tony still didn't know her name. Between games, Tony snuck wet kisses with Molly. Soon, the roommate disappeared and the Nintendo sat on the ground, shining a thin blue light on the wooden floor while Tony and Molly sipped wine.

"Show me your room," Tony said.

"Of course," Molly said with a smile.

Holding Tony's hand, she led him up a flight of carpeted stairs. Her room was large and cozy, and like the rest of the house, immaculately clean. The slightest cloud of tension was in the air. The ceiling was low, which made Tony feel giant-sized. Molly sat on the bed and Tony followed her, covering her neck with kisses. With each peck of his lips on her neck, she let out a loud sigh.

"I want to go slow, but you are making it so hard for me," she said.

Tony smiled. He rubbed her chest, teasing her nipples between her shirt. She had no bra on. In a few moments it was off. Her hands fell quickly to his pants, and his belt buckle. Tony glanced back at the door, which was half-open. As many times as Tony had done this routine, it never got old. He groaned with pleasure as her hands found their way between his legs. How many neighborhoods? How many houses? He pulled her up to his face and kissed her on the lips.

"I want you now," he said with a hiss.

He lay her down and kissed her more passionately. She writhed like a snake, and the soft covers of her bed crumpled into an indistinguishable wad. Then she stopped.

"What's wrong?" Tony said.

"I can't have sex with you right now," she said.

"Oh? Is it that time of the month?" Tony asked.

"No it isn't. I just can't have sex on the first date," she replied.

Tony didn't feel anything. There was never disappointment in the bedroom, only escalation. He lay on the bed beside her.

"Is that okay with you?" she said.

"Yes, its quite fine," he said, rubbing her arm.

He took off his pants.

"Would you like me to touch you?" Tony asked.

"Yes, I'd like that," she replied.

For Tony the sex didn't always matter. The sex would come. In a few minutes, in a few days, maybe never. It wasn't the sex that drove him, it was the moment. He slowly took off her pants, revealing a pair of black panties with tiny white clouds on them. She kissed his stomach, and he slipped his hand between her thighs. Then, Molly became an animal.

She pushed him on the bed, and took him inside her mouth. She worked feverishly, and for a moment, Tony felt like he was on a porn set in L.A with a seedy director behind him shouting "Yeah! Yeah!". He closed his eyes as she worked with practiced rhythm, eventually feeling the telltale sign of orgasm building in his stomach.

"I'm going to come," Tony said between sharp breaths.

Still going, she growled. With a *plop* she stopped giving Tony head for a second.

"You can go ahead it's fine," she said with a smile.

She resumed her duties and Tony came hard, shaking as Molly kept stroking, swallowing everything. They lay on the bed afterwards, chatting about movies.

"I'm a little nerdy," Molly said.

"Why's that?" Tony asked.

"My favorite movie is *The Willow*."

Tony laughed. He liked nerdy girls. She even said her favorite game was an Old PC-shooter, *Wolfenstein*. She offered Tony a ride home, and he took it. She drove an old Blue Honda civic. They drove back with warm breeze blasting their faces as "California Dreaming" played on the radio. The drive was mostly quiet, with Tony strumming his fingers on the door while Molly hummed along to the song. When he got out of the car, she waved at him. Tony waved back and watched the lights of the car fade into the distance as she drove off, and he knew he wouldn't see her again.

Chapter 20

The streets were black and empty. Everywhere was silent, save the muffled rustling of a strange noise in the background. His eyes opened in the dark, and he could sense her, somewhere nearby. His feet hit cold tiles on the floor and a smell crept into his nostrils. Something familiar, something foreign. His eyes ached, and his room was unfamiliar. His body felt light, like feathers falling off a mountain. He went outside. There wasn't a soul to be seen. Cobblestones on the road made a grid pattern that stretched into the horizon. The buildings were pastel with strange markings on them; written in a language he couldn't recognize. He walked forward, rubbing his bare chest with his arms, breathing in short breaths:

One, two, three.

A sliver of light broke across the sky, and a sheet of yellow spread across the rooftops, alleyways and door knobs. With this light came no warmth, and he kept walking.

One, two, three, four.

The familiar sensation hit the air again, a memory just out of reach. It smelled like a warm hotel room after a long shower; a sweet mixture of cheap body wash and carpet cleaner. He rubbed his arms some more, and then felt her again. She was close, darting through the shadows like a wraith. He ran barefoot across the cobbled streets, with an increasing sense of fear crawling up his back like a dozen spiders. There was still no one to be seen, he only heard only heard the roar of quietness. But she was nearby, somewhere. His feet matter spatter noises on the ground, echoing like the clapping of tiny hands. Then the sky darkened and he was afraid. The shadows around him stretched out in long and menacing, like tendrils. They moved in ripples and frantic bulges, rapidly expanding and contracting. Then he heard a screeching noise. Far away. Dark and menacing.

One, two, three, four, five.

He was still running, his heart a thunderous echo in his chest. Her presence was still nearby, just out of arm's reach, walking amongst the shadows. The sky was almost getting darker, the yellow sheet of the sun fading into nothing. The rustling noise he heard before started again, streaming from every crack around him. He tried to run faster, but felt himself slow as the darkness came closer to him. He tried to speak, but nothing came. Now, the sky was obsidian and the screech came again, a piercing shriek from the depths of hell. Around a corner a blur of movement made ice run through his arms. What was that?

Onetwothreefourfivesixseveneigh—

The light disappeared and Winston screamed, waking up and reaching out into the dark. He lay in bed with a pulsing erection, his heart running at a full gallop. His arms and chest were sweaty and he could still smell that smell, and feel the shadows around him. He clenched his eyes shut, gritting his teeth and grabbing his pillow with all his strength. She still felt close to him, somewhere out there in the shadows of the city, near the surface of the coming dawn.

Chapter 21

A blonde woman in a workout top wearing Bose Headphones ran by. Her bronzed body was a screaming paragon of plastic surgery and type-A workouts. Nearby, a tall man with a thinning hairline and gray sweats was pushing a stroller with a small child in it. The laughter of a few girls wearing linen summer dresses and tops from Express floated through the air. On the sidewalk, a few lazy leaves lay calmly on its clean surface. Bishop was sitting on a bench somewhere near his house in Georgetown.

Elements of Georgetown echoed upscale Jamaica; expensive properties, regaled social status and the envious addresses. Despite the plethora of big degrees and massive minds that populated this little D.C Utopia, few knew anything about where he was from, save the occasional yarn about violence or reggae music. Even those who had traveled on vacations knew little past the heavily incubated atmosphere of the all-inclusive hotels, white sandy beaches and hustlers ready to chase horny tourists. Here he was just a guy. A reasonably anonymous and artistic guy, a person who was most likely wealthy and who lucked out.

In America he was referred to as "Black", meaning possibly through some measure of good fortune his parents had gotten an education, utilized over a generation or two in the face of racism and prejudice, and made something of themselves. But Bishop wasn't African-American. He was Jamaican, and half-Chinese. The connotations of this observation are lost on the casual observer. With his ethnicity comes an entire swath of his society. Segregation, rampant colorism, even a common vernacular of the tongue. A lilt of the speech. In America he wasn't the son of one of the island's biggest businessmen. He was just a black guy who liked art. His mixed ethnicity sometimes drew questions from certain people. He normally had his hair short, but occasionally it grew out into a long set of curls. Once a girl asked him if he was Mexican, but then an African-American girl had said he was cute, and that she liked black guys like him. Then he met a person who though he was Turkish, something he had never heard before. Bishop simply identified himself as Jamaican, and in self-reference, Black. His entire family resembled him in skin tone and ethnic makeup. But he had seen real Chinese people, and they looked nothing like him.

He toyed with the idea of going to Europe. Maybe Paris for a few days to roam the streets and drink wine. He probably wouldn't though. Such random escapades were more the type of thing his father would do. The same mental circuitry that made him an expert at taking risks businesswise was an effusive part of his personality in other areas of his life. His father was a true alpha male with legendary exploits around town, despite being married to his mother for over thirty years. He could do the sweet dance between debonair and dangerous expertly, and it seemed his only weakness was his children. His success was theirs; they were free to roam and do whatever they pleased, living out lives as miniature versions of himself. Bishop's two brothers had chosen to stay in Jamaica, while Bishop went to D.C in search of new horizons.

Today, sitting on a bench somewhere in Georgetown was just an act of random chaos. He was bored. He had a membership for the local Bally's, but never went. His art, which showed promise when he went to American University, was slowly collecting dust in his studio. The man with the child in the pram walked by, and gave Bishop a cheerful smile. Bishop returned the gestured with a perfunctory smile and nod as he looked at the man, wondering if he too would someday have a child. A few years before, he had vehemently argued with Kevin about the value of marriage, and now, that moment in time felt lost and irrelevant, like arguing about Atlantis. The last few weeks had been a blur of alcohol and occasionally drugs. The power he felt on the cocaine was dangerous, but it didn't matter did it? Nothing in the world could transport him back in time, change his paradigm shifts and open the floodgates to how he used to feel. A piece of his soul was careening down a black, endless chasm, forever gone and irretrievable.

Suicide, he had read, does many things to the people it affects. It causes anger, trauma, shock, disbelief, (relief for some) and many other things. But mostly, the thing that hangs over everyone's head is the most obvious question. Why? When you ask the Why, you never get an answer. You can shout from the rooftops or postulate until plastic biodegrades, but the answer will be ever elusive. There were other friends Bishop had who had slowly degraded into acquaintances. As he slowed within himself, his emotions became more clouded. There was no real spark in the day, and everything seemed like a blank screen he was watching. Time was passing and nothing changed. Sometimes he woke up in a state of terror, wondering if he would ever feel anything, but since he started drinking, that hadn't happened. He didn't feel powerful with the drugs, just even. A little lame probably. A vibration tickled his thigh his cell phone. He pressed a small button. It was from Monica. The message made Bishop's chest feel odd.

Why do you wake up?

There was nothing else. This was the first message she had ever sent Bishop. He looked at the phone for a few moments and raised his hands to type a reply. Resting the phone back on his lap, he thought for a few moments again, and attempted to write a reply. After fifteen minutes he knew he didn't have an answer, and that was frightening.

Chapter 22

Another Friday night. Another foray into the madness that was D.C, its fused existence of power, control and jaded yuppies. Tony walked down U Street, half-listening to his iPod, half thinking. Life to him felt like a stream. A viscous splashing of circumstance, pain, regret and pleasure permeated by brief moments of euphoria, staggering moments of despair and always, a huge fucking question mark. If the city was dark, then Tony felt dark, obscured by its size and complexity, a culture that was his and wasn't his, a place where he could function but felt helpless at times. Only the night had some resolve, with its myriad outings in different locations, just enough to stimulate his mind and briefly chase away ghosts of the past. Everything he could want was in the city. Enough of his own culture existed there to integrate with the Jamaican community, various other cultures were there to expand his horizons, and of course, you can't beat living in the country where movies come out on the slated release date. But leaden weights still pulled at his feet, a noise in the back of his mind, a humming quite like—

"Hey man, can I ask you a question?" a voice said.

Tony stopped and turned around, pulling one ear bud from his left ear. In front of him were two young men, one tall and handsome in a movie star sort of way, the other shorter and plain.

"Yeah, what's up?" Tony asked.

"The thing is we are looking for something to do right now, and you seem like someone who would know what's going on."

Tony laughed. "Oh, really now?"

"Well you are dressed sharply and look like you might know what's up."

Tony thought of his outfit briefly, a pair of faded skinny jeans, and an even older t-shirt over a (possibly) older dress shirt.

"Cool. I'm headed to the Black Kat I think," Tony said, turning around.

"Hey, we know that place!" the taller one said. "And we have beer."

Tony turned back around, and the shorter fellow was zipping open a backpack. Inside were beers. Many beers.

"Wow, you guys are pretty serious," Tony said.

They walked across U Street, past a string of Ethiopian restaurants that took you to 14th Street, and took a left, taking you to Black Kat. Tony first came here to see an Indie Rock concert, amazed at his first glimpse of an American subculture. That night there were girls wearing pinstripe socks up to their knees, bunny rabbit ears and psychedelic clothing. Guys with cool haircuts, heavy piercings, platform shoes and tight pants were there in droves. Tony at the time was in the back, dancing a little but mostly watching, as the crowd worked themselves up into a drug-fueled, alcohol-laced frenzy of (at the time) epic proportions. The band was a gravelly set of guys who sang high in their noses who were drowned out by the speakers on stage. They were completely in band mode, with matching tight pants, long black hair and great body language. Tony never heard their name.

"Let's go here," the short guy said. "I came here once before, because all these boxes give good cover when you want to drink beer."

Tony nodded, remembering briefly in Jamaica there was no such law. Plus he had been drinking since he was thirteen. They stood behind the box of crates, which was beside a closed grocery store near the club, sipping beers. The two guys were brothers who lived outside D.C, somewhere in Arlington. They were young, idle and looking for some fun. The shorter one stashed the backpack behind a large bag that used to hold cement.

"I think that's good. Let's roll!"

In the few minutes they had shared a few beers, Tony was already seeing their sibling dynamics unfold. He could tell the shorter brother was slightly jealous of the other one, who was the splitting image of Michael York in *Logan's Run*. They walked into the club after being stamped. As a precaution, the two younger guys both got black X`s on their arms so they couldn't buy drinks. The older brother ran to the bathroom and started scrubbing his hands furiously. When he came out, a burly guy with a flashlight walked up to him.

"Let me see your hands," he said.

"Hey, why?" the older brother said with disdain.

The guy held his hand with a paw the size of a loaf of bread. Barely visible on his skin, were the telltale marks of the X. "If you wash these off again, I'm tossing you out," the guy said. He pulled out a fat marker, drew a new X on his other hand, and let him go.

"Damn, they have people watching the bathrooms? That sucks," the older brother said.

Tony wasn't listening. The younger brother was talking to two girls in the corner. The other brother joined the group and started chatting to the girls. One of them, a slim girl with brown hair was eyeing the younger brother with strong sexual signals, but he wasn't picking them up. Tony chuckled to himself, remembering himself from the past. The two girls morphed from white girls to girls with dark skin and curly hair. The younger brother transformed into him, a smiley-faced guy who wasn't aware of what was happening. Cluelessness is bliss.

He looked around. The bar was mostly empty, with a few people here and there. Some girls were at the pool table: three tall, model types. Tony didn't feel particularly like talking to them, but attractive women always knew what was going on in town. Tony walked over.

"Okay, which one of you is the hustler?" Tony asked.

None of the girls responded and one shot him an icy look. She was breathtakingly beautiful, with cocoa-colored skin, and heavy eye shadow that gave her a Goth look.

"Okay, fine. I was going to come up to you guys and say something lame like, 'Are you models?' But I thought I'd ask the real question before I start playing for money," Tony said.

"Who says we are playing for money?" one of the girls said, shooting Tony another icy look.

His face didn't show it, but inside he was smiling.

"Wow, and I didn't even get to say hello. I was just trying to be nice ladies."

Tony turned around quickly around and walked towards the two brothers. One of the girls was laughing and saying something about her t-shirt. He touched the younger brother on the shoulder.

"Go talk to those girls," Tony said, gesturing with his head towards the pool table.

"What? Those girls are really hot man, and they look kinda bitchy," The taller brother replied, his voice a bit slurred.

"Just go say hello. What do you have to lose?" Tony said, nudging him firmly in the stomach.

"Fine, Fine. Ladies, if you'll excuse me."

The older brother touched Tony and gave him a look that said, *What's up?* Tony just smiled and nodded. In the background, he heard the taller brother speak.

"Good evening ladies."

"Hey what's up," a girl's voice replied.

"Just saying hello. I must say you are quite beautiful."

He could hear the girl chuckle, and Tony almost laughed out loud. Dude was a bit corny, but he looked like an actor, and Tony knew the iciest girls are like a lot of women he met. Shallow. After two minutes he heard the guy calling him.

"This gentleman is a really cool guy from Jamaica. His name is Tony," taller brother said.

The girl with the dark eye shadow smirked. "Some of my family is from Jamaica."

"Really?" Tony replied. "I couldn't tell."

"So how do you know Phillip?" the last girl said. She was a leggy blond with heavily chiseled features and cold blue eyes.

Tony thought quickly. *Phillip? Who the hell is Phillip? Oh!*

"We met tonight. So what else going on tonight?" Tony asked.

"I heard about some house party. We might go there afterward," the blonde said.

Tony could see it already; the red cups, a mix of random people, music playing from a radio and lots of drunk people.

"First I'll play a game of pool with you. Then give me the details," Tony said, picking up a stick.

The blond gave him a cordial smile, while behind her, sitting on a chair, the girl with the dark eye shadow smirked a little wider. The girls actually were models. The girl with the dark eye shadow was Jennifer. One girl didn't introduce herself at all, and the blonde girl Tony spoke to first only referred to herself as "Ice". Jennifer had trounced Tony in four consecutive pool games. During this time, they had some friendly banter and shared a few hugs and high fives. There wasn't as much aggression in her eyes now, and after the games there was even the hint of a smile on her lips. The other girls had lost interest in the two brothers. They had wandered off after Ice had called the tall one a "fucking baby" and his brother a "stupid troll". Tony, playing a game with Jennifer at the time, had simply shrugged his shoulders. Soon afterwards, he saw them smiling and chatting with three short girls. Before he left the Black Kat, the taller brother had come up to him.

"They are from George Mason," he said, "One girl said she wanted to give me head tonight!"

His eyes screamed with excitement, and Tony had felt genuinely happy for him.

The party location was within walking distance of where they were, but Ice insisted on taking a cab there. During the cab ride she tried calling someone several times on her phone, cursing at no one and continuously redialing. After the cab dropped them off at the house, they stood on the porch.

"I have no idea where Rick is," Ice said, closing her flip phone shut and whipping out a cigarette in perfect sequence. The party was a dead affair; with a few bland people floating around, talking in hushed conversations. There was no music playing.

"Do you know Rick?" Ice said to a short guy walking past.

"Sorry, I don't," the guy replied.

She lit her cigarette and took and aggressive puff, her shoulders slightly hunched, her eyes like blue fire.

"Let's go to Adam's Morgan," Ice said.

The girl with no name simply nodded.

"I have to do something in the morning, but we'll catch up," Jennifer said, giving both girls a hug.

The fact that Jennifer didn't want to go to Adams Morgan didn't seem to bother Ice at all, and in no time she and the girl with no name hailed a cab, hopped in, and vanished up the street.

"I'm hungry, let's get something to eat," Jennifer said, waving down a cab.

Soon afterward, the cab pulled up to a pair huge of buildings facing a massive empty field with an old running track. Tony knew these buildings. They were simply known as "The Towers", two upperclassman dorm buildings near Howard University's main campus.

They stepped out of the cab.

"You are a student?" Tony asked.

"*Grad* student," Jennifer replied.

"Ah I see, but I thought you said you model?"

"I'm trying to do it part-time. I used to model more but it really fucked up my academic aspirations. I'm easing back a bit."

She said this without looking at Tony at all. He could see that, for some time at least, she had lived in a fast world of cold people and quick decisions. Turning quickly left, she started walking away from the buildings. Tony paused for a moment, then followed her, jogging slightly to catch up with her. She walked in brisk, long strides.

"Sorry, I'm crazy hungry. There's a McDonald's right here," she said.

A block away, the ever familiar arches of McDonald's glowed. A good number of people were inside for that time of night. There was a scattered array of Howard students, a set of hung over guys dressed in suits, and a sprinkling of sleepy attendants. As they made their order, one man stood out to Tony. He wore an old khaki colored trench coat that had more mileage than style. The weather wasn't cold by any means, but he was wearing gloves, earmuffs, a scarf and a thick winter hat. His face was clean-shaven, and his eyes darted left and right rapidly. He chewed frantically on a straw and held a large, empty McDonald's cup in his hand.

Jennifer ordered a chicken sandwich meal with fries. Tony got the same thing. As they collected their order, the strange man appeared beside Tony.

"My friend," he said with a deep southern drawl. "I saw the devil in a dream last night."

Tony nodded cordially.

"MY FRIEND, I'm serious," the man said, moving closer.

Tony could smell a bizarre amalgam of scents coming from the man; cheap soap, perfume and the slightest undertone of something malodorous. Whatever it was, the pungent odor hit him like a gust of wind to the face.

"I saw the DEVIL, you hear that?" the man said, gesturing with his hands in the air. He spun around, and pointed towards a small group of sleepy students all wearing grey sweat pants.

"You kids might NOT *know* the DEVIL, but I SAW him. Do you understand? I SAW THE DEVIL IN MY DREAM. He said that it was COMING. *It* was coming. HERE! SOON!"

For a second, Tony regretted nodding at the man. His simple acknowledgement of the man's statement seemed to have stirred him up into a frenzy. Jennifer squeezed his arm lightly and smiled at him, her cool, dark features crystal clear in the garish fluorescent light of the eatery.

"But the LORD, yes lil' man, the LORD," the man continued, gesturing at another student. The student smiled and cheered as the man raved.

"Preach! Preach!" the young man said.

Resting his gloved hands on his head, the man started humming. "Ohhhhh, lord, this is MYYYYYY time, this is MYYYY place… Oh lorrrrddd."

A few people laughed, and the rest of the patrons started to take notice of the man. A short security guard with thick arms walked over to him.

"Sir, if you keep making noise I'm going to have to ask you to leave," the guard said.

The tone of his voice was calm and flat, the statement expertly practiced. Tony imagined him saying this statement to the same man, or men like him day in and day out.

"Me? LEAVE? I have rights!" the man said, thrusting his cup into the air. "I'll show you why!"

He stormed over to the leftmost exit, and pointed at a piece of paper taped to the door.

"You see this? It says you can't bring your empty cup back INTO the establishment. Isn't this an establishment? I ASK you, is it not an establishment?"

In a tired way, the security guard nodded.

"Well, I paid MONEY for this drink you see? And according to the RULES here, I am a CUS—tomer. A *PAYING* customer. So I have rights. I have RIGHTS."

The man shuffled over to the drink fountain, and Tony was hit again with the pungent smell the man carried like a wave. With a decisive stab of his hand and a gleeful smile on his face, the man filled his cup to the brim with Orange Fanta, and sat at an empty booth near the exit. Immediately he quieted down, and began furiously chewing on the straw again.

"Trippy," Jennifer said. "I've seen this guy acting crazier than this, but they've never kicked him out."

She and Tony walked the block or so back to the dorm buildings. She nibbled on fries while Tony glanced over at the empty lot across from the buildings. Something about shadowy red brick buildings in their nighttime silhouette always had a touch of unfamiliarity to him; a far cry from the undulating roads and cement based structures in Jamaica. A few students were outside idling, and Tony saw the telltale profile of a few athletes; tall and well muscled.

"Just walk in with me. You look like you go to school here so we can just walk in," Jennifer said.

Tony followed her lead. A man sitting at the front desk stared Tony dead in the eyes as he walked past.

"My man, long time no see!" he said.

Tony smiled back at him. "Yeah man, you know how it is."

After passing through the lobby and heading towards the elevator, Jennifer looked at Tony with a smile.

"You went to Howard?"

"No, but I must really look like someone who does," Tony said with a chuckle.

They both laughed all the way to the sixth floor. Her room was clean and spacious, and a large set of bay windows gave a clear view of the street below. Tony stood by the window, again slightly lost in the nighttime vista of DC; the jagged architecture of rooftops and television antennas that meshed into a charcoal jigsaw puzzle in the horizon.

Behind him, Jennifer sat on an Ikea couch, finishing the last of her fries. She gave Tony a wry smile, the exact smile she made the first time he approached her group earlier that night at the Black Kat. Her dark eyes and chiseled face held a peculiar energy; he could see she was thinking about something, but it was hard to figure out what. He sat next to her, and kissed her softly on the neck. She let out a quick sigh, and her left arm trembled slightly.

"One second," she said, standing up.

She walked into the bathroom, and Tony could hear her brushing her teeth. Soon, she was back on the couch, beside him.

"I can't kiss a guy after eating McDonald's," she said with a smile.

Her breath was cool and fresh as she kissed him, and Tony didn't feel like reminding her that he had also eaten McDonald's. Everything Tony had imagined about her was even more vivid after her clothes were off. He admired gentle slope of her breasts, the long continuous contours of her body and the sweet taste of her nipples in his mouth. Her eyes, originally tinted with a glaze of subdued anger in them, now gleamed with a carnal energy. It was a wild and frantic affair. She scratched his chest and tugged at his hair.

"Fuck me!" she said louder and louder, straddling him like there was no tomorrow. Tony knew she had an agenda; she was *fucking him*. They rolled around on the floor, had a brief stint in the bathroom, and ended back up on the couch, where she came hard in reverse cowgirl, with her eyes closed and her body damp with sweat, her long arms clamped around Tony's neck.

Naked, they sat on the floor for a while, and she turned on the television. *The Late Show* was on, and they both laughed for a few minutes at some of the sketches. Jennifer walked into her room and Tony watched her go, her buttocks tight and flawless, barely moving with each step she took. Soon she came out, wearing nothing but a grey, sleeveless sweater with a hood.

"Do you like this?" she asked. "I got it in New York on my last gig."

She stood there bare from the waist down and did a slight pose, looking at an imaginary cameraman.

"Yes I do," Tony replied.

He took a sip of some of the leftover soda from his previous meal. Jennifer walked over and sat beside him, laying her head on his chest. She snaked her arm forward and stroked the small hairs on his calf.

"I have a boyfriend in New York," she said softly.

"I see," Tony said.

"He's a model too, and I heard he's been fucking half the lower East Side. Guys and girls."

She said this without much emotion in her voice, and Tony stared at the television, half watching another the skit as she kept stroking his leg. Something about how close she was started turning him on again, and she eased up off his lap and looked directly into his eyes.

"You kind of remind me of him," she said.

The statement held a weight that lingered in the air, dangling between them as she held his gaze, processing him. For a moment, Tony saw a flash of sadness appear in her perfect eyes. It faded quickly and the powerful, steely strength in them returned. She stood up and went back to her room. This time, she came out wearing a pair of large sweats with "JUICY" written on the rear end.

"I'm going to the library for a bit," she said. "You can chill here if you want."

Again, she said this without looking at him, and started putting some things from on top of a desk near the bedroom into a small knapsack. She walked past, leaned over and gave him a kiss on the cheek. Tony, still naked on the ground, nodded and sipped more of his soda. Her footfalls faded into the distance and the door closed with a *click*. After about ten minutes, he slipped back into his clothes and headed downstairs. The elevator ride down seemed to take forever. The doors opened and he walked back through the lobby. The man at the front desk area smiled at him and nodded. Tony nodded back, and walked outside, into the night.

Chapter 23

They are near a sliding door that leads to a small balcony. From an inverted position on the ground, Winston can see the glow of streetlights far below where they w reflect on windowpanes on an office building fifty feet away. His vision is inverted because he is tilting his head in ecstasy. It is wintertime and he is sitting on a small IKEA chair, naked and draped in a blanket. On the ground between his legs is Elsa. Her arms feel cool draped around his waist, the little chair creaking with his weight. He feels his lips on her, and a sigh escapes his mouth. A sigh that sounds more like a hiss. Somewhere below, the drone of a car passes and echoes. The light of the apartment is dim. In a corner a small laptop plays music. Winston doesn't know the band. Again. A hiss-like sigh escapes his mouth, and Elsa growls with delight. Her hands stroke his back furtively. Winston feels his stomach tense, his loins boiling with impending orgasm. Sensing this, Elsa throws off the blanket, exposing her bare chest. He looks at her for a moment, the dull glow of the city lights painting a faint silhouette on her shoulders. Her breasts sway with her work; she is beautiful in the night. She stops briefly, and looks at him, with her gray-green eyes, burning with desire. She resumes her duties. Winston can't hold back. He releases, each strike of the orgasm like a punch in the stomach. She doesn't move, relishing his taste, letting out little *hrmms* as he fights to control himself. The effect ebbs and slows, and his breathing is less labored. She is still enjoying herself. With a stained chin and chest, she looks at Winston. Again those eyes, again the smile. She is saying something, but no words come out of her mouth. The skyline starts to ripple and fade, the silhouette of the city lights getting dark. Her mouth is still moving, but her image, the apartment and the din of the music melt away.

Winston was alone is his apartment sitting on his bed, his blood still hot from the memory. His chest was tight. The smell of that night, the images, even the music all felt so real, so close. He closed his eyes and there she was again, saying something. He fought to remember the words, but all he received was silence. A bubble of intense regret ran up his arms. She *wanted* him to come. She *wanted* to taste him. Now Winston was fading just as the memory had faded. The room screamed at him in solitude, the walls echoing contempt. He hopped on a train and headed to Chinatown.

His iPod blasting music in his ears, he gritted his teeth, trying to ease the bombardment of memories in his head. After the train stopped, he walked down to the Regal Cinema.

"Welcome to the Regal Cinema. What will you be watching today?" a pimply young man said.

"Whichever movie is showing now," Winston replied.

Ticket in hand, Winston strolled into the cinema. It was dark and quiet. Winston liked the movie theater smell. That mix of carpet cleaner and warm butter made him twinge a little with excitement.

In Kingston, the theater that was all the rage was the Carib 5. The original had burned down in a fire when Winston was a kid, and they rebuilt it, made five cinemas and brought Kingston into First World entertainment. Upon going to the states, the movie theater scenario became a ritual. The anticipation of the booming noises from the speakers when previews started, the lull of audience conversation that slowly dissipated as the movie started; the hush of a tense scene, or the adrenaline rush of a well directed action sequence. These things were some of the scattered things that Winston could truly enjoy.

The theater was completely empty and Winston felt a brief spark of elation, hoping that he could enjoy the movie by himself. This illusion was soon shattered with the entrance of a young Asian couple carrying a huge tub of popcorn. Soon the theater darkened and the movie started. It flashes in a blur, end ends too soon.

He headed home and went to sleep, only to wake up at four in the morning, terrorized by another nightmare. Later, on the way to work, he looked at the *Express* metro newspaper. Winston saw that the movie "Annie Hall" was going to be shown on the Monument lawns later. He had been scouring the advertisements section, seeing what was out there to take his mind elsewhere. That evening, the lawns were filled with people sitting in a thick crowd near a massive portable screen. Winston sat on the outskirts some distance away. A sudden commotion startled him as dozens of people jumped up all at once. A brief panic hit Winston and he stood up as well. Then he saw that all the people who had jumped up were dancing. A very old HBO graphic floated across the screen, as low rate synthesized sounds played a horrible version of a pre-digital age jingle. Winston laughed at himself, realizing this must be some sort of ritual for the event. That was a good evening.

Amy had invited him to a poetry presentation at the Smithsonian but couldn't make it at the last minute. Winston went anyway. A man completely bald on the top of his head, with shoulder length hair hanging from the sides was the featured poet, along with a few other interesting characters. More than the poetry, Winston liked the building, its architecture and mystery. The intricate carpeting and old chandeliers, walls with secret passages and symbols that signified the origins of modern day America. He tried to imagine the various faces and people who would have passed through this very place; the variety of individuals, their purpose in life, their motives. How did they die? Curled up in a Georgetown duplex, dreaming of the America of today? Or were they simply in a world with similar problems and dreams minus the bother of smart phones and social media?

These thoughts came and went as the poets presented. Afterwards, there was some sort of reception. The usual gourmet cheese, grapes and wine selections were available. Winston helped himself heartily, even chatting briefly to one of the poets.

Two days later, a sample yoga class was happening at the field near Adams Morgan. He went there, with his mat and a crusty pair of shorts, trying oddly to balance while a buxom girl with a New Jersey accent gave the instructions to those participating. It was a fun, light-hearted activity, and Winston even met a girl there, Sarah, who went to George Washington.

He attended an art show at the National Gallery of Art, starting going to Potbelly's every now and then with some of his co-workers and thought of joining a gym. There were public painting sessions in Chinatown, art shows in Friendship Heights and the random volleyball game he saw at Marymount

College. It was a blur of events and places, and on one of those nights he came home, exhausted and fell into the world of sleep.

Then, he was in an apartment somewhere in D.C. It was one of those sub-level units. His feet were bare, and he could smell the faintest odor of wet carpet coming from the hallway. He was near a door, a large brown door. His feet seemed like stone and he couldn't move. Sounds started coming through the door. Softly at first, almost dull; the voice of a woman. She was moaning in ecstasy. He could hear her,

Yes, Yes, oh god, oh, oh god.

It was Elsa's voice. Winston tried his best to move, to no avail. Embarrassed and curious at the same time, he cursed himself for getting an erection. The moans went on and on, louder and longer.

Oh goodddddddd, Ohh yeeessssss

Winston frantically tried to move, images of the phantom man flooding his mind. How did he look? How tall was he? The screams beat at his ears like bats. The door started to creak open, and the moans became even louder. From where he was standing he could get the faintest glimpse into the apartment. They were near the door.

Ohgodohgodohgodohgod

Winston screamed. He sprung up in his bed, shaking and sweaty. Clenching his teeth, he gripped his feet, which were going through severe spasms. He held his head in his hands. "Please, please, please I want to stop thinking about this," Winston said.

It was three a.m., and he knew he wouldn't be going back to sleep. That was the first night he started running. He grabbed a pair of shorts and an old t-shirt. It didn't take long for him to hit U Street, running past patrons doing the nightly bar routine. He ran down 14th Street, past the Black Kat and the little pizza place, hit the roundabout near Logan circle and stopped a few blocks shy of Dupont. As he ran, he saw silhouettes of himself and Elsa in an eatery he knew. He took a rapid turn then took a turn up a residential street, running from the ghosts. The urgency with which he ran surprised him. His chest screamed for air, and he was sweating profusely. Finally, he stopped.

Wherever it was it was dark, quiet, and devoid of memories. Panting heavily, he sat on the ground for a while.

Chapter 24

The next few days, Bishop's fascination with Monica began. There was a very specific, very tangible reason why Monica proliferated his thoughts. Serendipitous circumstances aside, an essence of what *he needed* seemed to lay in her presence in his life. His world of late was a quiet one, his mind a buzzing hive of discontent, struggling to understand the chaos of life around him. Generally he questioned everything around him, trying to find merit in the smallest of things and meaning in the greater good. Humanity was an aging, failing bulwark of people with simple emotions and reactions in the dark and very unhappy Geoid space we called Earth. The genesis of these thoughts had emerged during his teenage years, humming just below the surface, tingling his skin like pubescent acne. Now as an adult, these thoughts were a significant part of his despair; the sense of utter loneliness in a world where people just fucking *leave,* and go to *that place* and never, ever come back. He knew this perception wasn't completely black and white, but for almost a year he had had no input from a friend, he'd had no contradictory voice or dissenting opinion on his state; no differing view to break the cycle of entrenched thoughts. Monica seemed to be that contradicting voice; the differing view. Lately they had been speaking online. Monica would message him with a question. A question that would strike him in the mental gonads. From what Bishop gathered this was Monica's usual *modus operandi* but she seemed to be an instrument of the universe, one sent to make Bishop talk, relate, and open up a bit to the beauty in life. Her most recent inquiry still rang in his mind:

Why do you wake up in the morning?

The question had slapped him in the face. It was one of *the* questions to ask; one he had always asked himself, but had never heard anyone ask him. Monica immediately became something else, something… pertinent. Given pause by this enquiry, Bishop had sat for a while, staring at the blue-green screen of his monitor, then told Monica to call him. Their conversation was lengthy and profound, filled with interesting anecdotes and things which made Bishop relate in turn, even laugh. He loved it: the way she floated in and out of random observations about the little things in her day; talking about how someone dressed, or her myriad experiences of being approached by odd characters in her day-to-day life. It was all fun, and all interesting. Her free-spirited nature was infectious, and it was hard to be mum and boring with her. Chatting with her, he felt the pull, an invisible rope tugging him inch by inch out of his dark room, a room he had grown comfortable in. But the more he spoke to Monica, there were days he didn't fight the rope. He walked with it. Even before Kevin's untimely demise, the *pull* had been there. He remembered an old flame of his. She had been beautiful, caring and gentle. Even with her, he had ignored the pull to be free around her. As much as he tried to be light-hearted and feign happiness, eventually she *knew*. She knew that there was something bubbling in his mind, something of great effect, which followed him wherever he went like a shadow. Eventually she slipped away into the hazy miasma of life, never to be seen again.

Occasionally, large crowds affected him, because within each of them, he saw eventual paths to death and destruction. He felt the lives of everyone around him like a black cloud shadowed by the Grim Reaper. He felt sad knowing they would die, sad for himself even. Would it be swift? Or would he be surrounded by family and friends? This accelerated delusion made everything seem more failure than progress. Love, friendships, career. Blur, blur, blur. Sometimes he wanted to cry, sitting in his artist chair alone in his room, riddled with guilt for reasons he couldn't comprehend. The tears never came. Only silence would greet him, and pain would console him.

For a while after the incident, he had visited a psychotherapist, which never helped. He always remembered every alternate Wednesday going to the man's office, somewhere near Shady Grove. The therapist's office was very neat, like, Martha Stewart neat. On either side of the walls, two identical black cabinets rose up into the air like bouncers at a nightclub. Carefully organized in their hollow interiors, were dozens of books ranging from subjects about basic neurology, motivation, and a few choice selections from Dr. Phil. The walls were a quiet, pastel color that Bishop couldn't name. There was nothing on the wall, save the doctor's diploma in a cheap frame directly behind him. The therapist's desk, large and billowy, was covered with papers, pens and other paraphernalia. As Bishop sat there, he wondered if the therapist had issues. Was he a guy who frantically masturbated to gay porn, liked wearing women's dresses and used to be one of those kids that ate dirt and gotten beaten silly behind school everyday? There was no way Bishop could figure this out. The therapist was a handsome man, with Charlie Sheen hair, a round but attractive face and intense eyebrows. His last name was Goldberg. But nothing had come from it, the man with he good hair and the interesting disposition.

Now there was Monica, the little paragon of convenient niceties: Laughter. Randomization and Beauty.

"Oh God, I have the ugliest Flintstone feet," she had said one day, when they had popped into an old thrift store. She had been giddy when she found a tattered pair of yellow Chuck Taylors with an indiscernible signature of the previous owner scrawled on the back.

"What do you think it says?" she had asked.

"No idea," Bishop replied.

"Definitely getting these," she had said, cradling the dirty shoes fondly. Other times she'd talk forever about tearing her pants, or some random online class she was taking for no logical reason. Every now and then she'd talk about her family, or question the purpose of her life. This is where he tried to ignore *the pull*.

He would poke at her habits, such as smoking and doing otherwise juvenile activities, to which Monica would always give him a strange, furtive look. She did this often when he jibbed her, pausing as she spoke and putting her eyes into a strange formation, with a slight frown in her forehead. The expression made him pause as well, and he would always get lost in the pools of her brown, fairy eyes.

That day, she had invited him to a poetry cipher. They met at the U Street train station but first she made a pit stop at an Internet café.

"Sorry, I get so *grahhh* when I'm waiting on e-mails and I can't check them."

For some reason, she refused to get a smartphone, and was relegated to operating in the modern uber-interconnected world with a very bruised Sprint Flip phone. They walked down U Street past a stream of identical looking row houses, and came to an odd colored building, with a set of stairs going up into what looked like a convenience store. They walked upstairs and entered a starkly clean space about thirty feet across, bristling cold with air conditioning and packed with workstations. A few young guys were excitedly playing some sort of board game in the corner. One waved at Monica. She waved back and started towards a terminal, then stopped quickly.

"Oh, I have something to give you."

She reached into her bag and pulled out a CD. On the cover was a drawing of a man with his brain half out of his head.

"Those are some of my favorite songs."

"Thanks," Bishop said.

She trotted over to a terminal and began furiously typing. Holding the CD in his hand, Bishop felt the tingle again, the tingle rising up from the depths of his mental dark room, slowly illuminating it with light. They weren't there for more than ten minutes. Outside, at the foot of the stairs, a young man in a black jacket was smoking a cigarette. This was Monica's friend, who was also going to poetry night. He had Monica-level energy, and he seemed even more excited than Monica to be going to *Latte Life*, the coffee shop.

The crowd was a mix of people from all walks of life. It was Bishop's first time. Monica had been raving about a particular drink that they had there. Apparently Bishop 'simply had to' try it, or Monica would spontaneously combust. Bishop went to get the drink (some Acai berry fusion or whatever) and stood in the center of the establishment. It was a coffee and food restaurant by day and on Thursdays the doors were open for eager poets and sometimes musicians to let it out in an open-mic fashion. Inside was a large room with a brown theme. When you walked through the door, to your right was a tray that contained sugar, non-dairy creamer, napkins and utensils. Directly in front of that was the cashier's area, which was also a preparation area for the drinks. Adjacent to the cashier were tables and chairs. At the far right of the room were booths that could fit up to five people. Near a booth closest to the front of the room, were a few familiar faces.

Monica seemed to know everyone, and it was a flurry of hugs, hellos and squeals of delight as she walked around the small space. Bishop stood where he was and sipped his drink. There was nowhere to sit. Monica and her friend headed towards a packed booth at the front and squeezed in. He stood and watched a few poets go up and perform their work. They were varied in their styles and delivery. Some came in ready to wow the crowd. They were loud and clear, with sharp, witty delivery, frantic hand gestures and wild eyes. Others came up, reading from a piece of paper, quietly and calmly, still engendering a good response from the crowd. Some were quite strange, like a lady who came up and started singing in a very low voice, quite off-key. She seemed to be in her own world. She had a frazzled head of hair, faraway eyes and baggy clothing. Nonetheless, the crowd received her well, albeit with scattered applause. Bishop didn't mind the poetry scene. He dabbled in writing poetry himself, but was loathe reciting it. Sometimes he wished he could go up there, and angrily vent about things he wanted off his chest and his mind. Then, the *pull* feeling came at him again, tightening him up, preventing him from breaking his mold. He glanced at Monica occasionally, watching her soft features from afar, wondering if she liked what she was hearing. She, her friend and a girl were talking excitedly and Bishop smiled, glad to have accompanied her there.

After an hour or so, Monica motioned for Bishop to come over to where she was.

"Do you want to leave after this next one?" she asked.

"Sure."

The next act came up, a lady with a sweet, booming voice accompanied by a shaggy guitarist who walked with an air of obvious superiority. After they were finished, they headed out.

On the way back, they spoke about where she was from a lot. Bishop didn't know much about her home state of Philadelphia and always asked her questions about what she did, where she went and the things to do there. Monica always seemed surprised when Bishop asked these questions, but she always had a response. They walked in no particular direction.

"So tell me something about yourself that almost no one knows."

Bishop smiled. *Always something provocative and quirky.* The only thing he started to realize was, that she would never answer these types of questions about herself, which put occasionally Bishop on the defensive. He tested the waters.

"You first."

Monica didn't bat an eyelid.

"You see here?" she said, pointing at her nose.

"I actually had a nose-job because I broke my nose playing volleyball, but no one can ever tell."

"Oh?"

"Oh, yes. Okay, now you!" Monica said, interlocking their arms.

He thought for a moment, watching a Lincoln car drive by noiselessly.

"Okay, here's mine. When I was about ten, some kid at school threw a stone and burst the back of my head. It left a scar, and when I was growing up people thought it was a bald spot and always teased me about it."

Monica seemed elated.

"Wow, lemme see!" she said.

Bishop bent over slight and she examined the back of his head. Sure enough, there was a faint, yellowish mark about an inch a half long on the very back of his head.

"Wow, if you had never told me that, I would never have known," Monica said.

"Well, now you know."

They laughed and kept walking together. As they neared an intersection that would lead up to Columbia Heights, Bishop slowed slightly. He wasn't completely ready to leave Monica.

"Hey do you want to crash at my place?" he said.

"Sure," Monica replied.

He hailed a cab.

At his place, Monica seemed to be right at home. She threw her bag on a beanbag in the corner as if she'd been doing it for years. The thin jacket went quickly on the floor beside the bed, and she flopped expertly on the pillows. Bishop paused as he took a good look at her. With her jacket off, he could see she had a nice shape, with a sizeable chest for her height, and curves he must have been blind to not notice before.

"Want to watch a movie?" Bishop said.

"Sure," Monica replied.

Bishop put his jacket on a coat hanger on the inner most part of the closet. He looked at Monica, sitting calmly on the bed.

"Hey do you need some shorts?"

Monica smiled at him and a twinkle of something mischievous flashed through her eyes. "Yeah, I felt like taking these jeans off anyways."

They started watching the movie, a romantic comedy, and eventually fell asleep in each other's arms.

Chapter 25

Winston's heart fluttered with excitement. On a random Wednesday, he had finally given Elsa a call. It was brief, and her tone was different, but she had agreed to see him.

"What are you doing three weeks from now?" she had said.

Three weeks? Winston had thought.

Regardless, they had made an arrangement. The maelstrom in his stomach made him a little worried, but he didn't care. The series of disturbing dreams that left him clutching his head in frustration, his clenched stomach, today maybe it could be resolved. He was in his apartment, rummaging through his closet. Outside looked bright and hot. There wasn't any need to dress particularly nice, but he felt like he should wear a nice shirt. He grabbed a soft white linen shirt and slipped on a pair of his favorite jeans. After a quick sweep of the apartment he was gone.

Elsa lived in Columbia Heights, about thirty minutes walking distance from Winston's house. Winston was right— the day was very hot—and in moments he felt a few dots of sweat form on his back. He stopped at the bus terminal and waited. He wondered what this occasion meant, if running into her in Dupont actually meant anything. The bus came, roaring up from a side street and stopped in front of him with a hiss. The doors opened and Winston was hit with a blanket of cool air.

"Hello," he said to the driver.

The driver, a massive bear of a man with thick braids that ran down to his shoulders nodded in reply. Winston took a seat near the middle of the bus and looked out the window. The trees glistened with dance of light of their leaves, the grass looked more verdant than usual and the sky was startling blue. There wasn't a cloud in the sky. Forgetting himself, Winston smiled. The bus came to a stop at Eleventh Street. This was as close as it would get to where Elsa lived, which was another eight or so blocks away. Winston felt his heart flutter again, and tried to calm himself.

"She's just having lunch with you," he said to himself.

Try as he might, this was very difficult. This wasn't some random chick he met at a bar and had bad sex with or some girl who turned out to be crazy and self-centered two weeks after hanging out with her. This was Elsa.

The blocks rolled along slowly with each of his steps, and he wished he had worn another shirt. He felt damp with sweat even though he wasn't sweating profusely. To the casual passerby, he looked normal. A tad shiny perhaps. He reached the street. There was the apartment building. It loomed in front of him like a beast from the past. It was a large brick building on a slanted street. It rose out of the ground like an oak tree, the roof partially hidden in thick foliage stemming from several large trees beside it. The area was quiet and had the thick smell of a forest. This was a little weird for Winston, because this was in the middle of the city, but it felt as if he had stepped into a little pocket that was hidden from everyone else. The mysticism was corny, but—

"Yap! Yap!" a little dog barked.

Winston would have surely fallen backwards if the bark—and the size of the dog—weren't both enough to warrant a laugh. The dog's owner was a large muscled woman with hard features and spotted skin. Something about her looked leopard like, but she spoke with a sweet grandma voice, the kind you'd hear in an 80's cartoon movie. "Sorry about that, young man."

She walked away and Winston watched them gradually get smaller in the distance. He flipped open his phone and dialed Elsa's number. One ring. Two Ring. Three Rings. Voicemail. His heart fluttered again, until his phone buzzed in his hand. Elsa's name flashed on the LCD.

"Hey, I'm here," Winston said.

"Oh," Elsa replied. She sounded disappointed.

"What's wrong?" Winston asked.

"It's just that… I'm watching this thing on TV and there are a few minutes left. Do you might waiting for a few minutes until I come down?"

Upon hearing this, Winston felt a quick rage fill his body. The three weeks he spent thinking about her, having his dreams and going through an emotional tailspin was all some stupid, childish fantasy. He thought about his actions earlier, as he rummaged through his closet to pick out a nice shirt. *Fucking idiot!*

"Oh… whatever," He said, and closed the phone shut.

He stormed off into the distance. Incredulously, he wondered what was happening. A television program? How important could a show be that she couldn't have invited him inside to watch it with her? He let out a sigh and found himself three blocks away sitting on a concrete block near a park. He gritted his teeth as he tried to imagine her, watching some inane reality drivel on the TV, doing the last retch into the toilet before she composed herself and came down to see Winston. He felt incredibly stupid. Stupid for talking to her at that damn party, and stupid for being so naturally hopeful and—

His phone buzzed. Elsa.

"Hello?" Elsa said.

"Yes," Winston replied curtly.

"Sorry about that just a few minutes left. You still outside?"

Her voice sounded sweet and endearing on the phone. Winston cursed the feeling of joy that sparked in his chest upon hearing her voice.

"I took a walk. Call me when you are outside," Winston said, and hung up.

He sighed, stood up where he was and paced around some more. After taking a few deep breaths, he headed back toward Elsa's. Elsa came out of her apartment looking regal. She was well tanned, and her hair, normally long and luxuriant was tied into a ponytail.

"Hey," she said.

Winston could barely respond. He was still very angry. Her beauty was like another slap in the face.

"Hey," He replied.

They didn't hug. As they started walking, Winston let out a soft curse.

"What's wrong?" Elsa replied.

"I have something for you," Winston said.

Indeed he did. In his hand, was a small brown paper bag. It had a few gifts inside. It was a tradition of sorts, however antiquated. Elsa didn't have a bag with her, so they had to go inside. Her apartment was filled with painful memories. It wasn't the same apartment he knew a few years back, but everything was the same: the small cabinet with her Barcelona knick-knacks. The flag she had from her trip to Brazil, the same set of books. They were all there. Then there was the bed. The large queen-sized bed that Winston had slept in countless times, the bed where Elsa had reached orgasm so many times from his careful work. This was the bed where she told him he was special, where they woke up and made breakfast in the mornings. This was the bed where he sat and watched TV while she was in the kitchen, baking salmon for dinner. It was the bed where they sat and watched a movie on her then-new television, holding each other. It was the bed where she had cried once after they made love: "I'm crying," she had said. "Because it was so good."

Now the bed was a monolith of the past, a devilish spectacle of what was. As quickly as he was flooded with the memories the bed brought back, he was equally flooded with a pinched sense of fear. This would probably be the last time he ever saw it. Elsa opened her gift, and her eyes widened with surprise. She had a look of appreciation tempered with the emotional restriction of someone trying not to look happier than they really were. She liked the gift, but she couldn't hug him, kiss him on the cheek or make too much of a fuss about it could she?

"Thanks," she said.

She took out the contents one by one, eying them carefully. "I love these," she said, not turning towards Winston. She pulled out a small brown bundle, wrapped cheaply in plastic.

"Oh, that's called coconut drops," Winston said with a smile. "A classic Jamaican candy."

"Thanks, I'm sure I'll enjoy them as a late night snack," Elsa replied.

Winston's smile paled when she said this. He remembered a night when he taught her how to make boiled dumplings, and she had said the same thing. That night, he never left the apartment. They had slept together, naked in each other's arms with their lips only inches apart until the sun broke through the blinds and ushered the night away. That morning, they had woken up at the same time, seeing each other's eyes as the first symbol of reality after coming out of the nothingness of sleep.

The apartment was becoming haunting, and Elsa looked as if she sensed the growing cloud over Winston's head.

"Okay, you ready?" Elsa said.

"Yeah."

As they walked for a few blocks towards a street that had shops and cafés, Elsa talked about her work.

"So they are working on a few initiatives to try and help out with some of the conflicts in Darfur. It's a long hard road, but I guess that's why non-profits exist, to make the smallest dent in the—"

Winston wasn't listening. He was happy just to be beside her.

"—A few weeks ago I had to travel up to Boston for a conference. It was actually supposed to be in New York, but at the last minute everything got changed, and boy! That was rough because I had sort of co-coordinated the whole thing and my boss was like—"

Occasionally he glanced at her as she walked. He watched her frame taking long even steps, scattering a few leaves with each step.

"—I like this area, you see that over there? That's getting turned into a dog park. But there isn't any grass and I wonder sometimes how all those dogs will cope with the dust—"

There they were, walking together again. It was a dichotomy of sensations. The last time they walked like this was in Barcelona. They were on a beach, the sun was setting, and she had looked at him with all the love in the world. Now—

"—isn't that right?" Elsa asked.

"I'm sorry can you repeat that?' Winston said.

"You weren't trying to get anything fancy right? Just some coffee or something? Somewhere we can sit and chat, no?"

"Oh…yeah. Anywhere you suggest is fine."

They went to a little café somewhere off U Street. Even though the day was hot, people sat at the tables outside, sipping large glasses of iced tea. People with large smiles, dark khaki shorts and sunglasses pulled back on their heads. Winston ordered a salmon sandwich. Elsa ordered the same. Their attendant was a friendly-faced girl with a soft southern accent.

"Would you like more bread?" she kept asking.

"Well, we could use some jelly," Elsa said.

Elsa was a hearty eater, and picky about her condiments. She could have five slices of garlic bread in front of her, but if there wasn't any jelly or butter around, an attendant just might get pissed off with her demands.

"I need some jelly. Do you think she heard me when I asked?" Elsa said.

"I'm sure she did," Winston replied with a smile.

Good, he thought. *I think I'm relaxing.*

"Why are you always hung up on the little jams and jellies? That's some nice bread there, you better eat up."

Elsa smiled and bit into a large piece of garlic bread.

"So," she said, wiping her mouth on a large orange napkin. "What's been going on with you?"

Winston went through the intricate details of the past year and a half. Naturally like any guy, he left out all the details about any women he had slept with (there were only two), the dreams about Elsa, and how empty he felt on certain days. Instead, he spoke about working in D.C, his cave-like office and bizarre co-workers. As he spoke, he felt his spirit rise. There were so many times he and Elsa had sat and talked just liked this. They had talked, laughed, made love. She watched him with a soft smile on her face. Her cloudy green eyes seemed filled with passion, and a bead of sweat formed on her forehead. She looked beautiful, in a sweaty summer way. Winston was feeling comfortable, but it was fleeting. This was his chance to tell Elsa he loved her, to declare it in an honest and proper way, even if it broke him. After all the introspection, the flakey girls and feeling empty, he had nothing to lose.

"Listen Elsa, there is something I want to tell you."

Elsa's eyebrow's raised and for a second she looked frightened, then her soft smile returned.

"I never was able to tell you enough that I love you. There are a lot of things I wish I could have changed... but I want to tell you now while I'm here."

Winston reached out for Elsa's hand. She clasped it awkwardly.

"Winston, you're frightening me. What's going on?" Elsa said.

"Nothing. Don't worry I'm not going to pop out a ring or anything. I'm just holding your hand because I'm telling you something serious. Is that okay?"

Elsa gave him an odd look, but she didn't withdraw her hand. Winston let her hand go.

"Look, I'm not trying to make you feel uncomfortable. It's just… I want to know if there is anything inside you that still feels something for me. Seriously."

Like a scene from a dramatic movie, Elsa removed the elastic from her ponytail, and her hair fell down the sides of her face, accentuating her features. She looked gorgeous.

"Winston, I thought I already told you that I'm not feeling that way."

"But Elsa, I don't know what happened. I mean, I think about you a lot, okay? And I care, I mean I really care about you."

Elsa's face filled with mixed emotions. "I'm sorry Winston, I just don't feel that way about you anymore."

The word "anymore" echoed through the hallways of Winston's mind like a bell in the Sistine Chapel. The noise traveled through the vast expanse of Winston's entire mind. All the memories they shared seemed to drop into a house-sized shredder. Everything spun around in Winston's mind for a moment.

"Winston?" Elsa said.

Winston was standing up. He started walking toward a small gate that lead out of the patios. Winston's chest felt like two hundred pounds of weight were strapped to it. He looked up. The sky was bright and beautiful. It seemed to be laughing at him. Elsa dropped a twenty on the table and walked behind Winston. Winston stood there, shaking his head a few times. The noise of everything around him had quieted, all he heard from the depth of his soul was:

I don't feel that way about you anymore.

It kept echoing inside him Echoing, echoing, echoing. His emotions sloshed around his body like a tidal wave caught in a well, and the water levels had started rising. His hands began to tremble, and his teeth started chattering. Oh God, Winston realized. He was about to start crying. Elsa stood quietly behind him. Winston felt the first tear break from his left eye.

"No!" he shouted in protest.

A mixture of self-pity, anger and hopelessness had enveloped him. He was about to have a major breakdown, or as his friends in Jamaica would say, "Bawl over a gyal". He walked a few paces towards the corner of the street and held onto a lamppost. Now the tears were running freely, and he felt his chest heaving. This was worse than his dreams, worse than his sexual frustrations. Now he was crying with the girl who no longer felt "that way" about him right there. Winston wanted to escape. He wanted to run away, but he couldn't move.

"Winston?" Elsa said.

Her voice sounded nearby, but she never approached him. As Winston crossed the street, and sat on some steps and wept, Elsa was always ten or fifteen feet away. Eventually this, more than the crying, would be the deepest blow. Winston occasionally looked at Elsa, and she wasn't looking at him. She walked around in circles idly. Looking off into the distance, looking at her cell phone, or just standing up. At no point did she walk over and say anything. Winston was a mess of words and actions. He started mumbling about how many things he lost in his life. He mumbled about being a loser, wanting to die and how he would never love again. This all came out in an incomprehensible mix of Jamaican patois and regular English. After fifteen minutes, Elsa said: "So, what do you want to do for the rest of the day?"

Winston stopped. What they were to do next? There was nothing next. Elsa was no longer a part of his life. The TV thing was bad enough, but this... coldness was new. She stood there, mute as a dead man, watching, waiting. Winston replied to this statement in the way anyone would:

"Don't you see me right now? Can't you see how out of it I am? If you want to leave you can go. I think I'll stay here for a while."

Elsa looked up for a second, as if processing what he said. Then she spoke. "Look, everyone goes through the same thing. Love hurts," she said matter-of-factly.

Winston almost laughed. Love hurts! It was blatantly patronizing. Was Elsa really that naïve? Did Elsa even know how much salt she was throwing into Winston's wound? Winston looked at the traffic. The crosswalk sign had a large amber hand on a LCD screen clearly displayed. Cars blazed back and forth, streaks of color in the hot summer sun. Winston saw himself getting up and running. He would run out into the road. He wouldn't' see the car. It would hit him in the knees, shattering his shins and twisting an ankle. The momentum would toss him upwards and his face would hit the windshield. The force of this impact hopefully would snap his neck and send him screaming into the black abyss, but if not the glass would tear deep grooves into his face, his shoulder bones would both splinter as his body found its way into the car and most likely, the driver would be gouged painfully by a shard of bone or a stray piece of glass.

Winston saw this play out in his mind beautifully, but knew it wasn't the best solution. He would die and Elsa wouldn't' even attend the funeral. She'd probably be sitting in her apartment, watching some dumb TV program and eyeing her cell phone, thinking, "Winston's funeral is today," and not even bat an eyelash.

Winston snapped out of his suicidal fantasy. Elsa was still pacing around looking at nothing in particular. Winston thought about explaining to her how her words had stung him, but he realized it didn't matter. If she had run over and hugged him and told him he'd be all right he still wouldn't be going home with her. No more would they sit and playfully argue about world topics, cook food for each other or take long baths together. In a split second, Elsa had gone from a fragmented thought to nothing. She had disappeared. With tears still in his eyes, Winston turned away from Elsa and started walking. He walked and walked, until Elsa was far behind him, still looking at her feet, as if wondering what to do.

Chapter 26

Tony sat in Adams Morgan at a French Café sipping a lukewarm latte. His head was spinning a little—thanks to last night's last minute party at some shady apartment near the Hill. A short attendant with greasy hair and a neck tattoo that barely read "requiem" brought his sandwich over. Tony made fast work of it and headed to Wonderland. It was relatively empty, with the exception of an extremely tall blond woman dancing excitedly with three other people on the dance floor. Tony nodded at a few regulars at the spot, realizing this also made him a regular. Those fellows were all faces and expressions, people he had never spoken to; members of the looking-glass dive bar world of D.C. Tony said hi to a few people and chatted with a new bartender. She'd lived in D.C for seven years and seemed to like it. Like many people Tony started to realize, she fit the formula of *comes-from-wealthy-suburb of X big city moved to D.C for X school's program to go to X school's grad program to work in X NGO.* She seemed interesting. Maybe in a few weeks he'd get a free beer or two from her. He felt a dull vibration in his pocket from his phone. It was a text message.

Come to the club, we have a guest hookup! ~ *Shyla*

Tony downed his beer. Before he left, he ran into another regular, but one he actually knew. He was a handsome guy of average height with dark brown skin. Tony couldn't remember his name.

"Dibs on the girl behind you," the fellow said.

Tony turned to see a dark-haired girl sitting at the bar with two other girls.

"She's Swedish," he said with a grin.

Tony smiled. *Euro girls*, he thought. A brief dialogue about European women ran on for forty-five seconds and then he left. A quick cab ride later, he was in Dupont. He hopped into a bar across from an Empanada stand and did a few rails, watching people in football jerseys excitedly rave about a re-run of a Redskins game.

Buzz.

Ah, man! My host is wilding right now and you have to pay to get in, but I have two drinks for you when you come in!~ Shyla

It wasn't a difficult decision. Dodging early night traffic, Tony stepped into the club, somewhere near the 18th Street lounge. He immediately recognized the girl at the door. She bartended at a restaurant she went to every now and then. After some light-chit chat, he went upstairs. The empty hallway downstairs was an illusion. Immediately he could hear the meshed buzz of a crowd. People packed the small dance floor and the DJ was playing some sort of drum and bass fusion. In the middle of the dance floor, twins in matching outfits were milking their coolness, raving and doing shots with girls. Tony went to the bar. Shyla was serving a client. She had a Beatles style bowl hair cut, a shimmering silver top and wore skinny black jeans. Shyla saw Tony and winked at him.

"I like your hair," Tony said.

"Thanks!" she chirped. "I cut it myself."

Tony smiled. "It's very a mod style."

She laughed and starting doing a variety of poses: "This is mod and this is the bod!"

She gave her *derriere* a quick slap and laughed again.

"Now about that drink," Tony said.

"What do you want?" Shyla asked.

"Anything is fine."

"Anything?"

Tony shrugged. "Well, recommend something."

"D you like light beer, dark beer or mixed drinks? What's your poison sir?"

"I'll try a dark beer," Tony replied.

"Russian it is!" she exclaimed.

"Russian?"

"Well most of the dark beers here are Russian. Don't worry, trust me you'll like it."

Shyla reached up to the third shelf behind the bar, her shirt rising up briefly to show a thin line of pale skin.

"Here you go," she said.

The beer was tall and dark. Tony had no idea what the label meant. It had a kick on his tongue when he sipped it.

"Gotta deal with some people now babe, just hit me up when you need another one!"

Shyla turned to two guys who seemed more than happy she was serving them. Tony took a stroll to the second level upstairs. A decent crowd was traipsing about. The DJ had switched to a tired selection of reggae dancehall tracks from the early nineties. Tony groaned slightly and sipped more of the beer. The twins were making a lot of noise, dancing happily without rhythm with their entourage. Tony made eye contact with one of them briefly. He made a beeline for Tony.

"Hey man, what's up!"

Tony smiled and raises his beer a la cheers.

"It's me, man, Eddie! Come have a drink with us!"

Confusion flashed over Tony's face for a split second. But only a split second.

"Edddddie! Of course!" Tony said.

They had a small table near the rear of the club. Twin number two is named Eric. Eddie gave an excited introduction to his brother who immediately waved to a nearby attendant. A fresh glass appeared and Tony had a drink thrust into his hand.

"What's this?"

"Never mind that!" Erick said.

Whatever it was, it was *strong*. The Russian Beer and the "twin surprise" were starting to have an effect. Both twins seemed like cool guys, both at the club with their girlfriends and a few other friends scattered around. Tony danced a bit, feeling a slight buzz cover him like a thin blanket. Soon, he went downstairs past a row of mannequins housed in glass displays. Each mannequin was in a different party pose; one was dancing, the other doing a shot and one was just staring straight ahead. Near the last mannequin were a group of girls. They all had a spray tan dirty-blond vibe. One of them was the splitting image of the actress who played the rock star in *Strange Days*. Tony chatted to Rock Star girl about the mannequin. She was surprisingly witty.

"Hey I want to take a picture of you and Wilfred," the girl said.

"Wilfred, who's that?" Tony asked.

"Wilfred is right beside you," she replied.

Tony turned to see the mannequin.

"How do you know its name is Wilfred?"

"It's a mannequin, it can be whatever it wants to be."

"But you want it to be Wilfred."

"And so it is."

"And the picture?" Tony asked.

"You look sort of like a model, so I thought it would be cool to catch the model and the mannequin in the same pose."

"I charge for pictures," Tony said.

Rock Star girl laughed.

"What's the price, superstar?"

"A kiss on the cheek," Tony replied.

She turned to her friend and whispered into her ear. They both started laughing. They had really good spray tans.

"Just pose already, beautiful."

Tony tried his best to imitate the mannequin. With a *click* the deed was done.

"You have a nice spirit," Rock Star girl said.

Tony smiled.

"We are going back upstairs. You should come with!" she said.

"Sure," Tony replied.

A new member of the team appeared, a short grizzly guy wearing a Kangol hat. Tony could tell he didn't know the girls either. He seemed quite comfortable with himself and moved with a very relaxed, practiced body language. He led the group to a back area with a small red couch directly beside a stripper pole. It was a revelation that Tony hadn't seen the pole beforehand.

"I have a dollar," Tony whispered to Rock Star girl. "Do something for it."

"Oh really now?" she said with a slight giggle. "Why don't you work with this?"

She pulled a hundred dollar bill from her purse and waved it in Tony's face.

"I give up! I know when I'm beaten."

Rock Star girl gave him a kiss on the cheek.

"Make sure I get a receipt for that," she cooed.

They sat on the couch and chatted some more. Her friends didn't seem to mind whatever was going on, and the guy in the Kangol was already very cozy with one.

"Here you go!" a voice said.

It was one of the twins, but Tony couldn't remember which one. He handed Tony another drink. Tony took a sip.

"Fuck, that's strong."

Kangol hat guy pulled out a vial of coke and did a hit, then offered it to the girls. Two of them took a hit, including Rock Star girl.

"You girls are going hard," Tony said.

"What do you mean?"

"I mean you party hard."

"I still don't know what you mean. We just got here."

Her face was clouded with confusion, and Tony realized that in her world, doing hits of coke with random guys was probably normal.

"It's no biggie," Tony said.

A few more hits of coke later and Rock Star girl was giving Kangol hat guy a lap dance. During the snort fest, Eddie or Erick had fished Tony another drink, and he started to feel his body get soft and light. Whatever music was playing was some weird Euro vibe, and the bass made the couch vibrate slightly. Flashing lights and the dark outlines of the increased number of bodies in the club all merged into a pulsing blob. Ice clinked against Tony's teeth as he sipped his drink. A feeling of a sudden release in pressure beside him brought him back to reality. The group had gotten up. Kangol hat guy was walking away with a girl in each arm. Briefly, Rock Star girl turned to him, and blew him a kiss. They soon faded into the blob; the only thing visible was the little kangaroo symbol at the back of the guy's hat, shining blue in the black light of the club.

Tony stood up, and a quick, wet feeling of fear went through his body. His left arm trembled slightly, and everything felt louder and brighter. The noise of the club was now a roaring melee of bass and voices. People seemed to be *everywhere,* closer and closer to where he was. Things felt hot. He briskly went downstairs, almost hitting an attendant with a tray of drinks in one hand. In the bathroom, he splashed his face with cold water, and tried to catch his breath. His eyes closed, and as the cold water slowly numbed his face, things started to calm down. He took long even breaths, and wiped his face with a few paper towels. Back outside, he walked to the bar on the first floor. Shyla walked over quickly.

"Hey I was worried about you," she said. "You okay?"

Tony flashed her a thousand watt smile. "I'll take that second drink now."

Still frowning slightly, Shyla gave a light smile and nodded, turning around. Tony let out another slow breath. Something wet was in his hand. He looked down, and saw that he was still clenching one of the paper towels.

Chapter 27

The plan was a movie at Lowe's Theatres. Previously they were supposed to catch some new flick at the E-Street Cinema, some modern day Korean horror movie, but Monica said she had a film she needed to see again. With Monica, it seemed many things were done in sets of two. She had recently attended two shows some local punk band had, went twice to an art installation somewhere in Bethesda, and now it was this movie she wanted to see again. Bishop had done some light research on the film. Some watered down story about a man's struggle to reach a friend through some family trauma or some junk. He didn't really watch movies, or much of anything these days. He was idling near a bus stop on M street. He had considered driving there but it was pointless. The theatre was only ten minutes away by foot and parking was atrocious in Georgetown. The hiss of giant brake pads sounded in the distance, and Bishop saw the tiny outline of the G2 Bus approaching. Soon, it came to where he was. A stream of people filtered out.

"Hey," Monica said as she gave him a light, firm hug.

The walk was uneventful. Monica spoke about some weird experience she had at the French Connection store back in the day. Bishop told her when he had a Lacoste fetish and bought so many Polos people thought he worked at the store.

"That's just like people here," Monica said.

"What do you mean?"

"To think you work at the store instead of just being a regular consumer."

"I don't get you."

"I mean, if you saw a white guy who always wore Lacoste shirts would you assume he works at the Lacoste store?"

"Well—" Bishop started.

"Exactly. Instead of someone saying, 'Hey man, I like your style,' or whatever, people assume that you are getting your shit discounted, on the cheap. The happy employee thirty percent off or whatever is it they get."

Bishop nodded nonchalantly.

"Is it like that in Jamaica?" Monica asked.

"The same kinds of assumption-based behavior you mean?"

"Yeah. Do people rock Lacoste in Jamaica?"

"Not really," Bishop replied.

"So what do people wear?"

"Well, its kind of chill. There are a few malls here and there where people shop. I used to buy a lot of Guess."

"Guess? You have a Guess store but no Lacoste?"

"Yeah."

"But I mean how do people *dress?* Like in the club or whatever."

"Ah, guys wear like, Polos and jeans a lot. Girls, maybe dresses or stuff like that most of the time."

"So people *don't* dress up to go to the club?"

"Well, the girls do. Not so much the guys."

"Weird."

They reached the theater. Immediately, the scent of the Potomac hit Bishop's nose. He casually glanced across the street. Behind an idling Maserati, a few families straight out of a Normal Rockwell painting were picnicking on the grass. In the evening, the sun coolly shimmered on the surface of the river. He grabbed the tickets. A huge attendant greeted them. He was a tall with a large head; a low cut Afro and big orb-like eyes. His mouth was fixed into a permanent smile and he had an uncharacteristically high and chirpy voice.

"Weellllllcome to Lowes theatres! Can I have your tickets please?"

Bishop and Monica gave each other a quick glance and a smile.

"Thannnnnnk you very much! Your movie theatre is number eight! Please have fun and ennnjoy the rest of your night!"

They chuckled to each other once they were out of earshot of the cartoonish attendant. They walked towards the movie theatre. It was around five in the evening, but the massive theatre felt quiet, almost tomb-like. The hallway was a good thirty feet across, with clean freshly steamed carpet snaking into all the rooms with screens. Theatre eight was almost empty, save two people sitting to their far right.

"Bathroom calling," Monica announced.

Bishop sat back and kicked his feet up. There was nothing on the screen yet, save some flashing advertisements. A noisy rock song ushered in the first wave of previews. Monica came back.

Halfway between the movie he lifted the divider that held his cup, and pulled Monica close to him. She lay on his chest, watching the movie at a somewhat awkward angle. Somewhere in between a long musical scene and the climax of the movie, they kissed. It was sweet and lingering. The touch of her skin and her smell flooded his senses; the noise of the theatre behind them shrouding them in chaos. Her tongue slowly encircled his, and her arms softly clasped his neck.

Bishop felt a sudden, powerful erection. His heart raced and his entire body felt rigid. The darkness of the last several months started falling like ash in front of his eyes. He had forgotten the taste and touch of a woman, and Monica's lips were a whiplash to his senses. They broke the kiss and she squeezed his hand firmly. She turned her attention back towards the movie, her head still on Bishop's chest. Bishop was still slightly rigid, his blood rushing fast, the intensity of his erection surprising him.

After the movie ended Monica took her second bathroom break, falling into her pattern of two's flawlessly. They left the theatre and walked back towards the bus stop.

"Oh man, I wish I didn't have to finish this project right now!" Monica said as the bus pulled up. She gave his hand a squeeze and kissed him softly on the lips. As the bus squeaked and disappeared into the distance, Bishop could feel the warm night air on his skin. He felt hot, charged with something. It snaked through his arms and legs. The slightest tremble moved his upper lip. Things felt clear, and sharp. His phone buzzed.

I want you tonight! ~ *Monica.*

Bishop smiled and started walking home, through the sea of shadowy Georgetown back streets. He thought of kissing Monica in the theatre again. The smell on her lips, the way her hands clasped his neck. Another raging erection came, and another instance of feeling like a hot rag was on his face. Whatever this energy was, it kept him going. He walked past the block that would normally take him to his house, up the cobblestone streets and past a few shops long closed for the evening. He walked across the bridge with the cycling path, and then he neared Dupont Circle. He stopped at the traffic light and idly glanced leftward and saw a pizzeria. A wet, cold feeling settled over him and he immediately felt his stomach cramp. This was where he had received the call. It was one of those nights almost a year ago. He had been with some people, the names and faces a blur. The tail end of some random Friday night.

He had been laughing for sure, someone had made a lewd joke, there was a girl on his arm or the prospect of one. They had all been smiling then his phone started ringing. The theme from 80's cartoon *G.I Joe* had blared into the night air from his phone speakers, causing the group to erupt into more laughter. Bishop had laughed too as he pulled out the phone, surprised to see a Jamaican area code on the LCD.

"Hello?" Bishop answered.

"BOOTY CALL!" someone behind him had screamed.

More laughter. A hand grabbed his ass.

"Guys!" Bishop chuckled.

"Bishop, how are you?" a voice said.

It was the gravelly baritone of his father's voice.

"Dad, what's up? I'm out with some people no—"

"Tell me. Was something wrong with Kevin?" his father said.

"Kevin? What do you mean?"

There was a slight pause on the phone.

"Bishop, I mean do you know if Kevin had any sort of issues. Psychologically?"

"Psychological? What? What are you talking about?"

The group jeered again, but Bishop waved for them to calm down. Another long pause.

"Nothing I'll call you back."

Then someone had said something, something he couldn't remember and they had stepped into the pizzeria. The faces were coming back to him now: a few friends from college and some friends of their friends. There was a cute girl that night showing him particular attention, a cute art major from Howard. Inside, they were sitting at a table, noisy and boisterous, laughing about everything and nothing. Then the phone rang again.

"Jesus Christ, man, she is PERSISTENT!" someone had shouted.

chuckled nervously and looked at the phone. It was his home number again.

He walked outside with the phone.

"Uh, hello? I don't really know what you were talking about earli—"

"Bishop. Why would Kevin do that to himself?" his father said.

"Do what?"

His father's voice came again, frantic and urgent. His father's voice had never sounded like that to him. Bishop's blood ran cold.

"Bishop tell me, WHY would Kevin do that to himself?"

For a moment, Bishop's mind flashed to the image of Kevin when they were driving to the airport. Kevin sitting tall and slumped in the front seat of the BMW, dark glasses on.

"Do what? Dad, I really don't know what you are talking about. Did something happen?"

"BISHOP. WHY WOULD HE DO THAT TO HIMSELF?"

Eyes already misty from the alcohol, Bishop felt something clamp around his chest. Little arms covered in barbs were grabbing his intestines. A powerful sobriety immediately washed over him. He racked his brain. What could Kevin have done? Unless…

"Dad are you saying he hurt himself?"

"Bishop… do you want me to say it? You really want me to say it?"

"Oh fuck. Oh Fuck! Are you saying he killed himself?"

Bishop hadn't realized, but he was shouting. There was another long pause on the phone. His father's voice came again, softer.

"Bishop, he shot himself this morning."

"He did-what? He shot himself?"

"Yes, they found him this morning in his house."

The phone had fallen, and he had immediately thrown up. The world turned red and the invisible things clamped his

entire body in a vice grip. The world had swirled around and around, and on the ground he could hear the tinny speakers of the phone and his father's voice saying, *Bishop? Bishop? Bishop....*
Bishop? Are you there?
Are you there...
Are you there....

Bishop was staring at the windowpane of the Pizzeria. It was currently empty and he could see the silhouettes of the past event. The people inside rushing out to see what was wrong. Him a few feet away, on the ground, throwing up and in a state of disbelief. He saw someone holding the phone talking to his father. Then saying, "Fuck."

The phantoms shimmered and vanished. At the same time Monica's image came to the forefront of his senses. He felt his blood rush to his head again and that feeling, that *charge* spread through his muscles. He turned around and walked home. Upon reaching his apartment, he went slowly into his art space. Dead center, a canvas stood idly; dusty and neglected.

They found him this morning in his house.

He took up the brush, and his painting board, dabbing a few drop of acrylics on it. The power he felt before was still inside him, the charge. Slowly, he started to paint. A dark blur of color formed slowly into a shape and texture. Bishop's hand moved with dexterity and swiftness. He splashed paint rapidly and quickly, spreading and forming. A form soon emerged as time passed, a tall figure sitting on a chair. The main on the chair was tall and slumped, in a room with a window. More details, more paint, more echoes of brush strokes in the late night.

They found him this morning in his house.

He painted faster, and the image became clearer. A man, tall and shirtless, sitting on a chair, looking out a window. A man in dark glasses. A man with skin the color of sand. A man like Kevin. Bishop fell to the ground, shuddering and choked, whimpering moans escaped his body. It was a brutal explosion of tears and it was not short. He lay on the ground, crying, as the man sat in the chair on the canvas, staring out at an invisible world.

Chapter 28

"We recommend these shoes for running," the attendant said, picking up a pair of ghastly silver and black shoes. "They help to prevent over pronation and provide good support."

Winston remembered his research on pronation—the way a person can run badly and warp their feet—and made a note in his mind.

"But it all depends on what kind of runner you are honestly."

"Thanks I'll keep looking around," Winston replied.

The running had become a consistent reaction to his nightmares, but Winston had found himself doing it more frequently and earlier. Something triggered a wash of good feeling after he hit thirty minutes of running. Endorphins, he had read, and it was the only relief he was experiencing of late. The nightmares still came fast and brutal, with no end in sight. Sometimes they were weird and incomprehensible. One dream had a fat, pregnant Elsa saying hurtful things to him, other dreams he would be in some place and he could feel her nearby, on a floor above him in an apartment building, or across a street ensconced in a throng of people.

The running had started to show its effects. The slight boyish plumpness in his cheeks was gone. His eyes seemed harder somehow. The sun had made his complexion slightly darker, even though he ran mostly at night. His body started feeling lighter and stronger. These side benefits didn't really do much for Winston. He knew the running was some futile attempt to escape reality, to run like Forrest Gump only realizing that no matter how far people run, they can't run from themselves.

The run had a very predictable crescendo. He would warm up in his apartment, doing light foot taps while listening to some music on his iPod. As his runs became more frequent, he had purchased an armband for the device. Then as the run started, he would like the feeling of whatever wind hit his face. He would take in the sights and sounds with his different routes. He'd run around the dam and by Howard University. He would run through Adams Morgan during the evening, feeling the stark difference from its nighttime bacchanal.

Occasionally, if his motivation flagged, he would stop, jog in place and do a series of overhead claps. Sometimes he would run until exhaustion forced him to lean on a wall, but there were times his legs were those of a horse, prepared for long unbroken runs of incredible distances. Musicians were his companions, the soft crooning of Coldplay, the roaring maelstrom that is System of a Down, or the 'cool ruler' Gregory Isaacs. These were the soundtracks of his runs; the soundtracks of his life.

Often, he wondered if he would ever see Elsa when running around the city. He didn't remember where she worked (and had no interest in running by where she worked either) but he wondered if one day, body sweaty with his white headphones on, if he would see her. Would she smile at him and wave, or simply pretend not to see him? It didn't matter, because as often as he ran, and as frequently as he changed his routes, he never saw her.

Today, he was at Pentagon City, in the DSW store. He had been looking at several pairs of shoes for a while, unable to decide. His legs and knees were pretty strong normally, and a doctor had once told him he had "perfect feet" so there wasn't too much worry about ultimate padding and protection. A pair of Yellow and black Adidas running shoes caught his eye. They had a hint of Jamaica in them and a style he liked. He picked up a size ten. An attendant at the counter ran his card and asked him if he wanted a DSW store card. He said no.

On the train ride back, he also thought about Amy. Lately she had been a sort of reprieve. They would chat on the phone intermittently, and he had accompanied her to a charity event at a primary school. She had just finished two years in the Peace Corps in Korea, and was in transition, looking for a job, preferably with a non-profit.
She told him to meet her in Dupont Circle this evening. He would run there.

Thirty minutes later, in a quick dry shirt and his new shoes, he jogged in place at the traffic light across from the block that led to the bookstore. Amy was standing outside, book in hand, dressed in a pair of close-fitting jeans and a simple shirt. She looked up as he came closer.

"Look at you Mr. Fitness!"

Winston smiled. "Trying a thing you know."

Amy closed her book. "You ever read any Murakami?"

"What's that now?"

"Murakami. A Japanese author. I sort of got into his work when I was in Korea," Amy said.

"No, I haven't."

"Well, you should. For some reason I think you'd like it."

"Well, any recommendations?" Winston asked.

" 'Norwegian Wood' is good'. Dude has some serious writing chops."

Winston made a mental note of what she said.

"What are you thinking of? We can have anything except Korean."

"Thai is good," he said.

They walked to Thaiphoon, two blocks away. She ordered Pad Thai and Winston had a spicy chicken dish. The banter was light and casual. Amy talked about Korea and all the cultural differences between an Asian country and America. She told story after story. There were one or two Korean guys who became obsessed with her, a narrow run-in with some gangsters because of some English teacher that had a coke habit, and a brief spell dating a guy from Australia. Now that she was back in D.C, she was "kind of" seeing her old boyfriend from graduate school. Winston took it all in, glad for the company.

"So enough about me. What about you? Any girl around these days?"

The mention of this made a brief feeling of uneasiness crawl up Winston's leg.

"Well," Winston started. Somehow it all came out. He started speaking about it slowly, how the relationship had dissolved without much bad vibes, but for some reason her re-emergence on the scene had affected a major nerve, he couldn't deal with the lost love. He didn't mention the nightmares or that he couldn't sleep and was running manically, but Amy face became very concerned. Winston paused for a minute and Amy looked at him, thoughtful.

"Why do you even care about this girl so much?"

Winston had no answer. "I can't put a finger on it."

"There's no other girl right now?"

"No."

"I'm really sorry to hear you are so unhappy. On the surface I would never have known. Is that why you've lost weight?"

"That's probably just me accelerating my running program."

Amy seemed satisfied by this. "Well, if you need someone to talk to. I'm here," she said.

"Thanks," Winston replied.

"In fact Greg was telling me about an event coming up this weekend. Some big party at a warehouse somewhere. We'll be going with some friends. You should come."

It had been a while since Winston had done anything like that.

"It's a plan."

They ordered some dessert, and Amy went into a few more war stories about Korea.

Chapter 29

Tony didn't understand. The young woman said she hated going into forests, but did some sort of non-profit work for a forest conservatory. It was a Thursday night, the day that orbits the weekend. This was at a happy hour in a quiet bar in the Northwest. He took her number and said they'd probably hang out soon, but he knew he wouldn't call her. Ben had messaged him earlier, saying that he and some people were hanging out at Bossa. It had been a while since he last saw Ben, and he was bored. He took the train to Dupont but stepped out of the wrong exit in Dupont Circle, putting him a full three blocks north of where he was supposed to go.

"Fuck. Fuck. Fuck," he muttered.

At the exact same time, a little child with the most innocent eyes ever walked by and froze in mid-walk. Then he saw the parent directly behind, eyes blazing with anger, grab the little girl and walk away quickly with her. For a second Tony felt embarrassed.

Welcome to the real world, little girl."

He didn't really feel like hanging with Ben and some people he didn't know right now, but there wasn't much else to do. It was like his intermittent aversion to the Dupont North exit, it happened without his control. At Bossa, Ben was chatting to a mixed group of students from American. Tony groaned inwardly. Sometimes they could be a tricky crowd.

On cue, one guy said, "Hi I'm Abe. I go to *American.*"

Tony nodded, shook his hand as he sat down. Whispering into his ear, Ben told Tony that one of the girls offered him her virginity while studying for some final recently.

"You really believe she's a virgin at this age?" Tony whispered back.

"A guy can always hope," Ben said.

Tony went to the bar to get a drink. A group of young, white professional women stood adjacent to the bartender. They snatched up their purses and phones as Tony stood beside them.

"Don't worry guys, I have my own phone and I left my purse at home. This is Dupont after all."

One of the girls laughed and asked Tony his name but he didn't respond because he was genuinely annoyed by their behavior. He bought a vodka cranberry and went back to the table. They were doing that highbrow college banter that Tony sometimes couldn't deal with, and he idly looked through his phone, wondering who 'Erica no. 3' was.

One of the girls is a libertarian and this is an issue with someone else in the group. Now they are chatting about Capitalism. One guy, wearing a crushed shirt with a shaggy head of hair raised his hand almost the way a professor would.

"Capitalism functions on being continuously expansive. To exist it has to keep using more and more resources," shaggy guy said.

"So are you saying if Capitalists don't keep expanding or spreading their interests, capitalism itself will fail?" another guy asked.

"No, I'm just saying it's expansive. Sort of like a virus. I mean, how many stores can you open? How many fast food chains or vehicles produced yearly does the planet really need?"

Another girl in the group made a weird grunting noise. She spoke, saying, "Well, Capitalism works because even in America poor people have cable."

Tony fought hard to stifle a laugh. He had heard these sorts of conversations over and over. A stream of ideologies overlapping ideologies from absolutist standpoints. Success was all about pulling yourself up by the bootstraps, making it happen "regardless", forgetting about *them,* the minorities and slavery. Forget about all of *them* institutionalized hang-ups and red tape, Poor people have cable. America is great.

After another drink everyone went to Science Club. Ben's friend Fox was there. Oddly, he is dressed exactly like Fox Mulder from *The X-Files.* They walk in, and to Tony's surprise, the crowd seems reasonably interesting and mixed. Ben told Tony he's "In" with the girl, and Tony nodded, throwing him a light smile. He eyed the crowd. A girl in a cute purple dress was standing by the bar. She had a short-sleeved tattoo on her upper arm. Her eyes were dark and mysterious. Tony walked over.

"Hi. Caught your eye and just wanted to say hello," Tony said.

"Well, hello to you too."

The DJ started playing an old dancehall song. The girl's eyes twinkled with an odd amusement.

"Whatever this is, I like it," she said.

"You've never heard this song."

"No, is that bad?"

As she said this, she held Tony's forearm in a way that suggested complete and pure innocence.

"No worries. It's dancehall music," Tony explained.

The girl's eyes lit up again with that odd look of excitement. Then almost as quickly, they flashed with a hint of trepidation as if she was a little child walking into a dark room.

"Can I tell you? I don't know what he is saying," she said.

"He is speaking Jamaican patois. Must be weird for you. "

The girl laughed softly. "Yes, a little strange. Can you translate some of it for me?"

He explained a few lines, which made her laugh. He laughed too. There were so many things about Jamaica's past and present embedded in dancehall music. There were political statements, violent sentiments and religious mish-mash, broken English mixed with Spanish, remnants of French and forgotten African languages. How could he ever truly explain this to anyone? He broke down the basics to her. He told her about some of the origins dealing with anti-political agendas in the early forms of the music, then the eventual evolution into the hypersexual party music it was today.

"Are you a musicologist?"

"Heck, no. Why would you ask that?"

"You seem to know your stuff very well... at least, how you explain it."

She bought Tony a drink. She held his forearm again, with that curious expression of innocence that made her seem like she was asking each question for the first time in her life.

"Do you like house music?"

"On occasion."

"I think there is an event you must come to. I am doing a little promotion for it, but I think you will like it. Some guys I know are throwing a big warehouse party."

Tony's heart beat a little faster. There was nothing he loved more than a warehouse party. A huge open space of raving debauchery.

"I will definitely be there."

"That is good," she said, her eyes shining with that weird twinkle again. "Take this and you don't have to pay or anything."

She slipped what looked like a green credit card into Tony's hand. It was blank with the exception of a weird symbol printed on one side and the address and date of the party in very fine print below it. In his peripheral vision, he could see Ben kissing the girl from American on the other side of the room. The others were there as well, chatting excitedly as they sipped on Bud Lights.

"Do you only promote parties?" Tony asked.

The woman smiled sheepishly and sipped on her drink.

"I do many things, I will tell you more later."

She definitely had some kind of weird aura, Tony thought. She squeezed his arm one more time.

"Some people I know are here. I will see you at the party yes?"

"Definitely."

"Until the universe brings us together again, Mr. Jamaica."

She walked over to a group of people Tony had seen walk in recently. He couldn't figure out why, but they seemed to have a similar, almost childish energy about them. He finished his drink and took a look at the green card again, feeling more excitement run up his spine.

Chapter 30

The guys from the Sushi spot had told Bishop about a party happening that night. They lived somewhere near Columbia Heights, and their spot was simply known as the Japanese house. It was always a good vibe, and Bishop had told Monica to come. At his apartment, he was ready. In a pair of black jeans, a blue Armani exchange shirt and a black trucker hat.

He arrived a little early, parking a block away. He walked up a small flight of stairs. Two people were sitting on a patio chair, talking in low-hushed voices about something. He walked into the living room sat on the couch, taking in the Japanese house. On entering, there was a huge picture of Nelson Mandela on the wall directly above a mysterious hole in the floor (a ten inch piece of floorboard is gone.) Bikes lean in a group by the entryway and the soft glow of yellow kitchen lights dribbles reluctantly outward. Brown floorboards stretch from the entrance hall to the kitchen; cheap brown carpeting sits on steps that lead up to the bedrooms on the second floor. In the living room there was a small television with an antenna on top. The antenna was merely for display; the house was equipped with digital cable television. The television rested on a small display case with two shelves. On the first shelf were a series of Japanese porn DVDs and a super Nintendo covered in dust. On the second shelf was a collection of old Japanese magazines. A rogue cover peeked out, its layout neon green with harsh Kanji characters and exclamation marks adorning its surface. A small round mat, a Persian hybrid, rested artfully in front of the television, appearing to worship the display case. A small glass table was directly in front of a gaudy khaki colored couch. Everything smelled of cigarette smoke. As it always had.

"Hey man, you want something to drink?" Shoda asked.

"Why not," Bishop replied.

He followed Shoda, who was dressed in a trademark cool outfit; silver sweat pants, a winter sleeveless vest, with a Jamaican-style mesh merino underneath. In the kitchen, the counter was packed with bottles of vodka and cases of beer. He reached into the fridge and pulled a beer out.

"Here you go man. So how is life? Long time I haven't seen you at the restaurant!"

"True, true. I'll make it there soon, I promise."

"Yeah, and make sure you bring some hot black girls with you!"

Bishop chuckled at this statement. Shoda always made this request without fail every time he saw Bishop. As he sipped his beer, he wondered if that question was only for him, or every black guy Shoda knew. The DJ was setting up in the usual spot, a large empty space that doubled as the dance floor in front of a small closet that had been converted into a makeshift bedroom with a hanging blanket for a door. He slipped some vinyl records on a set of two ancient turntables and old reggae started playing through twin speakers at either end of the room. People started rolling in, from all walks of life. Bishop saw some people he knew from American, mostly by face. There were a few cute Japanese girls who worked at other restaurants around town, and a skateboarder who was just going by and decided to pass through. Bishop had been to some wild parties here. There was something about people that worked at restaurants that gave people license to act crazy in their presence. Plus the Japanese guys went hard.

Bishop remembered a party when everyone was fueled on whiskey and cocaine and at some point people started tobogganing down the steps on a plastic serving tray. One guy even stood up as he did this, hitting the ground and flying into the bike rack. Everyone had laughed. He went back into the kitchen to get another drink.

"I like your hat," a girl with a cute face but a little too much makeup on said, patting his ass as she walked away.

There were so many stories here; in the little cracks and mysterious spots in corners and on the walls, in the cheap magnets on the fridge, random *kawaii* stickers that adorned old glasses and cups; flashes of moments in time. More people rolled in, and the energy started to build. It felt like the ghost of a Geisha tripping on acid, singing old love songs for Japanese businessmen, but instead her captive audience were college boys and yuppies looking at her Kimono and betting in *bro-speak* about who could take it off faster.

"Hey Bishop!" a voice said.

When he said it, it sounded more like *Bishoppu*. It was Makai, another affable member of the Japanese house. As he saw him, he remembered a party a while back, another epic one, with a haze of cigarette smoke burning his eyes, a cheap strobe light giving the basement area a club effect; his head spinning.

"What's good, man?"

"Not so much you know, just came back from work."

A girl floated over, a ridiculously sexy Japanese girl in a tight pink top. She said something to Makai and gave Bishop a cute wave.

"That's my new girlfriend," Makai beamed.

Makai headed outside, where he was aggressively hugged by a tall fellow with a massive Afro. The music was getting better and some people were starting to dance. Bishop headed downstairs to the basement. A guy with a Polaroid camera pointed to him.

"Him too!"

A girl who smelled like fresh pastry stood beside a guy wearing what appeared to be a World War Two pilot's hat, grabbed Bishop with surprising strength. The light flashed and hands patted his back and people laughed. Down here there was another kitchen and more alcohol. Shoda was in his room, searching for something with an unusual look of seriousness on his face, with a cigarette in his mouth. Bishop walked past and went to the downstairs bathroom. In the bathroom there was a small, garishly yellow mish-mash of terrible bathroom décor and ugly toilet accessories. The shower curtain was a semi-transparent sheet covered with a yellow rubber duck imprint. A beer can cut in two held toothpaste and a few toothbrushes. Above the toilet, a sticker read, "FUCK BUSH". On the floor, behind the toilet and wedged where the wall and the bathtub met, was a brown plastic ring with a red rhinestone. The men of the house bathed with Herbal Essence, Suave and Old Spice products. Behind the beer can, was a small Mecha toy. It looked like Voltron.

More people piled into the house. The rumbling of footfalls directly above was increasing. Bishop flopped onto a couch. Another set of speakers were setup down here as well, and someone started playing rave music. A hand touched his shoulder. Shoda.

"You good man?"

"Of course," Bishop replied.

Bishop watched a few people dance awkwardly to the rave music. The crowd was getting very mixed. Upstairs, on his way to the kitchen, he saw Monica. He felt it again. The heat on his face, the quick rush of blood to his senses and the threatening tension in his loins. She was standing with the guy from the time they went to the poetry cipher, who was laughing with someone else. They were both gay, with retro Bell Biv Devoe haircuts. He grabbed another beer.

"Hey! How are you?" Monica asked.

"I didn't know you were here."

"I thought I'd see you when I walked in. There are so many people here I know its pretty crazy. What are you drinking?"

"PBR."

Monica took the beer and took a heavy sip.

"This place is interesting," Monica said.

"It definitely is."

She mentioned what was above the Kitchen counter, a shelf filled with empty Maker's Mark bottles, proud trophies from dozens of wild parties, drug-laced nights of sex and debauchery. Each bottle told a story. Those bottles had seen people throwing up on blankets while sleeping on the ugly couch. They had heard petulant conversations between warring couples as they sat on the porch, high on ecstasy and smoking marijuana. The bottles had seen people sneak into a bedroom, and soon after heard their grunts and sighs of passion. Many people always wonder what walls could say if they could speak, but these bottles would be able to write screenplays, poetry and prose. Now they stood together and alone, a glass menagerie of the past, empty but full. Someone touched him with a face he didn't recognize. A short guy with red cheeks and blonde hair.

"I'm Scott, I live upstairs. Shoda told me you are an artist? Do you mind taking a look at something I've done?"

"Ok. I'll be right back, Monica."

Monica started pouring straight vodka into a glass and smiled, still chatting to her group. Scott's room was unusually clean. Everything was neatly arranged to the centimeter, and the mild scent of disinfectant lingered in the air, making the room feel like a classroom with a phantom janitor. Clothes were folded expertly, and nothing was out of place, save a small crack in the wall near the window, which blurred the image of perfection his room represents.

"I do oil paintings from time to time, and I like it when people can give me an opinion on my work."

Something about his energy was weird and frantic and Bishop felt slightly uncomfortable. On the bed was a painting resting on a white towel. It was an elaborate image of what appeared to be the D.C skyline.

"Uh, it looks good," Bishop said.

It actually was pretty good, but Bishop didn't care that much. He made a few choice comments just for argument's sake, then went back downstairs. A weird looking couple stopped him. The guy asked if he knew if anyone had speed.

"I guess some will show up soon," Bishop replied.

This answer seemed to satisfy the man and the woman, who walked briskly into the living room. Monica was still in the kitchen. When she saw him, she walked over and squeezed his hand.

"I was wondering where you were."

Her voice had a touch of something in it that made Bishop's face feel flushed again. They went to the dance floor. They eased up on a wall, behind a few writhing couples. She faced forward and moved her waist with intent, rolling it from side to side and upwards. Bishop ran his hand alongside her thighs, feeling their firmness through her jeans. She leaned back, resting her head on his chest, pressing on him even more. Bishop could feel himself getting aroused as he could smell her again, and her soft hands held onto his. He pushed her away slightly and laughed. He didn't want to become fully aroused on the dance floor. Monica turned around and pressed him against the wall. This time, there was no escape. Her large, soft breasts pressed against him and she rested her lips on the base of his neck. His blood was on fire. The power in the muscles was back, the raging tension in his pants. They kissed, and the party faded into nothing except the sensations of sound and touch. Her hands ran under his shirt and up to his chest. Fingers delicately squeezed his nipples and her breath was hot. Bishop pulled Monica directly into him and whispered into her ear:

"Let's go."

The BMW roared as the city flashed by in a haze. They kissed at every stoplight, hands roaming and searching. Then he was pulling into the garage at his Georgetown row house, and they were in the kitchen, limbs flailing and clothes flying. Then they were in the living room, their tongues swirling in a dance of bliss. Her fingers teased his belt buckle. Bishop's hands started to roam as well. She was wearing and old Joy Division t-shirt, and as it came off, he felt the *charge* again as he saw her breasts; perfect brown supple mounds. Bishop leaned over slowly and teased a large, brown nipple into his mouth. Monica sighed, and the tension riddled his body, the roaring clenching of muscles and heat on his face. He wanted her all at once, her entire body, and her mind. The tip of her nipple hardened and she clawed the skin at his neck, shooting brief spikes of pain down his back. Her pants were off, and he felt the crest of her labias through her under wear. They came off quickly, revealing soft, low-trimmed hairs. He slipped a finger into her wetness, feeling her buckle with the sensation then went down on her, almost exploding with excitement from the reaction she elicited.

The energy inside Bishop made him a raging piston. As he kept thrusting and groaning, Monica scratched his back and gripped his buttocks; sparks of white hitting his vision. The flatness of the last year had transitioned into an overwhelming reality, a slap to the tongue of life's pungent sweetness.

"Oh god, I'm close," Monica said.

As they came, Bishop felt almost every muscle in his body contract. His chest tightened and shuddered with the explosion between his legs. His breath left him in a *whoosh* and he buckled repeatedly, as Monica gripped him hard and fast, quaking in the aftershock of her orgasms. The world swam in a sea of white and then came back to color, and went out to sea again. Monica lay on top of him, with him still inside her. He was pulsing and throbbing.

"Wow, you are still hard," Monica said, giving him a soft kiss on the chest.

"I like the sound of your heart. It feels strong. I like how you feel inside me."

They lay there for a few more moments.

"I really like you," Bishop said.

Monica said nothing for a few moments. She eased up and looked into his eyes. Bishop looked into her brown pools and felt himself getting lost and even harder down there. She kissed him on the lips.

"I really like you too," Monica replied.

She started moving her hips on his hardness, and Bishop felt his readiness return. She raised her body up and moans echoed in the stillness of the apartment as they crashed on each other time and again, lost in waves of physical ecstasy.

Chapter 31

The Warehouse was somewhere near First Avenue. Already, a thick crowd was outside, laughing and drinking beers illegally in the open air. Winston was walking with Amy, her boyfriend Greg and two other friends. Amy and Greg held hands, chatting and laughing about past college situations. There was something a little bit weird about Greg. It seemed for him, everything orbited the college experience. On the train, his friends spoke about some wild times to a trip to Argentina, Greg brought up some incident at school (he went to UPenn but did grad school at George Washington) with some Argentinian girl that gangbanged most of the lacrosse team. Amy told Winston something about this article she had read about the Cirque Du Soleil possibly being in D.C soon, and how she wanted to see it. Greg reminded them all of a time he had gone to see the group when they were in Boston a few years back, of course, during a break from school. These types of relationships seemed profoundly American to Winston. To him, the prototypical white American male was masterfully able to mix two parts social awkwardness with one part confidence and one part randomness. Talking about how terrible you are at something, or telling anecdotes about near death situations that one chooses to get themselves in seemed to be the order or the day. Almost on cue, the other two in the group, both guys named Mike (both with beards) started talking about the party.

"Geez man, I'm not sure if I'm ready for this tonight bro," Mike number one said.

"Last time I partied here I met this chick, I mean she was SO hot, like Winona Ryder in Edward Scissorhands."

"Dude, she was hotter in Alien Resurrection," Mike number two said.

"Uh, Girl Interrupted, duh. I would definitely have done her in that movie," Amy said.

"Whatever, this chick was just gorgeous, I mean freaking gorgeous. So I'm walking over to her, right, and I'm not even realizing I'm fucking stepping on people's shoes and shit, fucking shit up. Then some dude hit me on the shoulder, and I'm like ' what the fuck man?' but its some dude I know and he gives me a beer, so now I'm drinking this beer and I'm getting even more wasted right. Then I finally go over to the girl and I say hi. She has these like, super sweet eyes right, and in that moment when she says hi, she asks me my name. She is seriously feeling me too, man, I can just feel it right? Then I forget my fucking name!"

"No way," Greg said.

"It was so fucked up. Like some kind of alien mind-freeze man. I'm wasted, I'm talking to this hot chick and I just kind of spazzed out and walked away."

Amy laughed. "So that was it?" she asked.

"Yeah man, I mean I met another chick that night, but I wanted *that* one."

"Dude, was that the same party with the skate ramp?" Mike number two asked.

"Yes!"

Both Mikes started laughing heartily.

"You think being drunk and forgetting your name is bad, try being drunk and skateboarding," Mike number two said.

"Screw that guys, imagine being drunk and driving a fucking golf cart." Greg said. "See this one time at school…"

Tony could feel the excitement. A warehouse party was like every 1980's B-movie about American life come true. Raging frat boys, speed-loaded guys from the Hill, coked out lawyers, frisky undergrads, the expat crowd and a plethora of random circumstances. Never a dull moment. As a kid he always thought it would be crazy to be in one of those summer camp movies where everything was about getting laid, being stupid and making memories for life. Tonight was a summer camp moment; a chance to morph into a shy young teenager, prodded on by a gaggle of horny friends with the same goal. Standing outside, he saw a throng of people. Many had backpacks, many were chugging beers and mysterious mixes in gym water bottles. He loved the sound of the laughter and the light smell of old concrete. The building was pretty large, and outside it was hard to tell exactly how far back it spread. The lightest throb of music spilled through a set of large doors that were covered with black plastic tape. In this middle of the door, in white, was the same symbol that was on the card the mysterious woman had given to him. Someone called his name. He turned to see on of the twins he recently met from the club in Dupont. He looked pretty stylish, wearing a black fedora, a vest and sharp black pants.

"This party is going to be sick!" he said.

"Looks like it," Tony replied.

They have drinks inside but they are also letting people do BYOB. "

"That's nice."

"Yeah man, if you want to make a pit stop at the premium bar, come through."

"Think I'll make a pit stop now."

They walked to the far left of the outside group. There he saw the other twin, with a few other guys. They were all pretty stylish, with vests, sharp pants and expensive leather belts.

"Eric, who's your boy?" one guy said.

Okay so he's not Eddie, Tony thought.

He was tall and well built, and spoke with the quiet confidence of a white guy who has slept with numerous black women. Another guy beside him, who was the splitting image of Blair Underwood, gave Tony a nod and a smile.

"This is Tony, a cool dude from Jamaica," Eric explained, opening a large black leather satchel. The leather smelled expensive. Inside, were a few bottles of Grey Goose and assorted chasers. To Tony these guys felt very Georgetown.

"Looks like he likes the party bag," Blair Underwood guy said.

"We don't have any cups yet, so you'll just have to take a shot and drink some chaser," Eric said.

Tony laughed. The Grey Goose burned his throat as he took a quick swig, happy for the cranberry that followed soon after. He found out all the young men were fresh out of Georgetown Law, earning God knows how much per year. They also had green cards with the strange symbol on them. Tony did another shot. The tall guy with the confident attitude clapped his hands together. It sounded like two steaks crashing at high speed.

"That's it, let's roll!"

The group moved in unison and Tony followed them. They walked past the door covered with black tape towards a narrow entryway. A solidly built man with arms like small tree trunks shined an ultraviolet light on the cards. A very elaborate 3D symbol appeared on the card. The man nodded and handed the cards back to the group. They walked through a large plastic chute, the kind that people use in nuclear disasters to create a vacuum. It was painted black with clear spots to allow light to pass through certain points. At a glance the dull visage of bodies moving nearby was slightly visible. Music that was just a trickle previously, roared. One of the Georgetown guys screamed a pre-party *LET'S DO IT!* Scream. Tony felt his heart race again. They stepped out of the chute and in front of them, the entire club unfolded.

Waves of bodies were jumping up and down. It stretched pretty far, almost as far as Tony could see in the forced darkness. There must have been hundreds of people there. The smell of perfume, liquor and cigarette smoke was strong. They were in a sort of lounge area cordoned off by a set of heavy metal bars. People were raving hard. Many had their own bags, just like the Georgetown group, but there was also a bar there. In front of it, three girls stood up, and one caught Tony's eye. She was tall, with dark skin and curly hair. She was powerfully attractive; with a low cut afro and a tall, model-like frame. In a form fitting black and white striped dress, she looked like Beetlejuice's hot girlfriend. Her eyes glowed green in the intermittent flashes of strobe lights. Tony walked over and said hello. They were all grad students from Howard.

"I guess you guys are part of the 'in' crowd," Tony said.

"Always," the girl said, slipping out a sly smile. "I guess that makes you a part of it, too."

Tony smiled. She smiled back, her perfectly etched face a mesmerizing image.

Bishop walked with Roy into the main entrance of the building. He was surprised by the size of the crowd just hanging around outside. Roy had texted him about the party. In fact, Bishop realized that Roy sent him texts often, he just had barely responded to any in the last several months. Roy had told him that this party would be "epic" and it was impossible not to get laid there. Bishop wasn't too concerned with the nature of the party, but since the other night with Monica, they had been meeting almost every night. The fury of their passion was almost shocking. They had hooked up in the car, in the alley behind the house, even outside some bar in Adams Morgan. Each time, Bishop had felt that fire fueling his body, a raging strength that bubbled to the surface whenever Monica touched him. Tonight was a more chill and relaxed party kind of vibe for Bishop.

It was ten bucks to go in. They paid and stepped through the large doors covered in plastic. A gust of air hit them in their faces. On either side of them, massive fans about six feet high were going full blast. A short walk around a corner, and Bishop saw the entire spectacle. It was chaos.

"Wow."

"Fuck yeah," Roy replied, looking at his phone. "My people say they are near the DJ."

They roamed through the crowd. It smelled thick with the heat of human bodies and beer. Bishop hadn't brought anything to drink. He and Roy went to the bar. The bartender was a cute girl with an almost full set of body tattoos. They got two beers and went to meet Roy's friends. The vibe was good. The girls around were *very* friendly. A hipster girl took a particular liking to Bishop, even though she was slightly taller than him.

"I like your eyes," she said.

"Thanks."

"I like Blasian boys," she said with a seductive smile.

Bishop chuckled.

"Wanna drink something? I wanna drink with my Blasian boy."

She pointed to a burlap bag nearby beside some shoes and a green army bag. It was in the thick of some more hipster girls. The bag was loaded with PBR and Heineken cans. Bishop took a Heineken. Heavy electronic music blasted in the air and the huge crowd growled in unison.

"Oh shit! I love this song!"

The girl started dancing and tugged Bishop's arm. At that same time, a light flashed a few feet away, and he saw Monica. She didn't see him. She and some guy were making out. The guy had his hand down her pants. In the flashing lights and the madness of the crowd, it would have been easy to lose them, or not even notice they were there. Bishop's chest clenched into a fist. The music faded slightly, with the exception of the voice of the hipster girl:

Hey Blasian boy....
Hey Blasian booooy......

Winston was standing in a corner, near the remains of an old, smelly refrigerator. From where he stood, the music was less loud, but still loud, fifty feet away through a series of narrow corridors. Amy and Greg had started a massive sloppy make out session a while back, and the two Mikes had disappeared. Winston had gone in search of the bathroom, and didn't feel much like going back in. The party was exciting, but something was off. He felt like going for a run.

"Jesus Christ, if I don't get some pussy, I must be gay!" a guy in a striped shirt said as he walked past. His friend, his face red with inebriation, gave a weak chuckle in reply. They disappeared around the corner. Then Tony appeared, holding a large red cup in his hand.

"WINSTON WILLIAMS! LONG TIME!!!" Tony's voice echoed through the narrow hallways even with the loud music.

"Why are you in here? The party well wicked outside," he said.

Tony had a way of looking at you where he seemed to be staring into your soul. His eyes were deep and penetrating, making Winston squirm slightly.

"Just taking it easy. Not a hundred percent on the party vibes right now."

"WHAT? NO MAN, TONIGHT IS THE NIGHT!" Tony made a smile filled with clear, white teeth.

"I don't really feel like partying that much boss," Winston replied.

"WHAT? OH, I'M SHOUTING. Sorry about that. Fucking loud in here. I have twenty dollars that says you can meet a girl tonight," Tony said with a smile.

"I don't need the money."

"Come on man, it was just a joke."

Tony stood beside him in the hallway, leaning on the wall. Two cute girls said hello as they walked past. Winston's mind blazed with confusion? How did he know so many people?

"I-I don't feel like any of these girls would like me," Winston said.

What you mean, man? Cool guy like you, you don't need anything else."

He said *anything* in way that made the word itself sound like concrete. Afterward he let out a soft, self-assured laugh. Winston envied it. He didn't hate Tony, but he hated how comfortable he seemed. He wanted just an ounce of that relaxed, don't-give-a-fuck vibe Tony oozed like a fat pimple.

"Tony, you deal with a lot of girls right?" Winston asked.

"Somewhat," Tony said

"I mean, you interact with a lot of women. What do you think about the meaning of a true relationship? You think its possible?"

In the background, the crowd roared, and the heavy bass made the walls throb. Tony glanced backwards for a second. He seemed conflicted, and with good reason. He turned back to Winston.

"Wow, we are having a TV moment man. Dissecting relationships at a drugged-up, no holds barred warehouse party!" Tony said with a smile.

"Just a question," Winston said flatly, staring at the floor.

"Okay. In all honesty, I try not to think about it too much. I just meet the next girl and see what happens there," Tony said, sipping on his drink.

A short guy in a hat walked past them. He raised his cup to Tony.

"PREMIUM BAR!" the guy screamed.

"PREMIUM BAR!" Tony screamed in reply.

Winston was flooded with confusion. *Premium Bar?*

Turning to him after a few seconds, Tony seemed to remember Winston was there.

"YOU WERE—I mean you were saying?"

Winston took a small breath. "Don't you ever feel that, you know there is more meaning to things?"

"Meaning?"

"I mean, like. A relationship has a purpose right? And people have connections, can we just turn those feelings off like a light switch whenever we feel like?" Winston said, his voice getting louder.

Tony stared at him blankly. *"What* are you talking about?"

Winston almost laughed. Tony knew nothing much about him past brief moments in high school. Even then they barely knew each other. It would be impossible to even begin to explain the Elsa situation.

"You have a girl right now?" Tony asked.

"No," Winston replied.

"You want one?"

Winston paused.

"Boss man, there are a million girls back there ready and waiting and I can't stand to see my *bredrin* looking like this! Here we are, chatting in the middle of this hallway, like a scene from a bad movie!"

Winston started to see why Tony was such a magnetic person. The more he spoke, the more he felt drawn to him. Even his mood had improved somewhat. Tony should bottle his blood and sell it. Maybe he was right.

"All right," Winston said, easing himself up off the wall.

"That's my boy! Now, there are these three Howard girls I met inside," Tony started to explain.

Chapter 32

Tony walked with Winston behind him. For a brief moment, he thought about Winston's expression and his questions. The guy seemed a little morbid. However, the Grey Goose and the beers had started kicking in, and that brief spark of curiosity about Winston's mindset faded as they re-entered the party. There was no point in being so *cerebral* at a spot like this. These parties favored the mindless types, the animals prowling around ready to pounce. Tony glanced back at Winston. He received a weak smile. Despite the sadness hovering around him like a hobo at a soup kitchen, his mood seemed a little different from when he was in the hallway. Maybe things were on the up and up.

A bouncer was in front of the cordoned area. Tony tapped him on the shoulder and pointed to Winston. The bouncer nodded and waved them through. Winston looked at the bars and the slightly more chic crowd.

"Is this the V.I.P?" Winston asked.

"V.I.P is whatever you make it man," Tony said.

Winston chuckled nervously at this statement.

"Let's go to Premium bar."

"Okay," Winston replied.

From the original group of five guys, only two remained by the bag. Their vests were open; the silk short-sleeved shirts had dark stains of sweat in the armpits. The Blair Underwood lookalike was very cozy with the Howard girl Tony had chatted to earlier. She stood in front of him with her hands on his waist as he leaned on a wall, talking into her ear.

"Dammit, these guys move fast!" Tony said.

"You were talking to that girl?" Winston said.

"Yeah, thought I was getting through too. No biggie."

Tony reached into the leather bag and grabbed a cup. (Some had materialized mysteriously). He poured Winston a strong drink.

"Drink this. *Quickly.*"

In fact, everyone in the lounge area looked a bit too cozy for Tony's liking. He scanned the crowd a few feet outside the barriers. A set of tall women was near one of the speakers, smoking cigarettes and standing with a relaxed disposition.

"I think I see some Euro girls. Let's get two more drinks for the road and head over there."

Half-sipping his drink, Winston asked him how he knew they were European.

"Dunno, Boss man. Something about their body language and the way they smoke."

When he said this, Winston seemed to remember something. His eyes got cloudy, and for a moment he seemed lost.

"You ever dealt with a European girl?" Tony said.

"Actually, yes," Winston replied.

"Where was she from? Germany?"

"No, Barcelona."

"WINSTON THE MAN HIMSELF!" Tony slapped Winston on the back and started laughing. Winston laughed as well.

"Let's see how our mutual Euro-radar works tonight."

Tony made sure Winston drank both of his drinks. After some more light banter and energy building they walked over to the girls.

Bishop had told Roy he was leaving. Roy could only give him the expression a man after ten drinks with a girl gripping his chest could.

"If you gotta go, bro."

An anger that went from the tip of his toes straight up to his head consumed him. It felt wet and dangerous. Whoever that guy kissing Monica was, he wanted to punch him in the throat, break his arms, and stab him with something. The rage was so thick, he could barely breathe. He stumbled through the crowd, immediately hating the mostly happy-go-lucky partygoers. People with glow sticks, girls making out with guys. Guys making out with guys. People on speakers, someone throwing up in the corner, frat boys with some poorly assembled beer pipe. Everyone seemed uproariously happy and this only made Bishop's vision redder. The degree of his anger frightened him; his heart was running and he couldn't stop it. His teeth clenched and his eyes were wet with something other than tears. He tried moving faster. There were so many people, and not that much space, he couldn't move very fast.

After what seemed like forever, he was outside in the BMW, its engine screaming as he headed back to his apartment. All the way there, the image of Monica kissing that guy played repeatedly in his mind, spinning like a carousel. His hands down her pants. The way her hips were tightly pushed against the guy's hand. The passion of their touch. She was feeling good; she was feeling something down there. *He* was making her feel good, not Bishop. Then, an image popped into his mind. Monica giving him head in his car, her lips wet and slurpy. People passing nearby; the exciting voyeurism, the exhibitionism. He felt himself getting hard, and cursed at himself. His eyes felt ready to pop. The car screeched in the alley behind his street, knocking over a large plastic bin. His fingers could barely control the gate remote. Everything inside him suddenly came to the surface. He retched in the toilet a few times. He went into the small art space, and sat by the wall, his eyes closed, asking himself why he decided to read Roy's text tonight. *Why did he read that text message?*

Chapter 33

The party pulsed and throbbed with a renewed energy. It was as if a pagan god had tossed a few Quaaludes into the social mix and topped that up with a double shot of Red Bull. Everyone was engaged in frenzied, sweaty dancing. The lights flashed, showing a sea of glistening necks of all shades. Hands were touching hands, hands were on waists, hands were on buttocks. On an elevated platform the DJ himself stood up like the deity of all that is cool, regal with his Sennheisers on his head, hair wet with sweat, his shirt glowing in the strobe lights. It had a picture of a classic Chinese take out box on its front. In a corner, a broad chested guy with a trucker hat that said "FORK" on the front, was passionately kissing a girl almost his height and size. Dozens of people were dancing and kissing. Preppy guys and hipsters blasted on chemicals raved. A few cute girls with nice dresses stood in a circle, faces flush with the redness of alcohol, their faces stained darkly with sweat, and a hint of desire. Somewhere in the middle of madness, Tony and Winston hung with the girls. They were from Europe, Germany they said. Winston had marveled at the way Tony had sauntered into their group, smiling and laughing with them. He couldn't hear exactly what he said to the ladies, but both girls had been paying rapt attention, then he had said something and pointed at Winston, then the girls laughed again, and then he had waved for him to come over. Winston was surprised by the striking looks of these girls. He rarely saw girls like this just hanging around, much less in an old smelly warehouse. Then Tony had spoken and gestured more, there were more smiles and laughs and then one of the girls, a dark beauty named Simone, spoke to Winston. Her German accent was barely there. She had come to the states when she was a teenager. Just before they had spoken to the German girls, another striking woman had stopped Tony as they exited the cordoned area. He said something to her briefly, giving her a kiss on the cheek before grabbing Winston firmly by the shoulder.

"I think I fucked that girl," Tony said with a laugh.

Winston's brain was in a different world. The girl from Howard in the black and white striped dress Tony mentioned earlier looked straight out of a Vogue magazine. Even though another guy seemed to have gotten through with her, Tony didn't seem to care. The woman who stopped him had a body that would make most men crumble. Winston started to feel weak in his presence. He stood a bit closer to the group, intermittently chatting with Simone. He didn't know her friend's name. He heard some of Tony's comments in snippets.

"—he's a great guy, in high school he was pretty cool as well."

"Oh? You both went to high school in Jamaica and now you are both in D.C? That is very—"

"Definitely and tell me more about your—"

"—Premium bar? What is that?"

"—cool guys from Georgetown, you can get some Grey—"

"—You are funny—"

"—I want to kiss you right now—"

Winston watched the blonde stepped close to Tony and kissed him slowly on the cheek. Her eyes were filled with a quiet desire mixed with explosive fascination. Something kicked Winston briefly in the chest. The alcohol, the scenario, something. Winston found his arm around Simone's waist and his lips close to her ear. He talked to her about random things. Stuff in D.C, his running, and even told a joke or two. Simone spoke to him as well, not seeming to worry about his arm, about how close he was.

A hand touched his shoulder. Tony.

"Premium bar."

Again, Tony spoke to the bouncer and they all walked in to the cordoned area. The girls began to fix drinks from the leather bag and Tony made Winston stop a few feet away.

"Kiss her soon, man. She likes you."

Tony started chatting with one of the guys Winston had seen earlier; one of the guys in the sharp outfit. The short guy from the hallway was there as well standing beside a guy that looked exactly like him. They had to be twins.

Soon, Tony was kissing the tall blonde, and Simone stood nearby, looking a little bored. Winston was making a drink, thinking. Everything felt out of his league. The expensive liquor, the beautiful women, the rapid way Tony seemed to penetrate their lives, all these different people. He took a quick glance at Simone. Quiet and dark; mysterious, as she sipped her drink. He found himself thinking about pushing his tongue inside her mouth cavity, feeling the sensation of her tongue on his. He wanted to smell her hair, to feel the touch of her breasts against his chest. He imagined this vividly as he drank another drink, feeling the world start to pulse in front of his eyes. Then he was actually in front of her, holding her close, her lips on his. She tasted a bit like cigarette smoke, but there was a softness to her lips, a curious tension in her body as she kissed him. Then her arms relaxed and raised up from his waist to his neck, and she was kissing him lasciviously. Her passion was magnetic, and he fell into the moment, not wanting to stop.

They lived somewhere in Bethesda, in a very modern building with a doorman and an access card. The doorman was reading the Washington Post, and didn't look up as the giggling group went inside. Tony didn't even seem to know that Winston was there. He and the blonde were in their own world of jokes, laughs and kisses. In the elevator to the fifth floor, as sighs escaped the girl's mouth while Tony was doing whatever he was doing, Winston held Simone's hand, his heart fluttering with both nervousness and excitement. She squeezed it back, giving him a sly look with her eyes. The elevator opened with a *swoosh* and smooth black marble that stretched forward for about forty feet became visible. The blonde girl, walking forward and holding Tony by the arm, laughed about something. Her heels clicked loudly in the hallway. Winston noticed despite her inebriated gait, she walked in the heels with a certain confidence, as if she wore them every day. Winston was a little drunk as well, but that lingering feeling of nervousness still lingered inside him.

The apartment was upscale and screaming with space. It had high ceilings, and that scent of freshness a new building gives off. A large flat panel television flanked by two black statues of small pit bulls stood in front of a massive red couch.

The floor was tiled; quite different from the usual wood paneled floor of row houses Winston was used to. The kitchen was large with bay windows that gave a clear view of the night. Simone lead him to the kitchen, and he saw the blonde girl (he found out her name was Lena) pulling Tony into a bedroom with a huge bed covered with small pillows and silk sheets. He saw her start pulling up her shirt, revealing a clear, bronzed back, then the door shut. Simone poured him some wine and sat on the couch. They talked for a little bit, chuckling occasionally as Lena's gasps floated into the room. On the couch, with Simone rubbing her hand on his thigh, Winston felt the nervousness drift away. They went into her room. It was almost a replica of Lena's, with a massive Sultan-sized bed, expensive silk sheets and an armada of pillows. Simone touched a button on the wall, and the room went from bright to a dull glow. Winston shut the door. In the dim light, Simone slipped off her clothes, revealing a firm, curvaceous body. Winston, feeling himself hard, took off his clothes and met her embrace, falling on the silk sheets, with the smell of her body and potpourri filling his nostrils.

Chapter 34

They sat in front of the television. On screen some reality show elimination round was happening. Beside Winston, was Simone. Beside her, was Lena in Tony's lap. They had just eaten breakfast and drank some more wine. No one spoke and the scripted music and canned situations echoed throughout the spacious apartment. Winston had surprised himself. Two rounds with Simone that night, and a quickie in the morning. She held his hand comfortably, another glass of wine in her hand. Tony had his feet on an Ottoman. The show ended and Lena said something about having work to do. She gave Tony another wet kiss, and a lingering stare into his eyes. She seemed to be processing him, questioning him. Tony looked right back at her with that penetrating gaze, smirking with a very internal mischief.

"Winston, you ready?" Tony said.

Winston wasn't really ready to leave, but he knew the cue. He had Simone's number, and over breakfast she seemed like a really nice person. There was a genuine quality to her, something he couldn't pinpoint. He would find out later perhaps. She gave him a hug and a similar deep, penetrating look into his eyes. Unlike Tony, he couldn't hold it as long.

"Do you guys always do this? You and Tony?" Simone asked.

"No. This is actually the first time I've seen him in several months."

Simone kept her gaze, smiling in a way that made Winston feel slightly uncomfortable. Then she stepped close and held his waist. "I'll see you soon."

Her expression made Winston's loins tingle. The same doorman was at the front, sitting quietly staring seemingly at nothing. If he didn't cough briefly as they exited the entryway, he wouldn't even seem real. In the morning light, they both looked a bit odd in their nightclothes. Tony more so with his thin leather vest, skinny jeans and boots. The train station wasn't very far. Tony sat heavily on a chair and let out a deep sigh. He smirked, then looked at Winston.

"Great night, yeah?"

"Can't complain."

Tony laughed and for a second Winston wondered if there was some constant internal dialogue with Tony, a genetically built in laugh track.

"I wonder if those two are call girls," Tony said flatly.

"You mean prostitutes?"

"Well, a call girl doesn't like to be called a prostitute, but yeah."

Winston's heart filled with fear. If men paid them money to do bizarre sexual acts—

"Or they could just be rich expats. That's another thing. I didn't really chat to Lena that much."

The train rumbled to a stop and some people came on. Someone sat beside Tony. He continued speaking as if the person wasn't there.

"I mean, she told me a *few* bits about herself here and there. But after all that Grey Goose most of last night is fuzzy."

For a second, Winston looked at Tony differently. There was an element of blankness to him in the way he referred to Lena, something starkly clueless. He seemed to be rolling through life without agendas or questions. Then he remembered that he didn't speak to Simone much either. Whatever they had chatted about was burned away from his brain by the last few glasses of wine the night before. The light of the day was bright on his eyes.

"Your girl was nice man. I actually prefer brunettes."

He said this matter-of-factly. A man beside him said something, and Tony started chatting to him about what he was reading. Just like that, Tony was gone again, lost in another situation. Winston's phone vibrated. He pressed a small panel on top.

4 missed calls.

3 new text messages.

1 new voicemail.

The missed calls were from Amy. Apparently they had wondered where he disappeared to. He checked the voicemail. He pulled the phone from his ear. It shrieked noise. This noise went on for a full two minutes, then he heard a muffled voice and it went off. Winston chuckled; Amy must have dialed him by accident. The texts from her were funny too.

1:03 a.m. Whare dd u ggo?

2:45 a.m. O$k have fl n

12:00 p.m Winston, hope you had a good time last night. I got totally wasted! Let's hang soon.

The train was nearing Northwest, where both Winston and Tony lived. They came off at the Shaw Howard University metro stop.

"I need some coffee or something man. You want to get a drink?" Tony said.

"No thanks, I think I just want to go home and sleep."

Winston watched Tony trot off in the distance, waving at someone before turning around the corner and disappearing from sight. As he turned down a street a few blocks from where he lived, he noticed that everything thing felt light and fresh. In only one night, his situation had significantly changed. His body felt different as well. His steps were stronger.

That night, he slept a quiet dreamless sleep. He woke up early before work and went for a long run, confident in his strides, enjoying the vista of the city as it rolled by, relishing the cool morning air. Work felt different as well. The office didn't feel like as much of a hole as it usually did, he had some interesting banter with Todd and he actually felt good that he worked in Dupont. The area felt brighter, and more progressive.

He and Simone went to a movie a day later at the E Street Cinema. She had recommended the movie, some film shot in South Africa. Her head felt nice against his shoulder as they watched the film. That night his apartment echoed with the sounds of their passion, and he awoke to the sound of the shower running. Tony was right. Simone's father was a diplomat of some sort, working with the United Nations. She was presently doing Graduate School at Georgetown.

Dinner with Amy soon after was filled with Winston's excited tales of the Warehouse party and the subsequent meeting. This time, they were at a sushi restaurant. In between sips of his beer and huge Alaska rolls Winston would mention different moments of the night, breaking down the details, talking about Tony's ridiculous magnetism and the randomness of it all.

"I guess it's a good thing you ran into me that at that coffee shop a while back."

"True, if I hadn't run into you, I wouldn't have met Simone."

He and Amy were planning a run. To him, she was an *actual* runner, doing 5ks and 10ks and any other number of grueling endurance tests. The light feeling he felt since the morning after the warehouse party had carried for a while. Three weeks had passed and he had no dreams. Simone was helping him to see things differently.

He met some of her friends, and a few times they all went down to the Monument, walking hand in hand, going to museums or having a small picnic. They went to small bars and little restaurants. He felt good inside. One day, after work, he picked up the phone and called Elsa. He smiled with himself. His heart wasn't racing, he didn't feel nervous. He felt quite calm.

She answered the phone.

"Hi," Winston said.

"Hi how are you?" Elsa replied.

For a brief moment, Winston felt that spark again, from the time when hearing her voice would excite him.

"I'm okay. I just wanted to say hello."

There was a slight pause. "Thanks for calling me. I am glad to hear you are all right," Elsa said.

"I was wondering if we could meet up sometime and just catch up," Winston said.

Another slight pause. "I—I am not sure if I can do that."

"Why? What's the problem?"

"Winston, you know I cared about you, so I don't want to—"

"*Cared?* What do you mean, I just wanted to say hello."

"You know it's more than that."

"No it isn't. I just wanted to say hello."

"Well, I can't believe that, and either way it doesn't matter."

Winston felt a hint of anger in his blood. He caught his breath.

"Why can't you stomach seeing me? Is it that terrible? I'm just trying to be nice here and I can't understand your attitude."

There was another pause.

"Winston," she said. "I'm getting married."

Brightly lit, the room got dark, and he could hear the glass house of his inner world shatter, scattering across the cosmos of his former self.

Chapter 35

It was cool inside as Bishop walked through the airport. Something felt different. The last time he came he didn't realize all the little tweaks of modernization that had been added to the airport over the years. Huge display panels showed flight information in waiting lobbies, trendy restaurants and an expanded booking wing, and massive motion sensitive doors that slid open as you approached them. Jamaica really was on the up and up. It made sense, Bishop realized. The last time he was in Jamaica, he was in a haze of confusion. The death of his friend, rapid funeral arrangements, the frantic to and fro of family members and friends. It had all been a blur, and Bishop could barely remember it. Now, it was Christmas time, and another year was coming to a close.

He had a one small suitcase, which he wheeled behind him. For a moment he thought back to the way the airport used to be. There was one major exit terminal, behind a series of bars. There you would wait until your relatives came out, and everyone was watching expectantly quite like a runway show. Like a fashion show, people often wore their most elaborate and expensive outfits, to let everyone know they were fresh from the states. People in ridiculous jackets, Louis Vuitton jeans and children dressed to the nines in some popular brand was the norm. Now it was different, more relaxed. People sat in different waiting areas. The exit area was now wider with a less narrow field of view. He stepped out into the warm air immediately feeling dozens of eyes on him. Near the curb a short man in a blue short-sleeved shirt came up to him.

"You need a cab, sah?" he said.

"No, I'm good, thanks," Bishop said, immediately noticing his perfect, clipped English.

In a few seconds, another person had walked up to him.

"You need a phone call?" this one said.

"No, its cool," Bishop said.

Bishop looked out on the horizon. The sky was breathtakingly clear, with a few wisps of clouds slowly journeying across its breadth. The air was thick with the smell of grass, and a slight breeze blew in from the sea. A car drove past, blaring loud dancehall music, and somewhere a man laughed in a high pitched-cackle. Someone walked past, happily gobbling a chicken patty wrapped in coco bread. A lady beside him wearing Dolce Jeans and Dior glasses spoke rapid patois into a huge smartphone. Coconut trees swayed near cars in the parking lot. Bishop was home.

A sleek black Benz came into view. The engine hummed quietly, as the came to a slow stop. Bishop felt his heart quiver with recognition. The tinted windows rolled down, and the large, handsome face of his father appeared. He was beaming.

"Bishop ma' Boy!" he bellowed.

He came out of the car, revealing his tall imposing frame. He exuded power, even in a pair of linen shorts and a polo shirt. His arms were sinewy and muscled, and his barrel chest barely accommodated his shirt. A few strides brought him immediately over to where Bishop was.

"Good to see you!" he said, his voice like a sonic boom.

"Yeah Daddy, good to see you too," Bishop said.

Bishop's father gave him a brief hug, and Bishop marveled at how powerful his father felt. He grabbed both of Bishop's suitcases effortlessly and put them in the car. The embrace temporarily brought Bishop back to his friend's funeral side, when his father had gripped him as—

"So, how's life in Washington D.C!" his father said with a smile.

The radio was locked onto *Fame FM*. His father listened to nothing else.

"Life is… its okay," Bishop said quietly.

"You dash me away man!" his father said with a laugh. In the same breath, his father said:

"You looking a bit slim though."

Something about that comment made Bishop feel briefly annoyed. A burst of memory from childhood, something hard to touch or see. Something irrelevant. The feeling dissipated quickly. As they drove away from the airport, he could clearly see hills of St. Thomas in the background, green humps far away. The car ate up the highway and Bishop leaned his head back and closed his eyes.

*   *   *   *

Winston was looking nervously at the baggage attendant. "Do you have anything to declare?" she said with a heavy accent.

"No, I don't," Winston replied. She was a broad woman, with massive arms and a short head of hair.

"Okay sir. Go ahead."

Airports always made Winston nervous. He didn't like security people, or the idea of people rummaging through his underwear. He wished he didn't even have to fly at all. Why couldn't people just teleport from place to place? He walked down a small corridor and walked outside. *Interesting*, he thought to himself. They had changed the exit area of the airport. He walked outside into a large group of people. It was the usual crowd; People dressed way too flashy for a simple airline flight, girls that had "I go to college in the states" written all over them as they stood up with their iPhones in their hands wearing flip-flops, and guys with fake New York accents trying to sound cool. A man walked up to one of the college girls. "You need a call?" he said to her.

She gave him a bemused look, then said. "No thanks." The man walked away and approached someone else. Winston pulled his suitcase off the curb and walked through light traffic towards the parking lot. In the back of the parking lot, beside a monstrous land rover, was Winston's car. It was a grey Honda Accord. Whenever he traveled, he would make the odd request of asking an extended family cousin to drop the car off at the airport. This way, he could drive by himself and not have to update anyone on the sordid details of his life. It took the joy out of meeting a familiar face at the airport, but it didn't matter to Winston. There was something about returning home to Jamaica for many Jamaicans that lived abroad. It was a mass pilgrimage of people from all territories: Jamaicans with investment banking jobs in New York, freshmen at school in the states and burnt out English teachers from Japan. During Christmas time, Jamaica echoed a signaling beacon telling everyone to come home like *E.T.*

Winston didn't really know why he was home. The last few months had seen an accelerated decline in his state. The brief situation with Simone had ended once his nightmares started again. She couldn't handle him getting up either screaming, or fighting the sheets. His running had gotten more extensive and frantic as his appetite had slowed. He was looking gaunt and stressed. But like thousands of other people, Jamaica's homing beacon had echoed in his consciousness, activating his pilgrimage software. He threw his suitcase on the back seat, taking in the stellar blue sky through the windshield. Jamaica had perfect weather as always. He started the engine and drove off.

Chapter 36

He knew the family ritual was taking place, some bogus gathering of people he didn't really want to see. The collective set of his brothers and probably a family friend or two. There was no avoiding it, but his annoyance about this was pretty subdued. For most of the twenty-five minute trip back home, cascading images of Kevin were on his mind. He couldn't enjoy the beautiful sky, or the great weather. His father must have noticed the cloud over his head because the conversation had long since ended. All he would say occasionally was something general, and non-specific. Bishop nodded to whatever he said, watching small tenements fly by the dark windows as they drove through Mountain View, then past apartment buildings and the low hilltops of Beverly Hills. The car noiselessly blazed through familiar streets, and despite his melancholy, Bishop smiled slightly. He had forgotten how powerful it felt to be in this vehicle, a huge ebony package of luxury and power. As the car turned onto Jack's Hill Road, which lead up to his house, the town disappeared, and thick trees, surrounding massive houses sprouted up into his vision. Then, in what seemed like no time at all, they were home. The house was a palatial beauty built on a precipice that overlooked all of Kingston. It was an opulent two-story building, with a three-car driveway and a pool in the back. It had four bedrooms, two balconies, three bathrooms and two offices, one of which had been converted into a storage room. The driveway was packed with cars of various makes. He recognized a fiery orange Honda, his older brother's. Inside, the lights shone brightly as if the house was on fire. Waiting at the door, was Bishop's mother.

His father drove into the driveway at no less than thirty miles an hour, narrowly missing a huge SUV parked precariously on the sidewalk near the gate. The car slipped between a bucket of dirt and a rusty old bicycle (it had been in that spot for years) and came to a halt in the first of the three garages. Before Bishop could exit the car properly, he was smothered with kisses.

"Bishop! So good to see you, baby!" his mother said.

"Mommy, please," Bishop said, unable to hold back a smile.

She looked at him with adoration and an equal dose of worry. "Good to have you home," she said, giving him another warm hug.

Bishop had more of his mother's attributes. She was small and slim, with tiny, almost birdlike features that made her look of an indeterminate age. Bishop had her skin tone, a warm tone the color of sand, and her nose. The rest of Bishop was all Dad, with a high forehead, round cheeks, and piercing eyes. Even so, he still looked like his mother. He gave her a light hug and went to retrieve his bags, but his father was already walking with them up the short flight of steps that led to the entrance of the house.

"Guess who's here!" Bishop's father roared.

Inside, a whirl of activity could be heard, and the forms of a few tall men appeared at the doorway.

"Bish!" came a familiar, booming voice.

It was Alfred, Bishop's older brother. Standing beside him, was Bishop's second oldest brother, Alex. He was one year older than Bishop. If Bishop looked anything like his mother, Alex and Alfred were splitting images of his father. They were both tall, well over six feet in height, and possessed the same, crowd-catching baritone voices as their father. At a glance they looked like twins. Another man appeared, slightly shorter than the two, but still over six feet himself. It was his father's brother, Jonathan.

"Come here, missa B!" he said with a broad smile.

Bishop smiled weakly as three pairs of powerful hands touched his shoulders, rubbed his head and slapped him on the back. Bishop walked inside and was greeted with the smell of home; the slight scent of Genie floor polish, antique furniture wood and freshly painted walls. The pleasing aroma of freshly cooked food streamed from the kitchen. As he walked inside, he nodded at a few friends of the family sitting down in chairs in different parts at the front of the house. His brothers had surprised him. Normally, after a hearty back slap, they would start teasing him about his outfit, or asking him why he didn't smile more. They would grab him and tell him to try and break their grip, or ask lewd questions about American women. Tonight, even though they had laughed and smiled, there was a quiet reservation in their eyes. The same reservation you see in the eyes of a man caring for a sick child. It was brotherly love. He knew why they had that look in their eyes. They were there the day that Kevin had died—everyone had known him growing up. In fact, they were one of the group who had actually seen him after he had shot himself. It was Alfred he had overheard one night, talking about how Kevin's head had been split open, and the body had seemed *different* as it was someone else, lying on the floor in a muddy pool of blood. They had seen Bishop go into fits near the graveside at Kevin's funeral as he clutched desperately at the coffin watching with tears in their eyes as their father held him back. Bishop was winded that day, blind with disillusion and disbelief and he eventually folded in his father's arms like a blanket, wailing loud passionate cries into the still evening. "That was my boy!" Bishop had wailed over and over. They had seen the eyes of the people around him, wet with tears for Kevin and for Bishop, his best friend. He knew why there were no laughs or jeers this time. They had seen him in a pain that no one deserves to experience, and for all their size and strength, they had been powerless to do anything for their little brother.

Bishop entered his old room, looking around awkwardly. The room was smaller than he remembered, but everything seemed to be in the right place. The walls were a sad yellow color, and his sheets had been changed. The window still had a small crack in it from several years before. He had covered it with tape then, and it seemed his secret was still safe. His suitcases were already in the room in a corner. He sat on the bed for a moment, and let out a huff of breath.

The room felt strange and tiny, a far cry from the row house in Georgetown. But it was home. There was the little desk he used to do schoolwork on, the dusty Prince tennis racquet, the remnants of some Anime poster. There was the storage box with the comic books and some porn mags. It was still here, somewhat fresh, but very old.

Briefly, Monica came to mind.

The thought coasted through his mind like a slow moving ship. He had ignored her for a while, and the subsequent flurry of confused text messages that had come afterward. Then they had met up and spoken at some point. Bishop had said he didn't know she was seeing other guys, she said she didn't think they were serious. It had turned into a huge argument and Bishop had called her a slut. She had tried to slap him and it got weird and then she had left in a huff, leaving a small bag of items behind. It was still at Bishop's place.

Sitting there on his bed in Jamaica the memory was cold. There was no heat on his face, no pulse in his blood. After the day she left his place, his painting had come back with a renewed fervor. He completed one piece or more per day. He had his speakers playing music as he did his work, completely lost. Monica was gone. The dots that had started to connect seemed blurry. Something had changed, and whatever embryo she had created within him was still there, but it was frozen. He painted to explore this, creating angry powerful images, or quiet introspective abstracts. He wanted the embryo to grow, but nothing triggered the feeling Monica gave him. He entertained the idea of seeing her again. Maybe she didn't get it all. She didn't know anything about Kevin really, and to her Bishop really was probably just some guy she was fucking. But then he would think about how powerful he felt, and how the white sparks had flashed in front of his eyes that first time they hooked up, and how happy he felt in her arms and how he would get lost in her eyes, then he would get angry. He would get angry, time would pass and he would hang out with Roy and do coke and drink and forget about Monica for a bit, and then more time passed and she didn't text and the days started to become cold. Then he was on a plane back to Jamaica, watching marshmallow clouds in the sky looking for any shaped like the Starship Enterprise.

"Bishop, come here! We have someone you haven't seen in a long time right in front of me!" his dad bellowed.

Bishop let out a sigh and walked outside.

Chapter 37

Modern transportation is so fast, Tony thought as he sat on his porch, looking out at the cool Caribbean nighttime. Just a day before he was in super chilly Washington D.C, and now he was back home, relaxing. A calm Christmas breeze blew through the yard, and the fat leaves of an Almond tree a few feet away fluttered like lips blowing softly. Tony's mother was inside the house, watching television. His father, as always was somewhere on the town, playing dominoes at a quiet bar, roaring with laughter with his friends. He would reach home around ten p.m. The day had been lazy and reflective. Tony relished the quieting feeling that being at home gave him. As he looked up at the bright, cloudless night sky, Washington D.C felt like a galaxy away. From the warm atmosphere, the dark, tree-lined streets and the slightest outline of the Hills in the background, he was truly somewhere else. There were no row houses in his neighborhood, just a series of small one-story houses with flat rooftops. Even the streetlights had a more subdued feeling. They glowed a dull amber, barely illuminating much of the street in front of Tony's house. He was shirtless, sitting on an old lawn-chair that used to rest under the almond tree, wearing a pair of shorts he owned since he was seventeen. His feet were bare, and cold tiles were under his feet. Tony sat and he thought.

Before sitting on the porch, he had spent some time looking through his old bookshelf. He had been a relatively quiet child, spending his evening and free time reading. Like most children, he read a lot of fairytales. Often he would request a trip from one of his parents to travel to the Tom Redcam library search for new books. He chuckled as he saw two books. One was about alien invasions, and the other, an illustrated guide to a magical forest. He had borrowed these when he was about six or seven, almost twenty years ago. His reading ability had been accelerated as a result, and he started reading novels around age ten. Like the fantastical worlds he read about, he had created unusually black and white ideals about life.

Any reading material was fine, and he also read several Bible stories. Internalizing concepts and phrases like "The patience of Job", "God's Wrath" and had a reasonably clear, albeit childish, insight into the moral ambiguities contained these stories. For a while, these stories gave him a certain comfort. To him the ideas of guardian angels, astounding miracles and a world fueled by the power of goodwill was an interesting way for humans to exist. Tony knew as he grew older that the world wasn't governed by these black and white theories. It is not a place of absolutes. A man simply isn't patient and his time comes. People don't fall in love and stay that way forever. The realm of the fairy tale, and many of the bible stories Tony eventually realized were the stuff of dreams.

The Star was a local publication that became famous in the mid 80's for a glamorization of anything violent in Jamaica. It wouldn't be uncommon to see headlines that read "Man's Head Chopped Off," "Headless Woman Found in bushes" and "Goat Thief Burned Alive". His father bought a copy every day, and as a child enamored by stories like Robinson Crusoe, Ali Baba and the forty Thieves, and Black Beauty, Tony wasn't the biggest fan of that publication. With its large black and red letters, graphic photos and tabloid prose, Tony was ushered into a reality his child mind wasn't ready for. It was a world of death, blood and gratuitous violence. The childhood books with their golden-haired heroes and stilted ideas became a very broken moral compass.

One summer evening, he and a few young boys in the neighborhood, going stir crazy and idle, constructed slingshots and spent the day trying to kill lizards. The entire day Tony had been unsuccessful, until near late evening. One lay perched on the wall outside his house, and he let a stone fly. It hit the lizard with the sound of a hand slapping an old leather couch. The creature had fallen to the ground, its head twisted at an uncommon angle, with blue veins and distended bones sticking out of its neck; its face masked in the grisly visage of death. Tony was depressed for weeks afterwards, and swore he would never hurt another animal. It was also the time when he realized that there was finality to life, an ending to everything that was inevitable. He told this to his mother, and as he stood on the same verandah speaking to her, he had immediately burst into tears, shaking and weeping with his mother quietly holding him in her arms.

Tony's youthful investigation of all things religious was assisted in part by a television show broadcast from the BBC. When Tony was five years old, Jamaica had been an independent nation for only twenty-five years. Like many countries that shed themselves of colonial rule, the indelible stamp of hegemony was still present. People used densely English worlds like "settee" to describe a couch. To this day some older men talk about shillings and pence. What Tony remembered as the most poignant was looking into the eyes of his former Colonial Masters through British television programming. There was only one television station back then, the Jamaican Broadcast Commission, *JBC*. On the JBC there were mostly English Documentaries, English movies and sitcoms (though the Aussie hit *Home and Away* was right up there alongside South Africa's *Generations*). There was a weekday program that dealt with analysis of mythology as it relates to religion. Tony would watch these programs, developing strong beliefs about what the host discussed. In one show, the host spoke about the legend of vampires. That evening, the image of a man, with 80's metal band hair, pale skin and huge fangs appeared on screen. The image terrified Tony. In another episode, he saw an artist's rendition of hell. This picture had that touch of a renaissance painter's hands. The bodies of the people who were all white (and who Tony assumed were all English) were a bit doughy. There were women with droopy breasts and men with tiny penises. The images had hundreds of people in various states of pain. Above, below or beside them were tall, demonic figures holding three-pronged forks. Many of the bodies were impaled on these forks. Headless corpses lay near tiny guillotines and in the background was a large, billowing canopy of red fire, reaching upward into an endless chasm. "This is hell," the announcer said. "A place where unbelievers will spend an eternity in pain and suffering."

With his personal revelation about *finality* after the incident with the lizard, this concept of *eternity* was morbidly frightening.

Tony wasn't sure what *eternity* really meant, but he knew enough to know that going to church and praying all the time—especially if you had the patience of Job—was a surefire way to not go to that place with the three-pronged forks, demons and chubby, screaming white women. That night he had the first of a series of recurring nightmares in which he was chased by the man with the metal band hair who waved a three-pronged fork, his teeth glinting in the light of the endless twilight of a dream night. He would scream, but it was always a scream like someone makes in the void of space, noiseless and empty. Then, he would wake up, frightened by the shadows around him, wondering if he were dead or alive. He would run to his parent's room after these dreams, banging his little fists on their door. His father would leap to attention and open the large white door and scoop him up into his powerful arms and say, "Oh! You have a little nightmare. Nothing wrong, man. Nothing wrong!" Sometimes this would assuage his feelings. Other times, he was so frightened that he would spend the night sleeping between his parents; their bodies like large mountains on either side of him.

Tony had smirked, thinking about his younger self as he closed the bookcase. Then he had walked to the porch and sat down. It was curious processing the evolution from child to man. The real change he knew, happened in high school. Like his father, Tony had some height, and by the time he was thirteen he was five feet nine inches tall. By Jamaican standards, this was quite tall. Most of Tony's classmates at the time were pushing five feet two inches or less. Of course there was the one fellow who was about six foot two at thirteen, and another fellow who was two hundred and eighty pounds in weight, but every school had those people. One really tall boy, one really tall girl, and a couple of fat kids. Between the ages of thirteen and sixteen he shot up to six feet two inches, and his features, soft and boyish, became those of a very handsome young man. His eyes, small and round became intense orbs that burned with intensity. His cheeks lost any baby fat that was left, and his jaw was strong and prominent. His frame was lean yet muscled, and his world changed. His quiet mannerisms oozed a confidence which was very sexual (thought he didn't realize it at first) and (also something he didn't know) many girls admired him. Even though he didn't speak that much, people gravitated towards him, and it all but seemed that the torments of the past were gone. Then Quasey transferred to the school.

Quasey was one of those kids with wild, inquisitive eyes and an unusually high self-confidence. He had no reservations about saying anything to anyone. This included the staff at school, his fellow students, and even his parents. He became famous one morning after his mother had dropped him to school and he stepped out of the vehicle, screaming. "I don't need any fucking lunch money!" He was short, about five foot five, but he had a presence that put all the other young boys in line. Within weeks, he had a small entourage of loyal followers. Young boys did his errands; they loved to listen to him tell raucous stories filled with sex. He bragged about having access to pornographic material on his home satellite system, and mentioned how he had fingered a girl at his last school. Quasey was also violent, prone to battles with boys twice his size, and getting into trouble with fellows in higher grades. One on occasion, an older boy named Drew, notorious for being a "bad man" at school, crossed paths with Quasey. Words were exchanged, and the two egos met like oil and water. Drew had thrown the first punch, splitting Quasey's lip and sending blood streaming onto his khaki shirt. Quasey had grabbed a stone and smashed it into Drew's ear. Drew had stooped down, clutching his ear, and Quasey had given him a solid kick in the testicles. Drew fell to the ground, and Quasey, with his shirt covered in blood, had kept kicking Drew until a few other young men and a teacher had pulled him away. It was the stuff of legend.

Tony had become Quasey's target from almost day one. Even though Tony towered over him, Quasey had no fear of him. His eyes shone with maddening contempt. His smile— almost evil in how self-assured it was—would be what Tony would try to avoid. Anytime Quasey smiled at Tony, he knew an insult was coming. He would tease Tony about his height, call him 'bighead', and go on about how dark his skin was. The teasing was unrelenting, fueled by the endless well of whatever dark confidence Quasey had figured how to rapidly develop. Tony was the same complexion as his father, a cool chocolate.

Many of his fellow students looked like Tony, with small variations in the shades of their skin. Quasey's skin tone was a lighter, almost yellowish skin tone. Some people said he was half Chinese, but Tony didn't see it. He had a chubby face, a piggish nose, and his eyes were like two small dinner plates. His eyebrows were unusually bushy.

Tony grew to hate him. It wouldn't have been so bad if Quasey was the only person that bothered him, but his venomous way of speaking was infectious, and it became normal for the intermittent Quasey joke to become regular conversational fodder. One day, he had sat near the football field watching some older boys play in the late evening. Their faces were glistening with sweat, and their dark bodies moved with calculated precision as they passed the ball to one another and shouted commands. As the dust swirled around them from the rapid movements of school shoes on the old, weather-torn field, Tony found himself feeling very alone. That day, an overriding sensation of nausea had come from the pit of his stomach and a thick stream of bile rushed up into his throat. The reaction was so quick and powerful, the foul tasting liquid even came through his nose. He had fallen to his knees, coughing and heaving as an endless stream of yellow liquid fell into the dirty ground before him, turning black as it hit soft pockets of loose soil. He didn't understand where the feeling came from, but he felt as if it represented how everyone felt about him; as if he was this object of ridicule, the butt of jokes, something wholly unattractive and unworthy.

As time passed he felt more withdrawn, and the nausea would build and he'd feel sick, particularly when hanging around large groups of people. A doctor eventually told him it was massive anxiety he was experiencing, and that he should focus on ways to relax. At the time, there was the worried face of his mother, the gritted teeth of his father who wondered aloud what brought this situation on, and some sort of medication, that made Tony feel drowsy and didn't help much with the anxiety. Every now and then, for apparently no reason, he would feel sick, his stomach turning in the opposite direction, with his chest tight and the world feeling like a blanket around his face.

Then, there was summer camp. He and several other highly energized teens spent three weeks in some place in the country. Tony's mother had insisted it would be a good experience. She was right. One of the counselors, a young woman in her early twenties, took a very quick liking to Tony. There was something in the way she had taken him with her eyes on the first day as he came off the bus, lanky and lean, with a duffle bag slung over his shoulder. There were activities during the day that were fun but menial. There were prayers in the evening and games during the day, and lots of free time in between. It started with brief visits to an isolated room in a storage shed at the rear of camp. She would get on her knees and take Tony in her mouth or jerk him off with expert technique. The boyish sensitivities that had bothered him at school immediately seemed irrelevant in the face of this brave, new sexual world. The world with the counselor with her small breasts that barely showed through her faded Polo shirt; the world where she relished him. His anxiety, ever lurking like a phantom, dissipated incrementally with each session. The sex came on the very last day, and that day Tony was ushered quickly out of the world of virginity. The long bus ride home was peppered with images of the counselor's naked body, the scent of her womanhood, the creaking of the wooden table in the shed and the explosive feeling of sweetness that ended it all. The following semester at school, Tony walked with surer steps; with the mental clarity of one who had left a major part of childhood behind. The first day, at a regular hangout spot, Quasey had come over, and in his usual fashion started saying a few choice words. Tony had walked over and looked him directly in the eyes, taking him in quietly. At the time he almost laughed. He towered over Quasey, and wondered why he had never realized his advantage of size.

"What you goin' do, eh Tony? Mi wan see you try sum'n," Quasey had said with his usual bravado.

The punch was swift. Quasey fell to the ground. He had recoiled quickly, his eyes flaming with anger and surprise. Tony was still taking him in coolly, not moving from where he originally stood. Quasey had run up to him, trying to knock him over, but Tony easily threw him to the side. Curses flew like rain from his mouth as he tried to rally some of the younger men around him to help, but they hovered quietly, as surprised as Quasey possibly, seeing Tony tall and resolute. The battle was fierce, ending with a punch from Tony that left Quasey winded and whimpering. The news spread around school. Tony was not to be fucked with.

Going through the vivid memories felt real. The smells of the night around him, the quiet whispers of breeze through thin blades of grass and the scent of mango trees brought it all back. Then, the slightest hint of nausea ebbed in the base of his stomach, and he could feel the little tendrils that so often had drifted up his arms, grabbed his stomach and chest come back. Tendrils that had made him throw up, and fight to breathe. Tony breathed slowly in and out, waiting for the feeling to pass. He took a long look at the night sky, reminding himself that childhood was gone.

Chapter 38

Outside, the sky was a perfect, cloudless blue. Winston stared from the window of his hotel, somewhere in the heart of New Kingston. The familiarity of everything hit him like a strong scent. One enterprising person that worked in the hotel lobby had told him about all the nightclubs only walking distance from the hotel. Winston had nodded and smiled, but he knew he wasn't in town to rage at parties and get drunk on rum. The pervasive emptiness was growing. Possibly, home held something that could break this cycle. He went outside and into his rental car. In minutes he was near his destination, close to a popular mall with a movie theatre.

Winston drove down Hope Road, watching dark bodies rippling with sweat in the midday heat float by in a blur. As he turned off the main road to Charlemont Avenue, a sense of dread hit him. It was the sensation he normally felt when he was coming home from school. It had been years since he had even been on this road, but to the mind, a memory is as powerful as a reality. After another minute, driving past a sign on the road that said "HUMP", he saw the house.

The yard was massive, and a thick collection of mango trees dotted the property, clustered at the front, and evenly spread towards the rear of the house. The grass was high and unkempt and dozens of half-eaten mangoes lay in various stages of decomposition on the lawn. The air was thick with the smell of rotting fruit. A small crack in the driveway, normally troubled with a tiny outcropping of tiny blades of grass, looked like a concrete Mohawk. Everything was overgrown and in disarray. Winston pulled the Honda up to the gate, with inches between the front bumper and rust covered bars. The gates were old, wrought in some blacksmith's backroom God knows how long ago. They had once been tall and black, with bars two inches thick, and a triangular pattern of arrowheads that rested atop a shaft of gnarled iron that resembled the inside of a moth's wing. Even with a heavy coating of red rust on it, Winston could still remember standing there as a little boy, thinking that one day the gates would come to life, devouring him while tearing him apart. There was a doorbell back then, a small white button on the right column by the gate, which had long since fallen out. A brand new padlock and chain were around the gate.

Winston stepped out of the car. There was the house. Tall and old in that Jamaican way filled with wood, antique furniture and bad memories. The roof looked battered, and mold grew on the walls from the base upwards, making the house appear as if it had lifted its skirts and sat in a bowl of green paint. Winston sighed and leaned on the gate, not caring for the powder of iron that now coated his arms. He looked down the driveway, and saw himself, smaller and younger, walking with his head down and his school bag in his hand, not wanting to meet their eyes.

Those eyes.

Winston's parents were a pair of young entrepreneurs that lived in the Barbican area in the late seventies. His parents, both armed with free degrees from the generosity of the administration at the time, sought to capitalize on the red scare in the seventies. Many people, fearing a communist uprising in Jamaica, fled to the U.S or Canada, taking all their money, and literally, left everything behind. Houses with high market value were sold for a pittance of their former price. Pretty soon, savvy, quick thinkers and smart businessmen owned several properties. When the communist threat ebbed, market prices went back up and many people got rich. Winston's parents had capitalized on that opportunity. Winston had come a few years later, bouncing into their lives in 1983. By that time, they had six properties renting steadily, and a few spots of land that were now worth millions. For young Winston, all he would ever remember of this golden period were brief trips to Devon House with his father, eating ice cream and choking at the taste of a Guinness Stout as his father laughed heartily in the background. The only image of his mother that he could remember was one of her in a white dress, the day they both took him to the house on Charlemont road. She had held him in her arms, all sixty pounds of him, and pointed towards the large mango trees and the yard: "That's where we are going to live," she had said with a smile on her face. That was 1986.

They were both killed in a car crash one month after they moved into the new house. His father, large and full of life, was taking his mother to a reggae concert. Winston, sitting on the couch with a babysitter, had waved nonchalantly as they walked away. He was focused on the large color television they had just purchased, marveling at the pictures and the sound. Two weeks later, *they* moved in. They were Winston's father's aunts, twins, on his mother's side. From day one Winston knew his life would never be the same. They had walked into the house with matching scowls on their faces, with eyes held in angry slits. Thick in the body and short of stature, they always wore ugly, billowy dresses that were too bright, even for Jamaican weather. Light pinks, sky blue and blood red dresses were what they loved. That day, they were both wearing bright purple skits with matching white tops.

"I am Miss May," one said.

"I am Miss Martha," the other added. "We are here to take care of you, you hear?"

Miss Martha had said it with an iciness that would later remind Winston of a bad hospital visit. They cursed a lot, and loved to pick on Winston.

"Winston, look at you hair! Real black people hair!" they would shout, cackling and gripping his head. The young Winston would scream. Their fingers, long and wrinkled like sausages, were extremely strong. They would yank at his hair constantly.

One day, the young Winston had lamented their treatment of him.

"Don't touch my hair!" he had screamed as one of the twins, Miss May, lunged after him.

That was the first day they started beating him. Winston had reeled in shock from the first blow. He had run to his room, not knowing that Miss Martha was walking behind him with quiet and sure steps. As he stood there, something went *thwack* on the side of his head, and his ears started ringing. He collapsed into a heap on the floor, and to his dismay, felt the tiniest trickle of blood on his forehead. "That will teach you some rass manners," Miss Martha had said with a hiss. Winston had rolled over from the floor, and watched her walk away with something gripped firmly in her hand. It was a hairbrush.

The objects got worse. There were wire hanger and little pieces of sticks they would find outside. They used smelly leathery belts too, but most of all they loved using their hands. They were chubby, but powerfully built women with hands hard from "yard work" as they would always say. It would take nothing to set them off, and Winston would try his best to hide or be nice so that they wouldn't whip him. It never worked. A day after they moved into the house, the TV was never turned on again. "A young boy shouldn't fill up his head with this foolishness. You tink I had TV when I was a child? Eh Winston?" miss May had said.

Anytime either of them, said "eh Winston?" he knew not to respond. The first few times he responded, he was smacked a few times with a wet rope. Now that the TV was never on, Winston spent most of his time in the yard, whenever the sisters didn't have him doing some odd chore. By the time 1990 had rolled around, Winston was eight years old and was wiping the floors, cleaning the bathroom and so quiet his teachers at school thought he had some kind of learning disability.

Winston read a lot of books, including fairy tales to escape his maddening environment. He loved Cinderella, because it seemed to mirror his situation with crazy overlord family members and never-ending torture. The twins were as cold as the future winters Winston would experience in the United States. The twins were staunchly religious and Winston never saw a man enter the gates. Every now and then, they would have some "church friends" over, and they would morph into the sweetest pair of people a young boy would ever see. Their eyes would lose their icy coldness, and they would constantly call Winston over to introduce him to some person.

"Winston, this is Mr. Andrews," Miss May or Martha would say. Then, either of them would rub his head fondly and then continue talking to her friend. In one of these instances, Miss Martha had looked down at him, and for a split-second, her eyes regained the coldness that would frighten a small animal, and Winston knew he was going to get a beating that night. He did.

There was an occasion that forever remained in his mind. It was an early Saturday morning, and Winston had nothing to do. He rolled out of his bed, tiptoeing in the early morning to go outside before the twins started harassing him. They normally woke up at eleven or so, but oh was he wrong this day! He walked past the bathroom, and the door opened. Standing naked in the doorway was his aunt. She was tall and obese, with multi-colored jelly-like flesh that shook like bread pudding with each step she took. Her breasts were long and hung to her stomach, exposing her enormous black nipples. Winston had paused in fright, but Miss Martha, she had screamed like there was no tomorrow.

Winston heard something different in that scream. The monster had been exposed. She had been humiliated. He hid in the yard for most of the day while they called for him, loudly proclaiming his death if he didn't come inside. He held out for most of the day, but eventually, hunger prevailed. When he came inside, he was beaten till he was bloody. Miss Martha whipped him so badly both buttocks bled and he pissed himself. Miss May had constantly pulled at his hair and ripped out little bits of it in chunks, laughing gleefully as she slapped his back with heavy hands. To cover up their crime, they had poured alcohol and salt on Winston's buttocks, covering his mouth as he screamed from the pain. That Monday, the freshly formed scabs broke in his pants when he went to Physical Education class. Winston was running up and down with the young boys, doing football drills. Then, a young man had said, "Winston shit him pants! Red Shit! Red shit!"

The young boys had all laughed, but Winston was mortified. The physical education teacher, a tall stern man of English descent, had sent Winston to the nurse. The nurse had examined Winston, and saw the marks on his back and his buttocks. "Winston," she had said. "Is someone doing this to you?" Winston had stood there mute as always. He was afraid to say anything. The wrath of his aunts was worse than the power of God.

There was no telephone where they lived; the twins had seen it fit to keep the phone line that came with the house off. The phone was a relic that sat atop the television beside a statue of Jesus on the cross. Winston never told the nurse what happened, but somehow the aunts found out. They had both taken turns beating him that night until they were tired and their hands were covered in a thin red film of blood.

Winston didn't know how to process what was happening. This sort of pain must be normal, he had thought. I must be a nicer person, a better person, he had said to himself. He tried smiling with the aunts, saying cheery good mornings and doing his housework with more gusto, but it never helped. The twins gave more care to washing their clothes and reading the bible than they ever did to Winston. It wasn't until one of the twins messed up—very badly—that things changed.

Winston took the bus home from school. He would hop on the bus at Half-Way-Tree, which would make the long journey all the way up to Old Hope Road, and let him off at the intersection where the new mall, Sovereign Center, would be built. There he would walk for half a mile and press the button on the gate to come home. One Wednesday, the bus simply wasn't there. There was some kind of incident, a strike. After waiting at the bus stop for an hour and a half, the sky began to darken. Winston had to walk the four or so miles home. He came home two hours later when the sky was shrouded in a dark cloak, sprinkled with the twinkling dots of the stars. That night the twins had raved about Winston's tardiness with enough energy to run a marathon. In some way Winston would later realize, it was their form of showing they were worried, that they actually cared. They went on and on about how dangerous Kingston was, how irresponsible Winston was, and of course how badly he would be beaten. Normally they would just go for the belt, the switch, or whatever was in reach, but tonight was different. They ranted for at least an hour, and Winston felt himself becoming more and more frightened. He wanted to just be hit and have it be over with. Their expressions, the strength that showed in the tense way their flabby hands moved had made Winston grit his teeth in fear.

The whipping that night had an unusual fervor. "Don't ever come home so late again!" Miss Martha had said while whipping him with a switch on her lap. Winston was almost so used to the pain he let out nothing more than a slight whimper. Then, Miss Martha had stood him up—this meant she would give him a few slaps in the face and say more mean things—

but instead of slapping him, she punched him full in the face. A bolt of pain shot through Winston's head and he felt something wet against the back of his throat. It was blood, and a lot of it. Miss May had squealed with fright, and then there was a flurry of activity. An old dirty towel appeared. A bowl of warm water. Their hands flew over Winston's face in a brown blur, and Winston had lain there, unable to breathe, almost choking on his own blood.

The next day, the school nurse sent someone over to the Charlemont residence. The twins were issued a warning for abuse. The warning was issued by an enormous police officer that looked a lot meaner than the twins as he stood beside them. After that day, they never laid another hand on him. The abuses became verbal in nature, caustic and grating, but Winston was happy to be pain free. The TV still remained off.

When he was ten, he resolved to make sure that no one would treat him badly again, by treating everyone as nicely as possible. "If I give myself freely to people," Winston had reasoned, "I should get the same result back

I should get the same result back.

Winston was standing in the same spot where he had made that statement, sixteen years prior. "If I give myself freely to people. I should get the same result back. Ah… youth." Winston said to himself with a painful laugh. Winston walked up the narrow steps that led towards the house. He stood at the entryway and he could smell the house, musky with the scent of rotting wallpaper, wet wood and soggy carpets. He didn't enter. He took a deep breath, walked down the driveway, and looked at the yard once more. Then, he refastened the chain to the gate, quietly started the car, reversed into the road, and drove away. As the house grew smaller in the distance in his rear view mirror, he took one last glimpse at the canopy of mango trees. He had never told anyone about this part of his life, not even Elsa.

Chapter 39

It was a stream of faces and places that felt dark and unfamiliar. The new generation of kids wielding their college degrees and reasonably above-average incomes were demanding more entertainment. People wanted more live shows, more bars, more restaurants and simply more to do. A few people who Tony knew hung out intermittently with him. The behavior at most places was the same: Groups of people standing face forward, staring at nothing and no one, music flying into the sky. But certain things hadn't changed much. At Devon House on a Friday the place was still filled with white and light-skinned Jamaicans, buying their above average priced drinks, intermingling in tightly knit social circles. Club Quad felt the same, with its dark skinned crowd on the first floor, who wanted their lighting dim and music loud. Young uptown and early twenty something's populated the second floor party. That place made Tony feel old.

On the streets, men lounged and idled at rum bars, cursing at each other while playing dominoes, or just relaxing on a sidewalk as music played in the background, sipping on white rum and slowly drifted into states of inebriation. These things filtered through Tony's system, making things feel slow and protracted. The dark venues, the people quietly standing up in close proximity working hard to ignore each other, the same musical mixes in the same patterns. There was something in the air, something thick with entitlement and a sense of purpose that permeated the attitudes of people at night, a groundswell of confidence mixed with conservative behavior. It was the pulse of island life, a place populated with sleepy days and a hemisphere that hovered within a smaller hemisphere. The customer service was brutal in some places. Harsh and rude attitudes in many situations were normal, Tony remembered. People didn't look at you and assume you were anything unless you were famous or of indeterminate ethnicity. Hot words were just as common as hot food in pots being cooked on alternate sidewalks. Here, Tony was hiding in plain sight, just another guy. He remembered that this vibe—no, this *inkling* was part of the reason he left. There was a lingering curiosity about the outside world that burned inside him. A desire to experience a paradigm of being that wasn't filtered through the post-colonial lens.

At the time the feeling had grown and grown, till he felt like he was bursting at the seams. It was then he felt that desire to experience *Americana*, its statutes of randomness and culture that had been sprinkled into so much of the media he would grow to know as a youth. The silly Pauly Shore sex comedies and campy action movies. Now he knew that it wasn't all lecherous women at summer camps, or super spies saving the day, but it was different. This was what he found hard to manufacture at home; a day he could not predict. In Kingston a man must revolve around a select number of bars and clubs because he is forced to. Men live and die going to the same bar for thirty years, and now it seemed, men live and die going to the same club week after week.

But it *was* shifting. It seemed the idea of "lifestyle" and "V.I.P." had invaded the Jamaican advertising consciousness. Every party had a V.I.P. section, all the flyers said things about partying with beautiful people, and the "it" crowd. It was an escalating scenario of self-delusion. Not every person can be the "it" person in a torrent of individuals that want to be *that* guy, or *that* girl. Too many guys acting cool create an inherent problem with the balance of things. Women get unrealistic basic expectations. They want the "it" guy. They model him based on simple factors that rule a contiguous environment. He must look wealthy, be known for something, or be famous. Partying here in a certain way took *effort*. The ideas of aesthetics and interest were vastly skewed. Looks were relative.

What do you drive? A girl had asked Tony.

"I don't drive," he replied

The conversation had eventually trickled to a near stop and she had soon walked away. This wasn't a pervasive mentality, but it was a *thing;* a thing with substance and weight, a measure of a man that was as clear as the smell of morning cooking. For the first few days of his two-week stay, Tony found himself mired in thoughts of old. The awkwardness of standing quietly in a dark corner, shouting over the speakers to barely get access to a girl nearby, the melting pot of color and class in close proximity. He had seen a gaggle of girls that looked familiar at some new bar off Hope Road. Party girls of old with ten years of mileage; faces showing the wear of endless sexual trysts, eyes flat and jaded. Theirs was the worst kind of looking-glass world; where men provided them with everything and nothing. They were objects, floating to and fro, getting drinks tossed down their throats and later other things tossed down their throats. These girls had meant something at some point Tony remembered; there was an ebb and a flow to them. He had probably even been friends with one. Then, time passed and they gained fame and attention. Whispers of their names floated around town. They popped up in magazines and editorials, the true mark of the Jamaican socialite. Then these girls had drifted away, they had transitioned into that upper atmosphere of the Jamaican social bubble, hanging with millionaires and executives, living lives free of responsibility. They were sirens that fed on the moment, basking in the timeless falsity of youthful beauty and perfect bodies, posing seductively in oiled up pictures on yachts. Now they were faded like the newspapers clippings that no doubt one of them had saved, blown out like bad cell phone pictures with no smart phone filters.

But Kingston had evolved.

The slothful crawl of technology that finally filtered through corrupted government programs and over-extended initiatives had started showing benefits. New rules for market competition had forced out some old monopolies and broken bad habits. People wanted service. They wanted style. They wanted more for their money. The Internet was blazing fast and there were new tech companies, and guys chopping coconuts were texting on smartphones. The world was everywhere now. Men learned *savoir faire* and changed the way they lived. It wasn't just about parties and bars. There were upscale restaurants and new expensive gym memberships, villas to rent and luxury cars to dream of. People worked on personal development and more people were trying to be artistic. Women exploded in education, raging through the universities in droves. Power and gender identity was changing from the ideals of the past; man and woman were now equal. The female was roaring, and she was being heard.

This wave felt palpable.

Kingston was no longer a den of falsely portrayed decadence, it was a destination. Foreigners roamed the streets, filled the guesthouses and invaded the dancehall events. So did the expats, short-term workers and interns, people with different dispositions and outlooks. Many figured these people were a way to escape the drone of the common. Tony would see the women that loved the expats. These were often beautiful women with chocolate skin too happy to be girl number two or three for some diplomat with a ridiculous stipend and loads of free time. Whoever that girl was, she could feel the wave too, maybe she had watched Pauly Shore movies and dreamed of summer camp, or wanted Han Solo in Star Wars. Maybe the old white guy with the thick accent was her version of Sean Connery, or just a glimpse into what could be, outside the borders of the hemisphere in the hemisphere; the endless rotating looking glass of familiarity and circumstance.

It didn't really matter at the end of it all, Tony reasoned. A city like any is filled with its intricacies and limitations. Its delicacies and its dangers. It has its heart, and it would beat continuously, long after he was gone, and the faceless women, the party girls, and the men chopping coconuts turned to ash deep in the ground, as the new generation roamed the streets, trying to get laid, posed for pictures, and woke up, ready to do it all again. Tonight, like so many nights in his life, he was getting ready to go out, to see if things were still predictable, or if Kingston would greet him with open arms, ready to seduce him with her new tricks, but he knew that it would feel and taste the same, like a glass of room temperature water on a hot summer day.

Chapter 40

There was some party going on. Amanda had told him about it. Amanda was a girlfriend from a very long time ago. She was one of those relationships that felt like a quick breath of fresh air, a flash in the pan of life that was neither good nor bad. She wanted to have dinner first. The conversation was a bit dull for Bishop's taste, and the food was bland. Something felt off with the interaction. Amanda had clear eyes and a pretty face, but there was something about her that didn't feel sexy anymore. It didn't really matter. She talked a lot about the scene and stuff happening with people Bishop could barely remember. He had grown up in a world of these restaurants and bland conversations, trips to Strawberry Hill and his father's villa in Ocho Rios, endless barbeques chatting in clipped speech, hiding in the cloud of the elite. When people spoke he knew how to say enough to seem interested. He could fake a smile, laugh on cue and chat about droll topics with gusto. It was all part of his mask, a mask he hadn't worn in a while. She chatted about some new bars that had opened up that people liked and chuckled about more things Bishop didn't care about. He knew where this was going. He laughed at another silly joke and then saw how her eyes were glancing to the left and he knew she wanted to leave. They would go to the party, go into some V.I.P. section and hang with all their friends from high school or whatever, then they would get wasted listening to dancehall music, some prissy party girl might give him attitude until she found out who he was, then she'd want his number and he would decide if he wanted her or not but then Amanda would be there and start dancing with him and the alcohol would unlock old memories and there wouldn't be much point to not do anything. They would go back to her place, and things would happen and she would cook for him in the morning. It wouldn't be weird because this always happened when he came back. Bishop was her illusion of something that would never be but was fine when he was there.

The party was at the New Kingston Golf Academy and it wasn't bad. They went into the V.I.P. section and Bishop saw a swath of people from high school and extended family members. He went straight to the bar, giving Amanda a cranberry vodka.

"I prefer white rum," she said.

"That's an old man's drink. Really?"

"Well, it's cheap."

"This is all inclusive party."

"Well, I drink it more these days."

Bishop chuckled and got her the white rum drink. They stood there for a while, and as the music picked up and the crowd got thicker, the fusion of location, music and liquor started to build, and Bishop remembered these parties with Kevin, the days they would dance and chase girls, laughing with eyes red from smoking weed and drinking shots. Amanda brought a few friends over. They were girls Bishop recognized from somewhere in the past, girls whose names didn't really matter. He gave a cordial hello. One girl, a striking girl of Asian descent gave him a lingering eye. He made a note of it and smirked as he heard Kevin's voice laughing at him.

You throw so much pussy in the rubbish.

Amanda came over and gave him a dance. It was light and to Bishop, unsexy, but she was into it and Bishop relaxed into it. Then he took a walk for a while and said hello to some people, being stopped every minute or so by someone asking him how long he was in Jamaica. One person mentioned something about Kevin, and Bishop gave him a nod and a smile, and got more drinks. More people were coming in and talking, and there were more handshakes and questions about how long he was in Jamaica, how life was in D.C. A vacuum was starting to form, and the music was turning into noise. He glimpsed Amanda, waving and looking cute in her nice top and white pants, chatting to some more girls that looked exactly like her. Then the DJ said something and the crowd went crazy, and streamers flew in the air and showered everyone. Bishop was slightly annoyed with the display, and went back to the bar. The Asian girl came over and introduced herself, putting her hand delicately on Bishop's waist, asking him how long he was going to be in Jamaica. He took her number and she floated away, giving him a lingering stare before disappearing into the crowd.

Then Amanda was close again, doing a similar dance this time face first, her lips close to Bishop's neck. They left the party and went to her apartment in Norbrook. She gave Bishop head in her car and then they had sex on her bed. It felt weird and functional, somewhere between good and okay. During the sex an image of Monica's large breasts and sensuous hips flashed in the forefront of his mind, for a minute or two, he raged slightly harder and Amanda had moaned with his increased tumescence and energy, then the image slipped away and Bishop came unceremoniously, flopping onto the bed with his head spinning slightly from the alcohol. Then Amanda turned on the air conditioning and put on an old Sade album and hugged him naked, stroking the thin hairs on his chest. He knew she was looking at him even though his eyes were closed.

In the morning, she made bacon and toast for him, looking nice in a pair of yellow track shorts with her hair mussed. They chatted about the future and some local stuff, mostly her annoyance with her insurance company taking forever to deal with some guy who had hit her vehicle and wasn't able to pay and then she mentioned going to Maiden Cay and Bishop told her he'd think about it. She dropped Bishop home and said hello to his parents. They gave the vague parental nod of approval. His father obviously didn't know who she was and his mother seemed to remember her, or someone who was related to her.

He messaged the girl from the night before and met up with her for lunch. She did some kind of modeling, which didn't mean much to Bishop. He told her he was an artist living in Washington D.C and her eyes had ignited with interest. He told her about possibly going to Maiden Cay and she asked if she could bring some friends. Bishop told her it wasn't a problem.

A bunch of people were on his father's boat. Friends from the past, some people who had tagged along and made sure to give Bishop a hearty hello. Bishop had nodded at a few people and the cute women. People drank heartily at the bar as the yacht pulled close to the small strip of sand that was the regular party spot. The Asian girl and her friends were really enjoying themselves, snapping pictures with their smart phones and getting drunk on Grey Goose. Amanda was there as well with two friends more than a little drunk and smiley-faced in a white bikini. Bishop wasn't drinking much, but enjoyed the touch of the sea on his body as he leapt off the boat at the Cay, narrowly missing some sea urchins on the sea floor. People were out and about, and as he took a stroll on the sand there were more handshakes and pats on the back. Questions came and went from familiar faces and acquaintances. The feeling from the night before was lurking somewhere nearby. The vacuum was threatening to return, then someone gave him some drinks and soon he was back into that place, the world getting dull around him, the throbbing echo of music from another boat making his ears tingle. The Asian girl was off the boat too, her body a dark brown from the sun's heat, giggling hysterically as some beefy guy splashed her with water.

Then they were heading back to port and Bishop, a little drunk and tired, suggested a few of them get dinner in Kingston. Amanda was a little too wasted to come, and Bishop went with Asian girl, her girlfriend, one of her guy friends and another guy he knew from school. The conversation was about nothing and everything; music, sex and high school. It was fun and light, Bishop laughed a lot and he knew where this was going. He would take the girl home and she would take a shower at his place, then she would come into his room and stuff would happen and he would listen to her speak about her life afterward, the things she wanted to do and then he would drop her home and call her some other time, probably going to some club with her and her friends while dodging Amanda for a day or two and then in a week, he would be back on a plane and then in D.C, his lips cracking and peeling from the cold, his body covered in a coat and his feet chafing from his leather boots.

Chapter 41

It was one of those nights, the kind that leaves you wobbly in the morning, filled with eighty percent smiles, ten percent regret and another ten percent of stuff that kicks in at a later date. Outside, the cold was light but obvious, the landscape manned by leafless trees dotting empty streets.

Tony was at the GIANT supermarket in Columbia Heights. In his shopping cart, were the building blocks of adult life; a bag of Tostitos, shredded cheese, oatmeal cookies, Raisin Bran and some spaghetti. His head throbbed a bit—the roar of Friday was still loud and clear in his mind—and he walked with a slightly off gait. He'd only been back in D.C for two weeks, and Jamaica was nothing more than a distant, sexless memory. Pushing the cart through the wrong aisle for the umpteenth time, he saw a familiar face. It's Dennis, otherwise known as Cool Asian Dude. Dennis gave Tony a once over and smirked. Dennis lived in Columbia Heights. Tony didn't. Dennis was wearing a hoodie with skinny jeans and old sneakers. Tony was dressed like he's ready for the club at ten a.m.

"I'm still drunk," Tony said.

"Nice," Dennis replied.

Tony gave a brief recap of the previous night's events. Girls kissing girls, him getting entangled with one of the girls who was kissing a girl, lots of drinking, hanging out with friends and eventually passing out on a couch in an apartment he'd never been in, about two blocks from the Giant. Somewhere in this carousel of thoughts, his friend Ben might have been present, but he couldn't' be sure.

"Nice," Dennis said again. He held a basket filled with party material; about four super cheap forty ounce bottles of soda, a stack of red cups and two bottles of vodka. "I'm having a little get together later. Pass by if you like," He said to Tony.

"Sure," Tony replied.

That would be the second slated party for the night. Tony promised himself he wouldn't drink. For what seemed like an eternity, he stared at a sign that read "Georgetown Valet." After paying for his items he walked outside, squinting slightly in the morning sunlight. He sat on his latest acquisition, a sleek road bike. The streets flew by in cold slaps on his face. Precariously balancing the shopping bag with his head spinning, he made it back to his place without serious injury. He tossed the groceries into a heap near his bed, and popped open the bag of cheese. After a few bites of Tostitos and shredded cheese, the world spun and Tony fell into the world of sleep. Hours later, after a quick shower and a booster of black tea and more Tostitos and shredded cheese, he went out. The first party was the Creation versus Evolution party.

Creationism is a term that relates to people who believe in a literal interpretation of the Bible. Some feel the earth was created six thousand years ago (dinosaurs and all), and these people are called Young Creationists. Others believe the earth and the universe were created by God billions of years ago, and these are called Old Creationists. For a creationist, the bible is the key to understanding their personal origins. Evolutionists are people who believe in Darwin's theories on the origin of species. They strongly believe that man descended from apes, and evolved over millions of years to develop rudimentary speech, use of tools, and eventually Pabst Blue Ribbon. Evolutionists are generally strong supporters of data that relate to genetics and several other biological phenomena. Paleontology, Thermodynamics and higher-level physics are also common points evolutionists will reference. Tonight the forces will clash. The creationist versus evolutionist party was the brainchild of Sally, a girl who lived near a bar Tony frequented. Like any small town or area, once you frequented a bar and lived nearby, you usually ended up knowing the regulars. Sally was often in the bar with glassy eyes and a funny disposition. This party, she said, was the true measuring stick for Creationism and Evolutionism.

"Each party will make a measuring stick," she said. "Each cup will be stacked one of top of the other. The group with the tallest stack, or longest stick wins."

"I like it," Tony had said. "But does that really prove one party is more correct than the other?"

Sally had stood close to Tony, inches away from his face. "Anyone who ever thought you could logically debate such things is a fool for trying. Alcohol always brings out the truth."

Tony agreed. These sorts of parties were fascinating to him. Was it a natural part of living in a city filled with academics? Or the offshoot of an individualistic, highly opinionated culture? Maybe it was more of that *Americana,* that randomness and unpredictability so inherent to his experiences thus far. Far away, across blue seas was his home, and in his home were his parents doing what they usually did. Where was his father now? Was he laughing with friends, slamming a heavy domino onto a table, or was he simply reflecting? Jamaica felt far in these kinds of moments. Moments when he found himself on some steps in front of someone's apartment, chatting about the nuances of the expression "Live free or die", listening to people give reasons for passionately hating writing critics, or guys high on drugs babbling incessantly about 80's cartoons. Tony knew many people like Sally, pseudo-friends who he ran into during his excursions around the city. He only ever saw these people at night, rarely during the day, and it was always somewhere random, like in an alleyway near an Arby's or at some public rally for a NGO of which he wasn't a big supporter.

The cold nipped at his fingers and Tony gritted his teeth slightly. This was this one thing he didn't like much about life in the States. The cold bed sheets, the irascible space heater in his apartment that made more noise than the comfort it provided, and the odd day when it was so cold a hot shower made going back into his room feel like he stepped into a deep freeze. But soon, he'd be at Sally's place, with people and warmth. As he rolled up, he saw some people on the stoop drinking beers. He brought the bike into the hallway, resting it beside three others.

Sally's apartment had a small entryway which lead to a room that doubled as a kitchen area and living room.

"Tony!" a voice said. "Get yourself something immediately."

Stooping below the counter fishing for glasses and plates, was Sally. She walked over and gave Tony a firm hug.

"You smell nice," she said with a mischievous smirk.

Tony chuckled and walked to the fridge. As he pulled out the first beer he had a flash of memory. They had almost hooked up once, on a night like this, when it had just started getting cold. He was pretty drunk and unable to go home, and she had said the bed was available. She had nothing on but an old college t-shirt and Tony was in his underwear. They had kissed slightly, but ended up asleep in each other's arms. After that things never went in that direction again.

A girl walked into the kitchen from the hallway that lead to the bedrooms. She was short, with an attractive face and a large chest. Sally introduced her as Agent M. She laughed at this.

"Which team are you on?" Tony asked.

"Evolutionist."

"Really?"

Agent M laughed again.

"Sally, it looks like Tony isn't a believer in evolution."

"Well I didn't say that exactly," Tony replied.

"No way, Tony," Sally said, wagging a finger in his direction. "Obviously humans evolved from monkeys. They share well over ninety percent of our DNA."

"So do dogs and dolphins. In fact I read that we are probably closer to a species of Tree shrew than monkey," Tony replied.

"A tree shrew!" Agent M shouted. "I need a shot."

Sally poured vodka into three fat shot glasses with small images of men with sombreros on them. They said cheers, and the clink of the glasses echoed in the apartment.

"So I met this guy," Agent M said. "He is such a Jew, and you know I love Jews!"

She chirped a cute laugh.

"Yes, you are a Jew lover. But you know his mother will never let you marry him because you are Italian," Sally replied.

"Ah, my Jew boys, I love them."

"What's his name?" Sally asked.

"Eli," she replied.

"Is he as Jewish as you know, Jesus?" Sally asked, pronouncing 'Jesus' as "Hey-soose".

"No, no, no," Agent M replied. "He isn't Mexican."

Tony laughed to himself, watching the conversation. Both Sally and Agent M had slightly flush faces, eyes burning with friendly intensity. Agent M explained her rationale for the guys she dated. Apparently, as an Italian, she wanted to rebel against her parents by dating more Anglo-esque guys. "I like pale, freckly boys with no hair," she said.

"No hair... you mean bald?" Tony said.

"No, I meant no body hair."

Tony laughed again. He really was a guy.

"Yes, every boy I've brought home my parents don't like. All these blue-eyed hairless boys."

Tony and Agent M went through a series of discussions about body hair, including information on how hairy her father is. She also said that her parents were "probably totally racist". On one occasion she told her mother she supported Barack Obama and her mother replied, "You know he's black, right?" Agent M said she then said: "Oh, he's half-black, mom." To which her mother replied: "That's half too much." She then started talking about her old neighborhood—Tony was drinking through the entire spiel—and images of the Sopranos kept popping into his head. During this time Sally had retired to the bedroom briefly.

She came out and sat on the kitchen counter.

"Don't you rebel, Tony?"

The girls fell into a discussion about some high school friend while Tony sipped a beer, thinking. Sally turned back to Tony in mid-sentence of her new discussion.

"You know," Miss M said, "That friend of mine, in high school she had a black boyfriend, that was her rebellion."

Agent M threw in a question. "Are you rebelling against your parents by dating white girls?"

"Well, I can't say I'm rebelling per se," Tony replied. "I've always been an equal-opportunist, and I think who you date sometimes depends on who you hang out with the most."

Tony realized he'd already had two glasses of wine and three beers in the space of fifteen minutes. Behind them, Tony turned to see a guy wearing a cheap cape holding a stick that was almost shoulder height. He waved it at Sally.

"DEATH TO THE HEATHENS!" he shouted.

Everyone laughed.

In an interesting demonstration, the cape-clad guy took a beer, chugged it and then shoved it on the stick, piercing the base. He slid the ripped can to the bottom of the stick.

"Creationists, one!"

A girl also wearing a cape gave him a high five. Soon more choice characters appeared, including a Charles Darwin lookalike, girls with witch hats and more people with Capes. Then a girl walked in, and Tony felt his breath stop short. She was tall, almost his height, with dark eyes and features that hinted at Mediterranean. Her body was tall with just enough curves. Standing over by the window with some people, Tony watched her. Then she laughed, and her smile made his face flush. For a second, her eyes caught his, and he felt a rush in his chest and looked away. He needed another drink.

The hours that followed were a slight blur. At least thirty people came to the small apartment, chatting about creation versus evolution, life and whatever else was on their mind. Several guys became "wizards" or "warlocks" and the night took an interesting turn as a major debate caused a few people to switch factions. The beers flowed like water, and at the end of it all four long sticks were stacked with beers from top to bottom. The tall dark-haired girl wasn't a lightweight either, she was on the evolutionist team, and more than once Tony observed her with two burly varsity looking guys throwing back shots of vodka chased with beer. There was something about her that made Tony pause. She glowed in the night, slightly out of place in the din of the party. He could see her on a boat or a beach, hair blowing in the breeze, perfect skin glistening on some midsummer afternoon somewhere he'd never been.

During this time, Sally shouted through a (fake) megaphone someone had brought that it was decided by everyone present that the entire company would head to Wonderland, only a few blocks away. Most of the inebriated party group, in capes and all, rolled in a noisy rabble to the bar, where people instantly started doing more beers and shots. Tony commented on the now brown hair of a bartender who normally had blonde hair. She winked at him and slipped him a beer. Most of the group headed upstairs and joined a sweaty throng of revelers already as drunk as they were. One of the wizards gave Tony another drink and things spiraled slightly, the floor vibrating a little with the movement of the dancers, the red lights a little bloodier than usual, spilling into the sea of flushed faces and glassy eyed patrons.

Tony stood by a wall near the main bar. Sally came over. They chatted about work and life in a very protracted way.

"You okay?" Sally asked, her eyes a mixture of concern and interest.

Tony knew this look. Once or twice he tried to act on it, and both times she had smiled and kissed him on the cheek and walked away.

"I'm good," Tony replied.

Sally vanished into the crowd. Tony surveyed the room, not able to distinguish many people. But there, standing near the DJ at the front was the girl. She was beaming that thousand-watt smile again, dancing with two other girls. Standing where he was, the room felt like a gulf. He felt that tingle in his chest again and shook his head and went to the bar. He bought another drink and sipped it while chatting to a girl with massive pigtails. She was a bit weird and he saw Sally and Agent M chatting to a guy in a ridiculous blue suit. Tony went over to them but the conversation was a bit boring, so he headed back to his spot at the wall. There were now a few girls in front of him. Two shot him a weak smile. Tony smiled back, and then the crowd erupted into a continuous roar of cheering and whooping.

"What's going on?" Tony said to the group directly in front of him.

A short girl who dressed as an Elf replied, "It's Kim's birthday!"

In seconds Kim arrived. Tony wished her happy birthday and she extended a hand to shake his.

"I don't shake people's hands when it's their birthday. Come here!" Tony bellowed.

He gave her a warm hug and chitchatted with her and her friends for a few. They seemed cool, and Tony could tell the elf liked him. Then, a hand touched him on his back. It was a girl he met two weeks ago.

"Tony!" she said, giving him a hug.

"Hey!" Tony replied with equal gusto.

By the time he turned around, the birthday group had re-entered the mob. More people were piling onto the top floor; the thick smell of beer, sweat, perfume and wood was becoming palpable. Back at the bar, Tony grabbed another beer. Someone behind him bounced into him, almost spilling his drink. He turned to see the tall girl from the party. He froze. Up close, she was beautiful. Her eyes were cloudy and green, her skin flawless. A bang of long dark hair hung between her eyes, and for a second the noise of the bar seemed to disappear.

"Hey I'm sorry," she said flashing a quick smile.

Rows of perfect white teeth threatened to blind Tony.

"No worries," Tony replied, realizing his heart was beating faster than normal.

What are you drinking?" he asked.

"Aren't you sweet. I'll have a Bud Light."

Tony did cheers with the girl and walked back to the wall. A hand rested on his shoulder. It was Sally.

"Tony that's Shannin. You should *totally* go for it. Kiss her," she said.

Shannin was still at the bar, chatting to a short guy obviously more drunk than she was.

Tony walked over.

"Sally said I should totally go for you."

Shannin chuckled.

"Follow me," she said.

Tony walked with her into the depths of the sweaty throng. Bodies dancing out of sync with the music bounced him mercilessly, spilling beer on his hands and back. Shannin's hand held his firmly. Adjacent to the DJ, in a dark pocket of space she stopped and turned to Tony, the blood red light reflecting on her face, enhancing her eyes.

She put her arms around his neck. "I saw you at Sally's party. I wondered why you didn't say hello. "

"Honestly, I didn't know what to say."

She removed one of her hands and jabbed Tony *hard* in his ribs. "Liar."

Tony looked directly into her eyes. "Well, there is one thing I've wanted to say to you all night."

"What's that?" Shannin said, slipping her arm back around his neck.

Tony felt his awareness become sensitive and a clarity form in his mind. "I think you're beautiful," he said. Shannin smiled. "I was going to say the same thing about you."

Then their lips locked, and once again the bar disappeared.

Chapter 42

Amy sat in the small chair facing an old TV in Winston's bedroom. She was in a long-sleeved skintight shirt with matching running tights. Over this she wore a small pair of running shorts. Amy had advised Winston that to run seriously during winter he would need to upgrade his running gear. After getting muscle cramps on their last run (he was wearing regular shorts and an old t-shirt) he took her advice. He too wore the running tights under his shorts, with a similar long sleeved running garment he wore under a regular shirt. The route they had taken that day was part of Amy's regular routine for her event training; a start somewhere near First Street, then a push through the city to Rock Creek Park, where they had run the entire route and then returned to Winston's place after grabbing some sandwiches from a deli near his apartment.

The run had been good, but Winston had been mulling over something as they had walked back to his place. There had been another conversation with Elsa recently, another weird phone conversation, this time he heard it from the horse's mouth. She flat out said she didn't want to see him.

He paced in the room slightly. "I don't get it," Winston said.

Winston walked around the small apartment with this shoulders hunched. His fists were clenched and his face twitched. He took a deep breath and sat in the chair facing the window.

"When I think of the nature of people, I think of the basic things. In life we like to make things so complex, so unnatural," he said.

"What do you mean, you don't get it?" Amy asked.

"I mean our associations come from learning about each other and creating successive levels of comfort with each other as time passes no?"

"I can see that," Amy said.

"So what I'm saying is, let's say all things considered, you have an amicable break-up with someone you care about."

"Like you did with Elsa?"

"Well, sort-of."

"Come on, don't act like this over-the-top analysis has nothing to do with you."

A tiny, soulless smirk appeared on Winston's face.

"Fine. So I was saying, what I find unnatural is the way we program ourselves to lessen the effects of all this mental work we put into each other. We meet, have happy times, great moments, evolve way past friendship, and for dumb reasons try to go back in time to a point where we just do hand shakes and barely even look each other in the eye."

Amy took a bit of her sandwich and looked up at the ceiling. After a few chews, she spoke.

"So don't you think that's normal? I mean, if you were to break up with someone, how would you deal with them being in your 'space' as it were."

"Like I said Amy, it depends on the nature of the breakup. I just don't like being treated like some idiot friend who's hovering around trying to get laid or something!"

"Okay, okay, no need to shout."

Winston stood up once more.

"It's the process of it all. It eats at me; it just sits within me in this way I can't process. Dammit. It's like when I went by her place and she wouldn't even invite me in, that's just not cool."

Amy rested a tiny uneaten piece of her sandwich on her plate.

"So why is this so important to you? Why does it mean so much if someone invites you in or not?"

"Because Amy, it shows me that I've fallen from grace. This girl who I've not only loved, and had vulnerable in my arms, won't even let me see where she lives. I didn't even get the courtesy of a 'Would you like to sit and wait until I'm ready?' comment. I'm sure some random fellow from a bar gets a free pass, but me, oh no, I'm so scary I can't get any of that!"

He was rigid with tension. Even after the long run they had done that day, Winston knew he might be out in an hour or so, watching the city go by in a stream of bright lights and cold wind.

"Listen, Winston, as it relates to guys, I've done the same thing. I mean, I don't think it really means she cares for you any less, but its just weird sometimes to have your ex in your comfortable place. I know it sounds weird but I mean, she's probably starting a new life, doing different things and—"

"So I'd taint her place is that what you are saying?"

"No, I meant—"

"I'm some piece of crap that would sully her surroundings?"

"Winston, stop!" Amy's face flushed red for a few seconds, and then regained its normal color.

"I don't know why you are doing this to yourself. This isn't healthy. I'm not going to give you a tough love speech, that's a waste of time. We all know what losing someone feels like and its bad for all of us. But as your friend I really don't want you to evaluate so much of yourself through this one girl's actions. Its just *one* person man."

Winston touched the blinds on a window, peering out at the city below. "A person I loved."

"Well, what can I say?" Amy replied.

She fell back onto the bed with a huff, her chest rising and falling with her breaths. Winston turned and looked at her for a moment. His eyes fell to the ground, and he let out a sigh.

"Amy, I'm sorry, I didn't mean to come at you like that. I guess it's just the way I think. I always had this notion that a person could at the very least get some simple affections from a person that says they care about him. In a way that transcends all the bullshit social posturing people do on a daily basis."

Amy, still lying down, asked, "What does that mean exactly?"

"I mean, wouldn't it be great if just once, people didn't fall into their own hoops? For example, I've realized Elsa has a way of saying to me that I'm 'a friend' now, or whatever. I think when she says that it's very associative with a sort of degenerative state of mind as it relates to me. Not only am I a friend in her mind, but this means she must also be colder emotionally, less willing to talk to me about basic things and have less of a desire to interact with me. After all, that's probably what she does with her other friends. It is so subjective and programmed, it's scary, but it's her choice, it's her posturing. Do you see what I'm saying?"

Amy folded her arms over her chest.

"We all have our paradigms Winston; ways we process our own information. What says her way is that bad? I mean as it relates to you it might be horrible, but another guy might not feel anything about how she's acting. In fact, he might be *expecting* it."

"Good point," Winston replied.

"I mean, the fact of the matter is, I think, is that your system for dealing with this stuff hasn't been sharpened yet. You can't process letting go as quickly as she has."

"I see."

"That's what I'm saying! I think you feel so wounded by these little things, it's creating some weird, spiraling, dark reality you can't escape from."

"Wow, someone's starting to get pretty deep," Winston said with a chuckle.

"I mean think about it, man. You are out of sorts about this girl for so long, knowing she doesn't want to hang with you, knowing she isn't even that comfortable around you anymore and she's probably fucking some stranger with half the depth you have—"

"Great imagery, Amy."

"Listen. So she's doing these things, and here you are, concerned about her welfare and wondering about how her apartment looks. You know you *care* and you *love* her, but you have no outlet for it. You can't very well tell her you love her at this moment can you? If you do, it would probably be a very bad thing, because like you said, she has you in this 'friend zone', so she's probably going to think 'Okay, he says he loves me. But he's a friend, so that means nothing, or he says he loves me, I don't need to process this.' Plus, she's getting married."

Winston watched Amy sitting on the bed, mired in thought. "I'm listening," Winston said.

"So, inevitably what happens is that you are this phantom outsider looking in. You want to be a part of her life but you can't. You want to love her and care for her, or at the very least get a hello once in a while, but you don't even get that, and it tears you up that some new guy, gets to see her, hang out with her, watch movies and hang out in her apartment. And you know, do *stuff* at night."

Amy continued.

"So, it's not just a case of unrequited love, it's a case of unrequited friendship as well. It might have been better if she just rejected you outright, because then you'd have the strongest reason to not want to see her. In fact, most people are rejected outright which sucks, but at least gives them a reason to hold on to. Something that says 'Yeah, the situation sucked, but now I have to move on'."

A brief silence fell over the room as Winston and Amy sat in their respective locations. For a moment, the echo of voices walking through the hallway outside slid under the doorway, and somewhere a dog barked. An ambulance siren wailed in the distance, followed by the hum of a large vehicle passing the apartment.

"You really hit the nail on the head," Winston said.

"Yeah, the situation really sucks. I have to say that I've had my bad breakup or two, but I've never told someone I want to be their friend and then not try to be friends with them. That's almost like a weird form of torture. I think it might help her state of mind more than yours. You say even talking to her seems weird right?" Amy asked.

"Sometimes," Winston replied.

"Well dude, I don't know what to tell you. I guess in these situations there isn't anything to tell, is there? The most I can say is that the sum of who you are isn't based on this person. I admit you are in an awkward social conundrum, but come on, this is life right? Would it have been much different if you guys had a typical breakup?"

"I don't know. I think I should have done the tried a long distance thing when I had the chance. Or at least fought a bit harder."

"You can't say that, Winston. It's not fair to *you*. You were in a place where you felt like she didn't even really love you, so you can't work on a bunch of 'what ifs'. That's living in the past, which is one of the worst crimes a person can commit."

"True."

"So, here's the deal. At some point you will have to get over this, because I'm really worried about you. You look thinner, and your eyes have this deep sadness within them."

"Really? I've been on a new diet. The unrequited kind," Winston replied.

"Sarcasm will get you nowhere, Winston. But seriously, I worry about you."

Winston looked over at Amy sitting on the bed. Her eyes were sincere, and he knew that should mean something to him. It should mean something to him that his friend was genuinely affected by his plight. She was affected by his pain.

"Amy, thanks, honestly. You see the weirdest part of this whole deal is that fact that so much of this is subconscious. I reach these points in my life where I think I'm over it, and I don't even think about Elsa and then bam! I'll have some intense dream about her one night and go through this weird spiral of longing and guilt about not seeing her. Then I feel manic, because to me it's completely illogical."

"Come here."

Amy moved to the edge of the bed with her arms outstretched. Winston sighed again and sat beside her. Her arms gripped him firmly around his torso. Winston eventually extended his arms around hers as well, feeling her hair tickle his forearms as they held each other. Amy broke the hug slightly and looked into his face.

"Winston. Don't let it get you down. If one person can love and care for you in that way, I'm sure another can okay?"

Winston looked back at her, into her green-blue eyes. Nothing in them held any vestige of uncertainty. Whatever it was that Amy believed, Winston prayed he could believe it as well.

"Okay."

Amy gave him a final hug. "Oh shoot!" she said glancing at her watch.

"What's up?" Winston asked.

"I have to go, I have an appointment right now!"

Amy hurriedly put her shoes on and grabbed her bag, in seconds she was gone.

Her presence left the room like a rolling cloud of fog, and Winston suddenly felt very alone. It was as if the emotion he expended was still there, and he was steadily inhaling its noxious fumes. *Elsa is gone,* he told himself. He walked back to the window, watching the cityscape. Somewhere out there, Elsa was walking around, probably making love to someone else.

An hour later, Winston went back outside dressed in his gear, feeling the bite of the cold on his face and ears. He started running down the street.

Chapter 43

Bishop wore a long sleeved pink and white striped Prada shirt, black skinny True Religion jeans and dark purple Varvatos boots. He was looking at a picture of three naked people in a pile of hay holding signs that said, "I AM REAL". Other pictures were on the wall as well. There was an image of a police officer in boxers with "I AM REAL" on a piece of paper pasted on his back. This was at some dingy gallery near M street, a converted junkyard that was now an art hub.

The hipster girl from the warehouse party a few months back had invited him to the event. He didn't remember giving her his number, or anything much for that matter except leaving quickly after seeing Monica with that guy. But he wasn't just a casual observer tonight. He had a few pieces in the show. He and hipster girl had had lunch somewhere, and once she heard he was an artist, she started contacting people she knew. A few calls and e-mails later, he was a part of the show. The setup was all right, but he didn't like his bio and the picture of him looked terrible. They over emphasized his Jamaican heritage as giving him some kind of ultra unique perspective on contemporary American reality. Whoever wrote his bio was a *tool*, Bishop thought. But it had been a while since he had been in that mental space, the space of the artist. Despite what people think, it is always cool to have people come up to you and ask you about your work.

He went to the bathroom briefly and took   a small vial of coke from his left pocket. He did a quick line and went back to his display area. He had four pieces up. "Man in Room" the image he made of the Kevin-esque man staring out at a blank cityscape, and a few more he had produced. One was a distorted image of a voluptuous woman with a demonic face filled with sharp teeth and then two abstracts done mostly in dark tones with red highlights. The art group that put on the event was called Epic Rage, a bunch of rich hipsters with nothing but time and money on their hands. Bishop chuckled slightly as he realized he fit perfectly into that demographic. A girl came up to his area. She was short with red hair and a heavily freckled face.

"This is disturbing," she said, gesturing at the image of the woman.

Bishop looked her dead in the eyes.

"What disturbs you about it?"

Looking away slightly, the girl said, "Well, you know, you have this really sexy body on this woman but the face looks so dark and evil."

"I think everything has both good and bad elements," Bishop said.

"I do too, but obviously you are making a statement here. Seems like some girl you hate."

"Why do you think it's someone I know?" Bishop said, raising an eyebrow.

"It's non-specific," The girl said.

"Meaning?"

The girl smirked. "Meaning if you had more than one piece like this then it would be part of a theme, yeah? I see only one picture so I'm figuring you painted this as some way to get back at a chick."

She put her arms in the air. "Call me fucked up."

Bishop laughed.

"Thanks for your perspective, it definitely is part of a series, I'm only showing one here today," he said, shaking her hand.

She nodded and walked over to a photography exhibit a few feet away. Bishop glanced back at the painting, the only one like that he'd ever done. The face was distorted, with black-red eyes and jagged teeth, but those breasts, the cool mocha skin and the voluptuous curves were all Monica.

He took a quick walk outside, rubbing his hands together in the cold night air. A decent crowd was outside, with wisps of condensed breath rising in the air from each huddled group like chimney smoke. There was a small bar outside. Bishop grabbed a beer and looked at the sky; streaked with blue-grey clouds that meshed into a brooding black coat. He walked to another section of the space, a blank area that was mostly smooth cement. A few guys with skateboards were doing tricks. He watched them idly, when a girl walking by caught his eye. She wore a shiny gray jacket adorned with large yellow buttons on the shoulders, a thin yet form fitting black vintage tee-shirt and a chocolate brown skirt complimented by long Cat-in-the-Hat socks. With a huge smartphone on her ear, she looked somewhat perturbed; a bit lost. Her hair was long and luxuriant, swishing dramatically as she walked. As Bishop looked on, she turned and caught his eye. A flash of familiarity hit him. It was Christina, the girl from the house party almost two years before. She held his gaze. A voice behind her made her turn. She squealed with delight about something and Bishop saw her hug a young man, also of Asian descent. He was much shorter than Christina, with a round face, spiky hair and gentle eyes. Bishop recognized the guy. He was the resident DJ for the night. More than once he had seen him in the bathroom, doing lines and for some reason, talking about Willie Mays the baseball player. His DJ name was Yoda. *Another tool*, Bishop had thought.

A few more people were near his exhibition, some tall basketball player types, pointing at the image of the naked woman with the devilish fangs. One of them snapped a picture of the images. Bishop had no interest in going over and saying anything to them. One of the Epic Rage promoters came over to him briefly and said something to him about an after party at his apartment in Georgetown. Bishop nodded nonchalantly. He could see Christina standing by one of the exhibitions, a semi-transparent piece of plastic with writing spray painted on one side suspended from the ceiling by black wires. As she squinted to make out what was written on the surface of the plastic, he took note of how her face looked like a beautiful mask. She flicked a strand of hair from her nose and looked at Bishop through the plastic. He coughed and walked over.

"Hey," he said.

"Hey to you, too."

"I like your style," Christina said.

"Thanks. Have you seen any of the exhibits yet?"

"Not really. I live near here and my friend told me to come by so I thought I'd pop in."

"I sort of like this message photo montage," Bishop said, gesturing in the direction of the photos with the "I AM FREE" theme.

They walked over to the exhibit.

"A bit strange don't you think?" Christina said.

"Nothing wrong with mixed messages," Bishop replied

"Mixed messages?"

"Yes, look at the cop in boxers. Is he free, or is he giving the person a second chance? You can't really tell from the picture."

Christina peered at the image. "I guess you could be right. What are you, an artist or something?"

"I might be."

"You certainly dress like one," She said with a laugh.

"It's the boots. All the rage these days."

Christina smirked.

They looked at various exhibits and schmoozed with a few of the Epic Rage crew before stopping at Bishop's paintings. Christina's face became serious.

"Something is really dark about this work," she said.

Bishop didn't say anything.

"I mean this lady looks so scary."

"Art is art," Bishop replied.

She let out a *hrrmmm* and pulled out her giant phone. "Mind if I take a picture?"

"By all means."

"My mother is going to freak out when she sees this," she said with a laugh, stepping closer to read the artist biography.

"I *knew* you were an artist! I see you on the bio here. That isn't a very good picture of you though."

"Same thing I said," Bishop replied. "You want a drink?"

"Sure," Christina replied.

Outside in the cold, Christina stood close to him as he got her a vodka cranberry and another beer for himself.

"Don't you just love places like this?" she said.

"Back alley junkyards?"

"No, places with this *energy*. You know, art, people and dirt all mixed up. Makes it feel more pure in some way."

"I think it's just rich kids trying to act like they know the street."

"Bah! You are no fun!" she said, punching him softly on the shoulder.

She smelled very sweet, some perfume or body wash Bishop didn't recognize. The DJ came over. He nodded at Bishop and turned to Christina. "A little club in the back has a dance-off going on."

"Oh! Let's see!" she said.

The "club" was more like a midsize storage room. A few gay guys were voguing. Music was playing from an iPod attached to small speakers.

"Let's dance, Bishop!" Christina said, tugging his arm.

"One sec."

Bishop retreated to the bathroom again. A guy with a thick red beard was weeping and chatting on a cell phone. Bishop did a quick line, and went back to the storage room. The vibe was weird but Bishop didn't care. Christina hopped around awkwardly to the barely audible music. DJ Yoda kept fist pumping. Bishop watched her dance, with her loud shirt, funky socks and hair swishing all around. It didn't make any sense, but it worked. She walked over and gave him a quick kiss on the cheek. Her lips were soft and tiny.

"Dance, Bishop!"

Bishop stood beside DJ Yoda, doing the fist pump with a childish grin on his face. Christina started dancing with the gay guys voguing and laughing out loud. Bishop felt himself smile on the inside. Something about her was interesting and childish.

Her place was a tall building with a dark brown color. In the lobby, a series of pictures of clouds on the wall lead to the elevator at end of the hallway. It was a new building, and the smells of recently finished construction were poorly covered up by potpourri and carpet cleaner. As they walked into the elevator, she turned to him.

"Did you sell anything today?"

"There were a few interested buyers. The guys will let me know if they sold anything later."

"Is it important for you to sell your work?"

"Not a big deal I guess."

They exited the elevator and went to her apartment at the end of the hallway.

A small ceramic cat was on a side table near the entrance. She slipped off her shoes as she went in. Bishop did the same.

"What's this?"

She smiled and ran a small finger between the cat's ears. "It's Maniki Neko. It's a symbol of good luck to ward off spirits."

"Where is it from?"

"Japan."

Bishop nodded to himself. Christina walked over to one of her windows and pulled it open. A gust of cool wind came inside. She motioned for him to sit beside her. From a little box resting atop a table facing her TV, she pulled out a small pipe and some small bags of weed.

"My grandmother gave that to me when I was a little girl. She was telling me some scary story from where she grew up."

She lit the pipe and took a few puffs, handing it to Bishop.

"Yeah, so she's from Tokyo and she told me this ghost story about the lady with the ten plates."

"Ten plates?"

"Yes," she said, taking another puff.

She looked out the window briefly, and Bishop watched her profile. Perfect nose; flawless hair; her tiny lips blowing the pipe.

"Back in the day lots of rich Japanese people had a lot of staff. A man, the owner of a *Ryokan*—basically a small hotel, had a prized set of ten rare and expensive decorated plates from China. One day a traveling dignitary came by and of course, they were preparing a feast for him. The master, wanting to impress the person brought out his ten prized plates to serve food with. The young woman, during the serving accidentally broke one. The master was so embarrassed and angry that he had the woman killed. Soon after that, people who lived in the house would hear a woman's voice."

Christina took another puff and handed the pipe to Bishop.

"She was saying *ichi mai, ni mai, san mai*... . It was the voice of a woman counting. She would could to nine and then start back. Soon someone saw her walking around the compound; it was the girl who had died. She was holding plates in her hands, doing the same thing, counting and counting."

For a moment, her face was masked in the slight shadow of her hair. She continued, "So if you ever run into an old Japanese woman walking with plates in her hand late at night in

Central Tokyo, it might be the woman, trying to find the tenth plate."

Her voice had a flat seriousness to it, and Bishop tried to image the woman plodding along through dark streets, forever searching for the tenth plate. He wanted to tell her about the Rolling Calf, a Jamaican legend about the ghost of a dead bull that roams the hills in the country, but her hand was already rubbing his face, her face closer. Her tiny lips touched his, and thoughts about stories vanished. She broke the kiss and looked him in the eyes. "You know you seem very familiar."

Looking back into her eyes, Bishop said: "I get that a lot."

He put his arms behind her back, and while kissing her, began removing her clothes.

Chapter 44

Tony sat in the chair, squirming slightly. It was constructed of a very solid wood, and the built-in cushion was soft velvet. The restaurant was somewhere downtown, far from the loud noises of Adams Morgan, seedy bars and late night pizzerias. Inside had an elegant décor. The entry way had a huge arch flecked with crusts of yellow paint. It felt Spanish to Tony, but he wasn't sure. There was this smell in the air slightly different from the food; an interwoven mix of perfume and *savoir faire*. The patrons were almost entirely white, many dressed in suits and evening dresses, clinking glasses of champagne. Shannin walked in soon after, stunning in a black form fitting dress, with dark heels to match. She gave Tony a smile through her eyes as she walked over. She gave him a wet kiss on the lips and sat down. The discomfort he felt being in the upscale establishment immediately went away.

She had duck and he ordered a chicken steak meal. They drank wine and chatted. It had been going like this for over eight weeks. The first night they had made love, it was days after Sally's party. The kiss they shared that night was a sort of revelation for Tony. Even though he had consumed quite a bit of alcohol, he had been lost in her lips and smell; the noise of the people around them and whatever feeling she had triggered. It felt *right*. Soon after she had invited Tony to go running with her, a serious challenge for him, a non-runner.

She had laughed when she saw him meet her in old Kappa Sweats and a sweater.

"I see you are wearing the swishers," she had said.

"Swishers?"

"They go, *swish, swish, swish* when you run."

She had been right and it had been a big joke. They ran from the National Monument to Georgetown, stopping at the Francis Scott Key Bridge. Surprisingly, Tony didn't feel as wiped out as he thought he would have. He occasionally lagged behind her, looking at her supple body, regaled in running gear that made her look like a spy or some futuristic Japanese animation character. Her body language screamed confidence.

"I thought Jamaicans were runners!" she had said between breaths, picking up speed.

"Fuck," Tony had muttered in a low voice, feeling icy wind dancing in chest.

"Jamaicans don't run in the wintertime!" he had shouted back, laughing at himself as his pants started to *swish, swish, swish*. She lived somewhere in Georgetown, in an apartment that to Tony looked like something from a gangster movie. It oozed opulence. Shannin had rubbed his shoulder and smiled at him, her smile like the sun in the sky.

"I'll make you some soup, you poor thing," she had said.

The apartment wasn't warm yet and Tony hadn't realized he was still trembling from the cold. He took a shower in her bathroom; a designer's black marble orgy. They ate soup and chatted about life. Her parents were pretty wealthy. Her father owned an insurance company and her mother was from *one of those families* she had said. Tony didn't press for any more information. He liked how she chatted about things, and the jokes she made.

She had held his hand and led him to the bedroom, taking his clothes off slowly. Tony was surprised by how toned her body was. Not a flaw to be seen. The sex had been incredible, and afterwards, spilling in silk sheets staring at an enormous overheard mirror, Tony knew he was in trouble.

There were yoga classes together, a few more runs and trips to places all over the city. Her friends were cool for the most part, but there was one occasion a fellow kept asking Tony if most Jamaicans lived in zinc houses, and he didn't believe Jamaica had a fully functional airport. The guy had gone on and on about third world countries, and referenced number of case studies on the nature of Third World economies (along with his own personal research during his travels to poor countries in Africa). Tony had just smiled and nodded as the guy spoke, listening and not saying much. Once or twice Shannin had slipped past, squeezing his buttocks with a firm pinch. It was at her friend's place somewhere on M street, another really nice apartment. That evening at her place he found her naked facing a stairway that led to the upper floor of her apartment. They never made it upstairs.

"You're beautiful," she would say to him. Tony resisted this moniker. The sincerity with which she spoke had a dangerous truth to it. He felt himself falling deeper into her arms in the mornings when they woke up. He felt himself laughing harder at her jokes, and feeling more annoyed if she was late to meet him somewhere. Women to Tony were mostly a bundle of jaded sensibilities, often confused and passively angry. Most women were simply a faded watermark on his life; shallow memories with barely a place to stay in his memory banks. But now, his stomach would tingle when he heard her voice, and if his phone vibrated, he would feel good if it was her calling him. Once, after work, he was walking home and the phone buzzed. It was from Shannin.

Smooch.

He smiled and shot back a reply. *Smooch.*

He was dizzy with desire to see her, and she was completely insatiable. Morning, afternoon and evening she would want him, looking deeply into his eyes just before kissing him.

"It's what you do to me, Tony," she would coo, sending sparks of excitement running up his spine.

On one of the nights she had come by his place, a little mouse had run behind a chair. She had raged about how disgusting the creature was. In a strange way, Tony felt like she was calling him disgusting as well. They had argued briefly about it. He lived in an older row house, which was impossible to guard from the occasional rodent. She had pouted for a bit, then morphed back into the darling of sweetness he had become accustomed to.

They were making plans for a trip to a cabin her family owned somewhere in Virginia. She showed Tony pictures of the cabin, and excitedly told him about the various trails they would walk and see, even a cave a mile or two away from the cabin site. As interesting as this was, Tony was brutally afraid of bears.

"Don't be silly," Shannin had said.

Tony couldn't get the images out of his head. Two young people, out in the woods, possibly sneaking a frolic in the bushes, when a massive black bear with a penchant for human meat would come charging through the underbrush and tear them to shreds.

"Bears aren't in that part of Virginia," Shannin said with authority.

She was probably right, but Tony also knew that bears were killing machines. They could run on land well over thirty miles an hour, they weighed hundreds of pounds, were excellent swimmers and could climb trees. Shannin had laughed and teased him endlessly about his bear phobia. Eventually Tony relented and said it might be possible to do this trip.

The weather had started to change, from the brutal cold of winter to the slightly more bearable chill of early spring. During this time, Tony had only spent time with Shannin, and he was happy. His birthday was in early April.

Shannin wanted to take him shopping, and she was spending money like rain. They sped through the large, posh Georgetown mall with quick steps. More than once Tony caught a few people staring at him. As they should, he thought. Shannin was a ten.

"I think these would look great on me. I think I'll wear them to this party I'm going to Friday. What do you think?" Shannin said.

Tony glanced at the shoes. Manolo Blahniks. Pricey.

"Uh, sure baby," he replied.

Shannin grabbed the shoes and walked briskly to the dressing room, almost hitting an attendant. In most situations Shannin was pretty relaxed, even a bit of a tomboy, but in a store with great interior decorating and underwear that averaged seventy bucks a pop she was a different person. The attendant shot Tony a dirty look as Shannin walked past her. Tony shot her a smile—the smile that always won them over—and gave her a delicate shrug of the shoulders.

Hey, the smile said. *That's how she is, what can I say?*

The attendant, a short brunette with a very round face and a pronounced nose smiled, revealing silver braces on her top row of teeth.

"Can I help *you* with anything, sir?" she said.

Tony eyed the attendant, easily imagining himself and her frolicking in a tiny room somewhere, the air hot and wet with their sex.

"Oh, I've been trying to decide between these. You see it's my birthday, and my girl there is getting me a gift."

Tony was looking at two very chic Prada jackets. Price tag, nine hundred bucks each.

"Why don't you try one on and I can tell you if it works."

He slipped the jacket on, feeling its weight hug his shoulders nicely. It was black suede with a delicate trim of soft material on the inside. It fit perfectly.

"Wow! That looks great!" the attendant replied, her braces like glitter on her teeth.

"Thanks," Tony replied.

"Try this."

The attendant stood close—a little too close—and handed him the second jacket. This one was pinstripe and had a dark army green color. For some reason it reminded Tony of a fairytale, or maybe something you'd wear at a party that Enya was hosting. This jacket had less weight and was made of a more pliable material.

"That looks good, too," the attendant said once more. "Have you ever thought of modeling?"

"No, never thought about it. I'll take it into consideration though."

He looked at her and smiled again. The attendant blushed and turned away. Shannin walked out of the dressing room with as much gusto as she had entered. The Blahniks were an off-gray color, with an aged but sharp look.

"You look great babe. You ever thought of modeling?" Tony said.

"Been there, done that," Shannin said.

"That's news to me."

"Ask a question, you get an answer," she said with a smile in her voice, facing away from him. She admired herself in the three-way mirror, temporarily in the middle of her own world. She said a few things about the shoes and what it might match. It was in this weird voice, almost as if she was speaking to herself, but Tony knew she was really speaking to both him and the attendant. She had drifted into the world of the upper crust versus the minions who dress them. Tony was an exception to that rule.

"I own twelve pairs of these kinds of shoes, and each time I get one I feel slightly more dissatisfied with the designer."

Tony nodded.

"You know what. It's whatever. Did you grab something?"

Tony held up the black Prada Jacket.

"Good choice. That second jacket would make you look like you were a part of the forestry service or something."

Still wearing the shoes, she sashayed to the cashier, doing a runway-style walk. She dropped a black American Express card on the counter. She tapped her fingers for a few seconds. "Ahem."

A large, sleepy-eyed attendant packing boxes onto a shelf turned around.

"I'll be taking the Blahniks and the jacket."

She walked back to the dressing room, her face flushed.

The attendant looked on Tony with a bemused expression. His smile said *I'd hit it too, bro.* He eyed the black card carefully before processing it.

"Having a good day?" the attendant said.

"'Tis' my birthday. Gonna try and make the best of it," Tony replied.

"I don't think you'll have any problems there buddy," he replied.

Tony smirked. Shannin returned from the dressing room. Her eyes were bright and she beamed an unusually wide smile. She held Tony's arm as they stood by the counter.

"And here's your order. Would you like the receipt in the bag?"

"Sure," Tony replied.

"And here's your card," the man said, handing Tony the card.

"Ah, you mean *her* card."

Tony suddenly felt like slapping the attendant, who was grinning sheepishly. Then he laughed. A rich, deep laugh that filled the store, causing a few browsing customers to look around in surprise. He walked out of the store, with Shannin on his arm.

"What's so funny, baby?" Shannin said.

"Oh nothing. Nothing at all."

They walked along the street briefly, with no particular destination. They were going to meet up with a few people later at a restaurant. Tony had invited Ben, Dennis and some people he knew. Shannin had a few of her friends coming as well. It was some ritzy new bar in Dupont. They strolled past the parking garage of the Georgetown mall and stood briefly at the small bridge with the Potomac running underneath. Tony realized he didn't like Georgetown all that much. He much preferred his section of D.C, the Northwest area. Filled with its dive bars, cheap restaurants and nicely tucked away mom-and-pop shops and thrift stores. Something about Georgetown seemed very plastic, like massive, Paul Bunyan-like caricatures of the Shannins and the Kellys hovering over the 4th ward like a pair of Nordstrom cardboard posters. The first time Tony had entered Georgetown, he had marveled at how quickly the obviousness of basic wealth changed. Streets were extremely clean and well maintained and the average store was more expensive. University students ran about with Georgetown shirts on, blue and pink Polo shirts and khaki shorts that was like a kind of uniform, and many of the girls wore summer linen dresses and cheap flip-flops. Gigantic SUVs roared across the cobblestone roadways, Mercedes and BMWs dotted the horizon like birds taking flight and the occasional super vehicle—a Maserati or Bentley coupe—appeared, quite like the prodigal son. Tony spent most of his time floating between the French Connection store, the mall and a tiny pizzeria whenever he made his trips to that part of the city. He rarely partied in Georgetown, as his only incentive more often than not, was a girl. Shannin was a perfect representation of the Georgetown elite, and Tony was its antithesis; a tall black man from *another country*. A cab rolled over to the curb. A middle-eastern man with a very neat beard and a smile that looked straight out of a Colgate commercial was in the front seat.

"Good day," he said. "Where to?"

"The Commons," Shannin replied.

They slid into the back and Tony felt Shannin's hand on his inner thigh. Slowly but surely, it traveled towards his crotch. Her hand lingered there for a while, and with a decisive stab of her index finger, started to massage Tony's most private of privates.

"Wait, wait," he chuckled. "I don't want to step out the cab looking like I did after leaving class at lunch break in high school."

Shannin erupted into peals of laughter.

Back in Jamaica, Tony had a teacher who was by his description, "insanely hot". Like many young men, after thirty five minutes of exposure to her generous thighs, breasts and lips, he would be rock-hard as the class ended. His trick was to walk with his bag over his crotch.

"I wanted to give you another birthday gift," she said.

Tony glanced into the rearview mirror and caught the driver looking at him the same time. He lifted his eyebrows, as if to say: *Go for it, my friend.* Shannin's hand reached his crotch again, and this time she grabbed his zipper. She slowly began to undo it, when the cab came to a stop.

"That will be $8.75," The driver said.

Tony looked at the driver's name: *Edward Jones.* He stifled a laugh.

Shannin handed him a twenty and they stepped out of the car. The Commons shadowed them, a tower of opulence. They walked inside and Shannin went to the bathroom. Tony looked through his phone briefly, seeing several birthday messages from girls he didn't know. Shannin called his name. He went upstairs and entered her bedroom. She was standing in front of the bed, wearing nothing but her new shoes.

"So this is the birthday gift, eh?" Tony said, smiling.

He kissed her on the neck and she let out an ecstatic sigh. She leaned back heavily on the bed, and clasped Tony around the waist with her legs. She pulled him forward. Once again, Tony could smell her, so familiar, and so close. They started kissing and she broke the kiss and whispered into his ear.

"It's what you do to me, Tony."

Chapter 45

Tiny buds were starting to show up on trees around the city, signaling the end of winter. It was April, still cold, but not icy. Occasionally Bishop could wear just a sweater outside. It was a Friday, and Bishop saw there were several messages on his phone. He listened to a message from his parents. They wished him a happy birthday and hoped to hear from him soon. There were also messages from Shoda and Christina and a few other people he had met recently.

"I guess there is some point to it all," he said to himself, as he stumbled into the bathroom.

Only a few days before, he went to New York to see Amanda. She was visiting some family in Manhattan for two weeks, and they had a few days together at a hotel. It was a furious, wild affair of mostly sex and light sightseeing. They had made a wild run of the lower East Side, blazing through bars and doing shots, making out in dark corners and in the cab on the way back to the hotel, near the ice machine and eventually did in the deed back in the room with the door slightly cracked, only feet from the bed.

Amanda was looking good; her body seemed more tanned and toned, her eyes had a brighter sparkle, and her hair was different. Bishop loved the New York City energy. That combination of the fast life, cab hopping and expensive nights filled him with a fire he hadn't felt in a while.

Everywhere he went with Amanda there was little dialogue and a raging need to touch, caress and explore. The hotel was fertile territory as well, and Bishop felt lost. Lost in her body, lost in the coke, lost in the alcohol. It was bliss.

"I hope you have a happy birthday," she had said, as Bishop was about to take his bus back to D.C. He had given her a kiss and waved as she left the terminal. Back in D.C, things felt lighter and slower. It was warmer, but that pulse wasn't there. Georgetown was brutally quiet, and the only thing he could hear in the distance was the light hum of a city bus.

Now it was his birthday, and he could feel the fingers of time grabbing at his insides, quickening his steps towards the abyss. He took a shower, and after drying himself off saw a new message on his phone. It was from Monica.

It read: "Happy Birthday! I hope you are doing well!"

For a second, his mind was jolted with memory. She had told him about how she spent her last birthday, going down to the Archives Navy memorial with a few friends, laying on the grass and eating mushrooms. This led to a random night of screaming at lampposts, dangerous skateboarding and three stops at different fast food franchises. Monica had told the tale with her usual gusto, making every detail sound like the best thing *ever*.

"Oh my god we ate so much food," she had said. "I looked like an enchilada when I went home that night."

Bishop had laughed at the time, looking into her eyes and glancing at her generous bosom. He picked up the cell phone, and looked the message again, then pressed *delete*. On a small shelf near his computer was a little bag that belonged to Monica. It was a small green leather pouch. Inside were some old compact discs, makeup and a cheap plastic toy. Bishop picked up the bag and threw it in the trash.

Shoda had mentioned two other birthdays happening around the same time, all being celebrated that weekend. Bishop flopped on the bed, looking at the ceiling. A few new works were on the wall, a painting of a girl wearing a small orange jacket with nothing underneath and a colorful abstract he had painted after his first night with Christina.

There wasn't a plan really. Christina had told him about some new Sushi restaurant near Columbia Heights. Coincidentally, Shoda had also mentioned this sushi place to him. Thankfully, the day went by quickly.

Inside the restaurant resembled a green emporium. Blue-green tiles decorated its countertop. He was surprised to see Makai.

"I didn't know you worked here," Bishop said.

Makai grinned at him, and gave him a brief fist-bump.

"*Tanjoubi omedetou* Bishop. Happy birthday!" he said.

Bishop thanked him. Makai pointed towards a set of tables in the back. A crowd of people were there, a mix of girls and guys that Bishop didn't know. Another guy there was also celebrating his birthday. His name was Michael.

"Hey Michael, it's Bishop's birthday too," Shoda said.

"No way!" Michael replied.

Michael was a handsome man with a sharp buzz cut. He carried a quiet air about him; one of wealth, status and power. He extended a large hand towards Bishop.

"Hey man, happy birthday."

He winked at Bishop, which Bishop questioned briefly. There was a touch of effeminacy to Michael. He didn't seem gay, but you never know.

"Do you have plans for later?' he asked.

"I'm not sure," Bishop said, glancing at the bar.

He saw Christina walk in and say hello to Makai.

"You should hang with us man, totally. We can celebrate our birthdays together."

He said it with a quiet insistence with a practice that bordered on perfection. Bishop recognized this was a guy who could get almost anything he wanted from anyone. Bishop was powerless to resist.

"Okay, it's a plan," Bishop said.

Christina walked over and gave him a kiss on the cheek. She said hello to the group and sat down. The group was a mixture of different people, including a cute girl named Becky from Boston who beamed at Bishop when Shoda told her he's from Jamaica. The drinks started flowing for both birthday boys, and soon enough Bishop, Shoda and Makai were in the bathroom doing blow. It was ridiculously cramped.

"Where's your hot girlfriend?" Bishop said to Makai.

"Ah, we broke up. She was such a skank," he said with a laugh.

He made skank sound like *skankoo*.

They headed back outside. Makai was still working, and said he'd meet the guys later. At Michael's insistence, the group was ready for a brief stop on the Adams Morgan strip.

"Listen, you should really hang with us tonight. We are going to party at this hotel later, I would really appreciate it if you came with," Michael said, as as if it wasn't the fourth time he had asked Bishop.

Bishop nodded, feeling his charm flow everywhere like a wave of invisible energy. Christina was a little drunk and flirting with one of the guys at the table. Bishop, a little annoyed was chatting to the girl from Boston, Becky. She was leaving the next day and seemed quite open to something. Her eyes were very insistent and her questions a bit too heavy with sexual innuendo. She looked nothing like Amanda, but there was something familiar there, something Bishop couldn't place. Michael came over and rested a massive paw on Bishop's shoulder.

"We are heading out in ten minutes. Did you drive here?" he asked.

"Yeah," Bishop replied.

"Okay. What's your number? I'll text you the address," he said.

Bishop gave him the number and glanced at Christina again, still talking with the guy from the party. He got a double shot of vodka, feeling his throat warm with the liquid. Shoda came over, almost trembling with excitement.

"I think I have some girls that want to come to the hotel," he said.

"Nice," Bishop replied.

The girls were two fresh-faced Howard sophomores. They were cute. A few more beers and birthday cheers were made, and the group headed outside. Makai was with them, and Bishop wondered at what point he had come to the bar. He was hopping up and down in a strange way. "I have to pee pee," he said with a chuckle.

A very attractive woman (Shoda said she was Iranian mixed with something else) came up to the group and gave Michael a hug. Apparently, this was his girlfriend. There were three cars in the group: Michael's huge Ford Explorer, Shoda's Honda Civic, and Bishop's BMW. He pulled up to Bishop's car.

"Nice ride," he said, beaming a smile. "By the way this is my girlfriend. Mary."

Mary waved at Bishop with the same casual energy as Michael.

In the car, Christina was quiet.

"What is your problem?" Bishop said.

"What?"

"You and that fucking guy, chatting all night."

"I don't get what you are saying. We were just talking."

"*Just* talking, yeah? My birthday and you spend the whole evening chatting to that loser."

"Why are you so angry?" Christina replied.

Bishop didn't reply. Instead, he turned on the radio and blasted rock music. The hotel wasn't far away and he parked nearby. Silently, he followed the group to the doorway. Christina held on to his arm as they neared the group. It was a weird sight; about thirteen people, mostly drunk and high heading into the hotel. The hotel had light colors and a very retro theme. Inside the hotel room, there were a few books lying by a wall covered in mirrors. A large LCD TV attached to a large swivel arm on the wall faced a set of couches and large pillows. A table in the left corner was filled with DVDs, bottles of water and small snacks. The group filed in. Shoda was happily chatting to his two girls; both with the look of very curious party girls.

A few of the guys from the table sat on the floor with an empty, glazed look in their eyes. Weird music started playing from somewhere in the room and the TV screen came on, showing a repeating montage of bizarre music videos. Mary came out of the bedroom wearing nothing but a large yellow t-shirt, holding several bottles of vodka in her hand.

Everyone seemed to be waiting on something, even Bishop. Christina was still holding his arm; the slightest touch of her breath on his shoulder. Michael was sitting in the middle of the room with a large book on his lap—The Large Book of Breasts. He pulled out several baggies from his pocket. In them were a series of small pills and vials. He opened one bag and started handing out pills.

People popped pills and the liquor started flowing. The music got louder, and soon a small group of people were sitting in front of the television, transfixed by the images on screen. Shoda was with his two girls in a bubble chair.

"Bishop," Michael said.

He handed something to him. It was a small purple pill.

"What's this?" Bishop asked.

"Who knows man, it's Tylenol," Michael said with a smile.

Bishop slipped the pill into his pocket and went into the bathroom and looked into the mirror. His face looked a bit tired, but his outfit was sharp. He pulled out his vial of coke and did a quick line. He splashed his face with water. Back outside, Christina came over and gave him a kiss on the cheek. She had a drink in her hand, and she rubbed his chest.

"So soft," she said.

Her eyes look funny, and Bishop realized she must have popped one of the pills. *Fuck it,* Bishop said to himself, tossing the pill down his throat. He chased it with the rest of Christina's drink.

Michael walked around to everyone saying "Are you good? Are you good?"

There were two guys sitting by the mirror, nodding out of beat with the music. Bishop stood near them for a while, listening to the weird music playing through the speakers attached to the TV.

"Bishop, you good?" came Michael's voice.

"Yep," Bishop replied.

The phone in the room rang a few times. Through people near him, Bishop heard that they were threatening to kick everyone out. At some point, everyone went into both bedrooms, hiding in closets and under the bed, expecting hotel security to blaze in with guns drawn, but no one ever came in.

One person had a camera; it was a large metal relic, definitely not digital. Flashes appeared frequently accompanied by cheers. The room seemed larger for some reason to Bishop, people's eyes glinted with brightness, and the sound of the music made each of his teeth shake. A hand touched Bishop's shoulder. He turned to see Becky, looking directly at him. Her eyes had the same weird look as Christina's. He realized his must look the same way, and started laughing.

"What's so funny?" Becky said.

"Everything," Bishop replied.

Becky came close and kissed him, her lips smeared with vodka. Bishop felt her tongue rush into his mouth, searching and probing aggressively. He pulled away and smiled, the world brighter and more colorful. He heard a small commotion beside him. Michael stood in the center of the people sitting in front of the television. Bishop realized there were many more than just thirteen people in the room now. At least twenty people were hanging about, a mixture of girls and guys with glazed eyes and slow body language.

"Thanks for coming to my birthday party," Michael said with the same warmth.

"Actually thanks for coming to me and BISHOP'S night!" he said, pointing at Bishop.

A few people clapped.

"Since we've all had a few drinks and *Tylenol* for our headaches, let's really get the party started."

He pulled out another baggie filled with more pills. These were white. He handed them out, and people swallowed them eagerly with more shots of vodka. Another hand touched his shoulder. It was Christina. Her face was red and she was smiling.

"I saw you kiss that girl," she said. "Are you still angry at me?"

Bishop didn't have time to respond, he was lost in her eyes, light brown pools that seemed to stretch into the horizon forever.

"No," he replied.

Then she leaned in and kissed him. She was more passionate than usual, her arms gripping him tightly. He heard Michael's voice.

"Here she is," Michael said.

An attractive woman with auburn hair was beside him. She was also wearing just a yellow t-shirt. To his surprise, Bishop saw she wasn't wearing any underwear. Michael put his hand around her shoulder, slightly pulling her shirt up, exposing the slight fuzz of pubic hair.

"Thanks to everyone again for coming here. IS EVERYONE GOOD?" he said.

YES! came the resounding reply.

"Awesome. Now the party really starts."

Michael gave the girl a wet kiss on the cheek. He winked at a guy near the TV who nodded and fiddled with an mp3 player attached to the speaker system. The music changed to light house music.

"Let's ESCALATE!" Michael shouted.

He turned around and grabbed Mary, and started passionately kissing her. The girl with the auburn hair still stood there, and slowly lifted her shirt, showing hints of a firm body. A young man in the room, handsome in a grizzled sort of way stepped toward her, a drink still in his hand. She started kissing him, licking his face and running her hands all over his body. From somewhere, a light came on that projected circles all over the room. Another projector was activated, and the images from the TV were now everywhere, casting a ghostly pallor on everyone's face.

The girl with the auburn hair eased the guy to the ground, forcing three people to move away from their pillows. They maintained a contiguous position near the couple. On the ground, the girl fiddled with the guy's pants. The music throbbed and a weird blanket of attention fell over everyone. The escalation of the evening had a pulse, and Bishop felt it tingle in his fingertips and in his lips. Christina seemed to feel it too; her face slightly red but her eyes sober and intently looking on the couple, her lips slightly apart. His heart was racing.

The girl fiddled with the guy's zipper frantically, making strange noises. She whipped out his manhood and took it in her mouth, spilling her hair all over the man's stomach and legs. Like ghostly orbiters, everyone quietly watched. Knowing she had a captive audience, the girl growled and put on a show, licking, spitting and jerking with frenzied attention. Bishop glanced to his left briefly, seeing one guy by the window openly masturbating, oblivious to anyone else around him; lost in his onanism. The pills and the coke made everything sharp. He could *feel* the girl's hair on his body as well. He could *feel* the sound waves crawling over his arms and tickling the hair follicles on his head. His silk boxers felt like he was wrapped in cool fabric. He touched Christina then, feeling his fingertips shoot sparks as he made contact with her skin.

The girl was naked now, revealing a tight, runner's body. She mounted the guy. Still wearing his shirt with beads of sweat on his forehead they—

Christina turned to Bishop and kissed him, their lips feeling fused, with an orchestra of ecstatic background music. Images from the weird music videos filled his vision while Christina touched him, running her fingers under his shirt, and pushing her hand into his pants. She bit his lip slightly when she felt his hardness, sending pulses of complex pleasure into his brain. They fell onto a couch, splashing in a pool of leather softness; the hotel room a distant memory. She was everywhere and nowhere, a blur of sense and touch. She had ten fingers and ten hands, all of which swept over his body like eels dancing in a cake box. He teased a nipple through the thin fabric of her top, feeling her entire body shudder. She closed her eyes and sighed, a sigh that sounded like a gust of breeze on a dark night. Then their lips met again, and they spun around in the leather pool, giggling and horny. He felt hands undoing his belt, but Christina's hands were still around his neck. It was Becky, the girl from Boston. Her eyes were glazed and a smile like fire was on her lips. Christina kissed him again, and Bishop felt Becky take him in slowly, her lips like warm foam.

They spun around in a dance, and then he glanced leftward and saw the girl still straddled atop the man, her auburn hair flying in slow motion. The music thumped and time slowed. Bishop locked eyes with a guy watching the girls blow him. The guy smiled and raised his beer. Bishop looked at the ceiling, seeing spinning images in the dots, little faces and hands pointing and turning, wildebeest running across a desert horizon; a fat man taking a dump on a toilet seat; a half bitten apple. Then he glanced down, his lower body lost in a sea of hair. Becky and Christina had blended into one person, a woman with four hands and two lips; roaming, searching.

Then it seemed, they floated from the couch, through a narrow hallway and into one of the bedrooms. Their naked bodies floated to and fro, dancing to the rhythm of their pulses. The music outside dulled, the echoes of more sexual acts drifting through the crack in the door. Christina clutched him, her taught body showing the slightest outline of abdominals while Bishop thrusted, her hair spilled out on the bed like a scarf. The bed disappeared briefly, and Bishop was airborne, entwined with both women in various positions, lost in a cloud of gasps and grunts. He took Becky from behind, tugging her hair and scratching her back. Christina bit him on his shoulder. Two guys stood in the corner, watching.

Bishop felt like a piston again; a piston flying through a tunnel of violet light, with everything spinning and calm at the same time. For no reason, he glanced at the window. At the windowsill, was Kevin. He was smiling and saying something Bishop couldn't hear.

A flash of fear went through his system, and then he felt Christina's lips on his neck and her hands scratching his back. He looked back at the window, and Kevin was gone. He pulled out from Becky and turned to Christina, she lay on the bed, her slim body tight with anticipation. He entered her, and she scratched his back while Becky scratched his back. He could feel everything and nothing; skin and fingers everywhere, swarming and spinning. Now the ceiling was close to his face, and Christina's lips were on his and he exploded, feeling his body shatter into pieces and reform. The world became the bed and the bed became the world. Christina clutched him, rocking while moaning a suppressed orgasmic murmur, her thighs shaking in irregular spasms.

He finished Becky with his hand, watching her convulse and her eyes roll over. They lay there for a while, with the noise of scattered conversations around them, the occasional snap of a camera phone here and there. Christina started crying as she put her clothes back on, her flawless face stained with running makeup. Bishop was staring at the ceiling, still on the journey, drifting and spinning. He could hear Christina leave the room, and Becky teased him down there, her fingers tickling and probing.

"What do you do?" Becky said.

Bishop glanced at the window, wondering if Kevin was still there. He was gone. Outside, D.C was black and cold, dotted with lights.

"I'm an artist," he replied. "Just an artist."

Chapter 46

Tony hadn't heard from Shannin in a week and a half. One weekend ago she went to New York to meet up with some friends, giggling and video chatting with him on the airport Wi-Fi, telling him to lower his voice after he had said something lewd. She had said goodbye and texted him another *smooch* and then that was it. There weren't any responses to his texts, e-mails or voicemails. Another day passed and when Tony woke up and looked at the LCD of his phone it was still blank. The week drifted into the weekend and still nothing. Out of boredom, Tony went to a Bar in Mount Pleasant. It was a bit dead, and he went to the strip at Adam's Morgan.

The bars were a blur. He wasn't drinking much at first, just standing in the corners at the various establishments, people watching. Couples kissed, large groups of girls shouted at each other over the music. It had been a while since he was in this mish-mash of chaotic social dynamics, and the slightest twinge of familiarity tickled his fingers. To his far left a tall blonde girl strolled in, followed by a friend with super curly hair. The tall one had piercing blue eyes and a face fit for modeling. They disappeared in a throng of people near the bar. Tony took a quick stroll around the premises. Some girls gave a passing glance, others a lingering stare. The two girls returned and were standing near Tony, the blonde talking to an attractive guy who was short and hairy. He had a self-involved look that shined like a bulb. Tony got an image of him and the blonde together at some later date; her long legs wrapped around him while he was a thrusting fuzz ball. Upstairs, at the other bar, two girls were standing near a high table having drinks. Tony said hello to a girl with dark hair and a pretty face. For a second, he had a flash of memory. She reminded him of someone—a girl from last year—but he couldn't remember the name. The girls are from Fairfax Virginia and Pittsburgh respectively. One bought Tony a beer: a Delirium. It was strong and sweet.

I'm falling into that place again, Tony thought. One of the girls, with a spunky energy and mocha skin, talked about beer. She said she made a great homebrew, and told Tony to try it sometime. Tony laughed, saying he might do that. Behind him, two leggy bottle blondes appeared. They were standing by the bar for a while.

"Wow, you guys have been waiting so long to get drinks?" Tony said.

"The people here are *so* rude," one of them replied.

"Come on, its not that bad," Tony replied with a laugh.

The second girl smiled at Tony. She was pretty, with a sort of actress-meets- surfer-babe vibe. Conversations mixed between both groups. The blondes were with a tall guy with a soft voice. The new group was from Michigan, and Tony dropped a few questions about Michigan into the conversation. He could only remember one name, Lisa, the cute blonde. Eventually the group walked away and Tony resumed chatting to the girl who liked to brew beer (Marsha) and her friend (Caroline). They both worked on the Hill and hated it. They now had two fresh beers, in huge jugs that would make any lumberjack proud.

"Do you want one?" Marsha said.

"Sure," Tony replied.

The beer was good, and the slightest hint of a buzz started to form. Tony wasn't in the mood to get drunk, and headed over to a small water cooler. Sipping on a cup of water beside the cooler was a slim girl with an early 90's Winona Ryder haircut. Tony smiled with her.

"Why are you standing here by yourself?" he said.

"Oh, I just like to," she replied with a smile.

"Well, I know one thing for certain about you, and that is the fact that at least ONE person tonight has told you they love your hair."

She smiled.

"People always tell me they love my hair," she replied.

"Well, I'm talking about tonight."

She laughed. She looked at Tony with a hint of defensiveness. It looked like she was happy to just listen to music and people watch. She was Tony an hour before, at the first bar. He told her to have a good night and returned to the two girls. They wanted to go to the dance floor, but Tony realized the blonde hottie from the Michigan group might be available. He broke ranks with the group for a second, touching her on the shoulder She really was pretty.

"I'm displeased, I never got to speak to you at length," Tony remarked.

"True."

He cut to the chase. "I like this—" he said, running a hand through her hair.

He touched her hair, and he rubbed her jawline briefly. She didn't flinch. Her friends were busy chatting to a few other people, and then she turned around.

"Wait, you are leaving?" Tony said with a soft laugh.

"It's my friend, he's bitching because he wants to dance. He wants to go to Dupont Circle right now."

"Then we have a dilemma. We should hang out sometime. Would you like that?" Tony asked.

She paused while taking Tony in for a few seconds. Then she grabbed her purse. "Possibly."

She punched her number into Tony's phone and walked off. On the dance floor, the two girls have disappeared they are back at the bar.

"After party?" Tony said to Marsha.

"Always," She replied with a smile.

Tony looked at her face; cool brown skin with intriguing dark brown eyes, full sensuous lips. They headed outside in a group and walked up the strip, through the rabble. A feeling of guilt landed like a cool wave over Tony. He paused near a pizzeria.

"Marsha, I just remembered I have to do something in the morning. Can we meet another time?"

In his mind, Tony knew this was a delicate balancing act. Not going home with a girl could come off like outright rejection.

"Sure," Marsha said, exchanging a glance with Caroline.

She gave him a kiss on the cheek. It felt slightly weird. He watched them walk up the top of the strip and turn the corner. Then, his phone buzzed in his pocket. It was a message from Shannin.

Hey sorry. Can you come over? I will pay for the cab.

Something felt ominous about the message, particularly the timing.

Tony was brooding in the cab. He knew something was off. The cab pulled up in front of the apartment building where Shannin was already waiting outside. She wore dark sweat pants and a black cardigan. She paid the driver and hugged Tony. Just seeing her again made Tony's heart jump slightly, even dressed down she was stunning. She gave him a kiss on the cheek.

"How are you?" she said.

"You tell me," Tony said, looking into her eyes.

She squirmed slightly with the intensity of his gaze, and looked away. "Come inside."

They were in her kitchen. A kettle was boiling some tea. Tony sat on one of three black stools that faced a large central stove. He hadn't removed his jacket.

"You want some tea or something?" Shannin said with her back turned to him, fishing through the cupboards.

Tony said no. Tea had become a ritual for them lately. She had taught him about many different varieties she was interested in, how to steep them, cold teas, herbals and teas that tasted good with milk. Most times they went anywhere to eat she would have some tea first, and many times in her apartment they had both sipped tea from large his and her mugs while watching TV.

Tony watched her carefully, watching her body language. She seemed relaxed, but there was a tension in the air.

"So I was trying to call you and you kind of vanished," Tony said.

"I know. I—I thought you'd probably be worried but I didn't know what to do."

"Do about what exactly?"

She stopped looking through the cupboard and turned around. She looked at her feet for a few seconds.

"Well, it's about the New York trip, I mean I was hanging with some people and I ran into an ex-boyfriend of mine. We were seeing each other before I met you and—"

"You slept with him."

"Tony, it wasn't like that, I mean this was like… some deep stuff that was way before I met you and I honestly don't know what happened."

Tony sighed.

Shannin came over to his side of the counter.

"This is the first time I've done anything like this. I couldn't process it. That's why I disappeared. I didn't even know what to tell you."

Tony stood up, as if in a trance. "You didn't think this would hurt me?"

"Baby, I'm so sorry!" Shannin said.

Her voice was cracked. She held him briefly, and for a second, her scent, so familiar, wafted into Tony's nose. Gently, Tony eased her off him.

"You know, I haven't seen anyone else since I've been seeing you. I mean…" Tony trailed off and walked towards the staircase, staring blankly at a large painting on the wall.

I didn't realize we were in a monogamous relationship. I— I'm sorry if I hurt you," Shannin said.

"But we've been seeing each other for almost four months."

"I thought you were seeing other people."

"How? I spent so much time with you."

Tony was flooded with confusion. He walked over to one of her windows, sighing slightly and leaned on the ledge.

"I'm so sorry!" Shannin said again.

She started crying and Tony looked at her blankly. In his mind it seemed he was right; most women were just a bundle of jaded sensibilities shrouded in a ball of confusion. A light anger began to spread through his system. It felt strange and invasive and his left arm started to tremble. He couldn't remember the last time he had been angry.

"I'm leaving," he said, walking away.

"Tony, please don't leave."

Ignoring her, he walked down the staircase, hearing his footfalls echo in the massive expanse of the apartment. His arm was shaking now, and his chest felt tight. Shannin was saying something, but he couldn't hear it. Blood rushed to his head and ears and things around him didn't seem clear. He didn't remember leaving the apartment or walking outside. Georgetown wasn't close to where he lived by any means, but the streets ebbed and flowed with his internal confusion. He didn't realize it, but tears were also on his face. In what seemed like no time at all, he was at home, half-frozen from the nighttime chill, and flopped into his bed. Thoughts spun in his head like a frightened school of fish. Images flashed into his memory of her atop him, wearing her heels and the cheap blond wig, them at the restaurant with her in the black dress; their first kiss at the bar. Each image slapped him in the face. The memories felt like a violation; some rampant aberrations in the rhythm of his life. His hands were still shaking, and as he lay there, the room, normally frigid, felt very hot. He started wheezing and coughing as the tightness in his chest turned into a sharp, splitting pain. He stumbled off the bed and walked awkwardly to the bathroom, accidentally slamming his shoulder into the doorway. Wincing, he quickly opened the bathroom mirror cabinet. There it was; a small bottle of Xanax. Tony gulped for air with shaky hands. The tremors were so strong he could barely open the bottle. He took three of the pills and swallowed them with some tap water and immediately turned on the shower. Tony leaned forward headfirst, the stream of cold water hitting his face with a constant *pitter patter*. He stood there for a while, until the tightness in his chest eased up a bit, and the images weren't racing as quickly in his mind. The noise of the shower cleared this up a bit, and slowly, he started breathing normally again. He flopped into bed, still damp. A few images were still at the forefront of his mind, and he fell asleep seeing Shannin laying on her bed, naked with her heels on, echoing her favorite sentiment:

It's what you do to me, Tony….

He woke up the next day, feeling frayed and tense. Outside was a dull purple, almost night. Tony had been asleep for almost fourteen hours. He went for a walk by U Street. There was no purpose to this stroll, but the apartment felt dead. He was sure there might be a message or two from Shannin on his phone, but his hand trembled slightly and he decided it would be better not to turn it on. He walked a few blocks, past a few small restaurants and shops. At a small intersection near a pharmacy, he saw a figure approaching him. It was a person wearing sophisticated running gear, similar to what Shannin would wear. As the person came closer, Tony recognized the face. It was Winston. His heart sank. Winston was emaciated.

His eyes looked more sunken into their sockets, and his face, normally round and flush, was flat and dull. Even his running gear, meant to fit tightly, seemed loose. Winston paused as he saw Tony, removing an ear bud from one ear.

"Tony, how's it going man?" he said, running in place.

Tony didn't answer for a second. It was strange to hear Winston's voice coming from this body. He didn't seem like Winston at all. He looked like a walking cadaver, escaped from some funeral home with a fresh leash on life.

"I-I'm fine. Winston... is everything okay?" Tony asked.

Winston let out a loud laugh. It was a laugh deep from the recesses of his soul, but frighteningly empty. It sounded like a tire letting out a whoosh of hot air, mixed with the cackling of a witch. Winston's chest seemed to strain with the force of his laughter.

"I'm good man, I'm good," Winston said with a weird smile.

"I don't believe you. Jesus, man, you lost a lot of weight."

"I guess."

"What's wrong, boss?" Tony asked.

Winston shuffled his feet nervously and looked down and to the right. A flash of memory surged through Tony's head, and a twinkling of déjà vu ticked his stomach. For a brief moment, he saw Winston, shorter and more plump in high school. That look he made—downwards and to the right—was something he did when he wanted to avoid uncomfortable conversation.

"It's nothing. Nothing you would understand anyways," Winston said flatly.

Tony felt a frantic concern overwhelm him. Winston still kept staring at the ground. He looked at Tony for a second, then walked directly under a tree nearby. Tony followed him.

"Listen, man, we go way back. You know you can talk to me right? What's going on? Please tell me."

"It's nothing, Tony," Winston said forcefully. "Go man, just go and do whatever it is you are doing."

"It looks like you could need some help."

"What? I don't need anything."

To Tony Winston's body language said otherwise, but there was an abrupt coldness to his voice.

Tony reached forward and touched Winston's shoulder. It felt like bone.

Winston took a step back. "Don't touch me," he spoke hotly.

"Boss I'm just trying to—"

"Get AWAY FROM ME!" Winston screamed.

His voice was a harsh shriek, coming from somewhere inside him that Tony couldn't even imagine. It was the sound of emptiness and utter dissolution mixed with rage. Winston spun around and slipped the ear bud back into his ear. He took off in a slight run, heading up the street. Tony instinctively pulled out his cell phone to dial him. Then as Winston's body became a small dot in the horizon, Tony realized he didn't have Winston's number.

He never had.

Chapter 47

That damn Tony! He hadn't expected to see anyone today. Today he had decided to do it. After more nightmares and a frantically developing paranoia, Winston knew what he had to do. He would take one last run. Everything was empty now.

He stopped at another intersection and rubbed his temples. He had been getting headaches as well as nightmares, and one threatened to start now. The throbbing in his frontal lobe ebbed and quieted. He took a quick look around at the city. Everything for him represented an obstacle. Every outing and interaction felt cloudy, like a cup of water mixed with milk. He felt faceless, literally like a *thing*, an odd construct. There he was, running through D.C, nature's fucked up amalgam of circumstance and sensitivity. Oh, how he wished he could say "fuck it!" like Tony, and just barrel through life screwing girls, doing drugs and getting lost in different couches night after night.

He knew it wasn't enough. At the heart of his pain, deep within his subconscious, was a skyscraper-sized question mark. A question mark that had been growing inside him for years. The Elsa situation was merely a catalyst, some sort of emotional enabler that started the erosion of his reality. There was no need to party; no need to listen to music; no need for sexual interactions. All that was left was his running, and even that was getting tiresome.

He lived in a city of fighters, people who championed causes and tried to evoke goodwill from those around them for the lives of their fellow men. But there was something odd, and distinctly disturbing about the undercurrent of social conditions in this atmosphere of change. What is it worth if the people around you would fly to Africa at the drop of a hat to help a nameless person, but never call their friend to see how they are doing? What is it worth, to fight for the rights of a person on a picture, if you won't even try to fight for someone you love?

Did she feel his pain as tears ran down his face on that warm summer day? None of their interactions warranted a friendly touch on his shoulder, or even a hug? Where was the love she had claimed she had for him?

Now he was running through Dupont Circle, the last vestiges of sunlight vanishing in the horizon. In the cold evening a few people were sitting on benches, close together for warmth. They seemed to be simple images in a menagerie, all on mute.

Winston thought about the dichotomy of human existence, where we live outside ourselves, attracted like moths to the flame at all the big things happening around us. Some celebrity has a baby and everyone talks about it. A country goes to war and everyone is in an uproar. A hero dies and the nation mourns, but do we ever pause and look at ourselves?

Of course we do, Winton thought, gritting his teeth as a gust of cold breeze stung his skin. We do when we're old, and we realize that life is in the moments, not in the fleeting desires we think we want in our youth. It is when we sit back and look upon the world with wizened eyes that we realized that inevitability comes with it a certain clarity. The young feel they have endless opportunities, that their immortality is a thing hidden amongst the folds of their clothes in their closets.

But one day we all wake up, and look at the world in a different way. We realize we are mortal, and that our time here is truly precious, and no matter who we have hurt, who we want to save, and how far we want to travel, it must all come to an end. In this end we reflect on that which we have truly cherished, that which we have felt, and that which we have loved.

Winston felt as if he was too well attuned to this mode of thinking, as if he somehow lived outside the cold, emotional spectrum that everyone seemed to bask in. Why did he feel the need to fight for beauty? Why did he feel so wretched when so many went on with their lives to easily?

Why?

Amy was right. Her question rang true. *Why do you care about this girl so much?* When a person dies, gets shot, is severely ill or infirmed or narrowly escapes death, then people appear. They rally around, happy to know that the number they never call in their phones still has meaning, that their lives are brighter because you are still in it, despite how miniscule you may be. This was what Winston was for Elsa. He was a detail, a speck of paint in the picture of Elsa's life that was almost blotted out.

But perhaps it wasn't Elsa. Images flashed once more in his mind of his abusive aunts and their meaty hands, eyes hot with rage and his skin burning with pain. There was the void of his parents; the empty reality in a huge empty house.

It was time to drift off into some other place. To leave the world as we know it. He was not doing this to "get back at her" or destroy himself to win her sympathies. It was his spirit fighting with his mind, and a myriad emotional complexities he would never be able to figure out. It was a battle for meaning, one of those things that people who champion causes know all about.

He was fighting for that hug, that little touch that someone would give to a friend. That smile from a person you don't know, the warm handshake a salesperson gives you. That's all he ever wanted, just a touch on the shoulder, a look in the eye, and a whisper of "it's going to be all right". He just wanted to know that he was human.

The groundswell of emptiness was now a raging maelstrom and all he had as a dinghy and nowhere to hide. He was the proverbial sad Care Bear with his accompanying cloud.

It could all go away, with a rush of cold water, the frantic spasms of his arms and legs as his muscles gave out, then a drift into endless black.

He could answer the question about what lies beyond that *undiscovered bourn* from which no man returns? In a few seconds, with a flash of light in his eyes and the blinding sensation of freezing water in his lungs, he could answer the question. He could be absolved and leave it all behind.

The sky was dark now, and he approached his destination. A bridge running over the Potomac, near the Abraham Lincoln memorial site. His heart raced and even in the cold he could feel drops of sweat on his brow. In front of him, stretched quiet, black water.

He put his hands on the railing. Gripping it firmly.

Had he lived? He had felt the painful joy of love. Its nimble fingers had run all over his body and massaged his soul. It had penetrated him like a virgin in so many backseats. He wasn't a fucking ostrich hiding his head in the sand from the perils of the world. He had faced them head on, and they had screamed right back. Life *is* tough. Life is a shit storm of happenstance and *whachimacallits*.

He took a look at the ripples on the surface of the river. Threads of light from some unknown source danced across its surface. A flurry of small white dots, flapping about near the river banks a hundred feet away. Little blurs in the distance. *Ducks?* There, a mile or so away, the movement of lights horizontally in the blackness. A car.

Winston stared out at the blackness of the night sky, and for a moment he was on Hellshire beach in Jamaica again. In front of him, frothing white and dark green, was the Caribbean Sea. Clear, white sand stretched for miles in front of him, and in the distance rocks dotted the horizon, as massive waves echoed their crashes through the quietness of a summer day. In his mind's eye, he saw himself and Elsa. There they were, walking on the beach hand in hand. Then, their embrace would break, and Elsa would run into the water. Winston behind her, would follow, and they would splash and laugh, then end up sharing a salty kiss. The sun's rays would fall on their skin, highlighting the contrast between Winston and Elsa, and little droplets of water would shine on their bodies, glamorizing their embrace. He heard a voice laugh, the deep laugh of his father, and turned around to see no one, but the empty beach. The image faded, and the coldness of the night returned. What did the vision mean?

Life was constant and ongoing, and Winston was a participant. Feelings or not, his exit, self-inflicted or accidental, would not send a tidal wave throughout the cosmos. No one would mourn him, and he might not even get a mention in any papers. Would anyone truly shed tears, or shout angrily at the sky at his stupidity? Whatever his bizarre reaction to Elsa had meant, it had shown him the purity of his existence. It had shown him that deep inside him resided an energy that was strong enough to send him over the deep edge into an abyss of no return. As threatening as it was to his existence, it also reminded him of it. Quiet showers remind him of the rivers of liquid that ran down her body when they shared a moment, and sometimes from nowhere, her laugh would echo in his mind. If ever he were to experience bliss, or a lovely dream, she would say his name. The words would flow off her lips gracefully, like a ballerina moving in slow motion. *Winston*, she would say. In this dream he would smile, and her words would wash over him like waves on the rocks that jut out to sea at the Edge of a mysterious cliff, somewhere out there.

In front of him was the blackness of the dark water and its depths. But behind him, was the rest of his life. Maybe that was what humanity really was. Maybe everything is fucked up, and we are all living in a caffeine-laced pseudo society of cheap makeup, politically influenced wars, bad food and magazines that give you 100 reasons to break up with someone you love. Maybe there isn't as much hope as there used to be. People are probably different, with different priorities and different ways of interacting with each other. But we are still people. We fight to get our meals, have a place to sleep and wake up each day ready to do it again.

Maybe that's what I'm meant to do, Winston thought.

When I sleep, he thought, *I have nightmares and I'm flooded with memories of what could have been, but when I wake up, I'm alert, and ready to face the battle again.* He stood there for a long time, his fingers burning from the cold. Something cold and wet was on his face. Tears. He clenched his teeth and closed his eyes.

Maybe this time, he thought, *when I wake up, I'll win. If not, I'll just keep on fighting.*

Winston took his hands off the cold railing of the bridge, and turned towards the lights of the city. A passing car flashed high beams into his eyes, and he squinted for a few seconds, as the excess light on his retinas created a temporary cloak of dazzling white. This quickly faded into dark spots that rejoined to restore his normal vision. His teeth chattered, and his fingers felt numb. He was cold, hungry and far from home. But he was alive. Fucked up, but alive. He let out a deep breath and took his first step towards the city. It waited for him with outstretched arms and bright fluorescent lights in its bosom, ready for the return of its prodigal son.

THE END

ABOUT THE AUTHOR

Marcus Bird is a writer, filmmaker and musician from Kingston, Jamaica. He is the author of several books, including *Naked As The Day*, *Kingston Nights* and *Ahab's Whale*. His short story *An Elephant in Kingston* was shortlisted for the 2018 Commonwealth Writers Prize and is the title of his short story collection of the same name.

Questions? E-mail Marcus at: marcusbird@gmail.com

AN ELEPHANT IN KINGSTON

The same talent that scored Marcus Bird a shortlist nomination in the highly competitive global Commonwealth short Story Prize competition, is on full display here in *An Elephant in Kingston*, his first collection of short stories. In these stories a man avoids suicide by partying with a fallen angel; a magical stranger offers someone the ability to remove memories of his ex girl friend; and a man becomes obsessed with the mysterious appearance of an Elephant in Kingston city. Named after the story which was shortlisted for the 2018 Commonwealth writer's prize, *An Elephant in Kingston* goes from the fantastical to downright hilarious, a multicultural, twisting ride into new realities and back.

KINGSTON NIGHTS

In a Kingston where every night you compete for the attention of young women with world famous athletes, reggae superstars and millionaire businessmen, a young promoter named Indie battles with traumatic issues from the past while trying to stay afloat in the choking social atmosphere of endless parties and casual hookups. As he falls deeper into a growing malaise, he meets a girl who seems to be his only salvation out of the Kingston fishbowl. Or is she? Kingston Nights takes us into a dark, edgy modern day Jamaica far removed from quaint beaches, all-inclusive hotels and countryside hideaways.

Ahab's Whale

Hearing about the fierce reputation of the legendary and infamous captain Ahab, a young man desperately seeking to expand his horizons sets out on a quest to find Ahab and learn from him the ways of the world. Follow him on a fantastical journey, where he learns many principles about life and reality, while facing great challenges and dangers as he follows the captain in his search to find and vanquish a creature known only as "The White Death". Set in a magical time of monsters and magic, *Ahab's Whale* is a story that is sure to enchant and inspire you.

Naked As The Day

A young man finds himself in ragingly cosmopolitan Tokyo, haunted by memories of the past, facing an uncertain future. When a typical twenty-something year old English teacher in Japan develops severe physical and psychological aversions to his daily routine in a small town, he decides to move to Tokyo with a few months worth of savings in search of more stimulating horizons. As his physical symptoms remain, and now hit with the demands that come with living in one of the world's most expensive cities, he must take a fast track course in both survival and self-actualization from a host of characters including libidinous transients, self-proclaimed celebrities and kleptomaniac supermodels. Armed with few skills in the face of an uncertain future, Naked As The Day takes us on an occasionally humorous and poignant journey of human choices and ultimately, their consequences.

BOOKS AVAILABLE ON AMAZON